"*Feels Like Summer* is the perfect beach read full of characters to root for and a mystery that unfurls like a sail catching a breeze. There's heartbreak and triumph in this poignant family drama that will have you racing through the pages to reach a highly satisfying conclusion."

—Jamie Day, bestselling author of *The Block Party*

"Filled with secrets, intrigue, lovers, and betrayals . . . extremely well written and enjoyable."

—*New York Post* on *Feels Like Summer*

"If you're looking for a breezy beach read featuring memorable characters, shore settings, and an intriguing mystery, *Feels Like Summer* by Wendy Francis fits the bill."

—*First for Women*

"Wendy Francis's book thrilled me like a ride in a race car along the coast with the top down. It is everything a summer read should be."

—Elin Hilderbrand, bestselling author of *The Perfect Couple* on *The Summer of Good Intentions*

"At a glamorous hotel by the ocean, four people face up to truths that can no longer be hidden. *Summertime Guests* is compelling, surprising, and a wonderful summertime read . . . I devoured it."

—Nancy Thayer, bestselling author of *The Summer We Started Over*

"Francis shines as a master storyteller. A must-read for anyone who could use an escape."

—Kristy Woodson Harvey, bestselling author of *A Happier Life* on *Summertime Guests*

"A smart, probing drama that skillfully unravels the complex emotional lives of an ensemble cast . . . A reflective, deeply engaging, and suspenseful story with many threads sure to ensnare the attention of rapt readers."

—Shelf Awareness on *Summertime Guests*

"Riveting . . . A smart read with plenty of meat for book clubs."

—Barbara O'Neal, bestselling author of *When We Believed in Mermaids* on *Summertime Guests*

"Wendy Francis has created both a family and a story I did not want to leave. These three sisters on a summer vacation display the strong ties that can both hurt and heal a family. Filled with the sweet, briny air of Cape Cod, this extraordinary tale shows that, together, we can weather all the seasons of life."

—Patti Callahan Henry, bestselling author of *The Secret Book of Flora Lea* on *The Summer of Good Intentions*

"A tender and vivid portrait of a family by the sea, of three unforgettable sisters and the tidal pull of their love and secrets."

—Luanne Rice, bestselling author of *The Shadow Box* on *The Summer of Good Intentions*

"So much more than a beach read, this very real, poignant, and funny novel will make you look at your own family in fresh, new ways."

—Lee Woodruff, author of *Those We Love Most* on *The Summer of Good Intentions*

"A great summer read for fans of Jennifer Weiner and Emily Giffin."

—*Library Journal* on *The Summer Sail*

Betting on Good

ALSO BY WENDY FRANCIS

Betting on Good

A NOVEL

wendy francis

LAKE UNION
PUBLISHING

Published by Lake Union Publishing, Seattle

www.apub.com

Amazon, the Amazon logo, and Lake Union Publishing are trademarks of Amazon.com, Inc., or its affiliates.

EU product safety contact:
Amazon Media EU S. à r.l.
38, avenue John F. Kennedy, L-1855 Luxembourg
amazonpublishing-gpsr@amazon.com

ISBN-13: 9781662523014 (paperback)
ISBN-13: 9781662522994 (digital)

Cover design by Alison Impey
Cover image: © JacquiMoore / Getty; © Diane Bondareff / Shutterstock; © Kathy images / Adobe Stock

Printed in the United States of America

For Peter,
1979–2024
Gone too soon; loved so much.

Keep your friends close and your bourbon closer.

—*Old Kentucky proverb*

OFF TO THE RACES

Prologue

NATE

This is it.

Nate can feel it in his bones, right down to the marrow. *Glory Days, for the win.* The harsh Kentucky sun beats down on his skin, but Nate would be sweating, anyway. It's not often that he gets to place a bet at Churchill Downs, especially when he's sitting on information pointing to a huge victory for a certain horse.

Despite being saddled with 15–1 odds, Glory Days has been clocking impressive times in training all week. If she wins the esteemed Kentucky Oaks today—the mile-plus race around the track for fillies only—she'll capture the champion's garland of lilies and the winner's purse of $1.5 million.

If.

It's a big *if,* Nate acknowledges, but as they like to say at the racetrack, he's got a feeling. How can a horse named after a Bruce Springsteen song do anything *but* surge to victory? Glory Days has the look of a winner: a beautiful bay with a shiny brown coat and black accents, as if someone has painted her legs, mane, and tail in ebony. A distinct white starburst emblazons her forehead, and Nate discerns a certain cockiness to her carriage as the trainer parades her across the track in the traditional "walkover" to the paddock.

It's Friday, May 2. The Oaks race is the precursor to the Derby tomorrow, a kind of equine tease. But Nate fully intends to cash in on his hunch a day early, hopes to pocket a stack of crisp hundred-dollar bills in his seersucker jacket. He doesn't dare tell his wife, Drew, how much money he has riding on this race (no need to worry her unnecessarily). Nor will he share it just yet with Graham and Leslie, their friends who are joining them in Louisville this weekend for Drew's fortieth-birthday celebration.

Because that's what this trip is all about, Nate reminds himself. Not about winning, but about making sure Drew has a fabulous time. Whatever misgivings his wife might have about turning forty, Churchill Downs should sweep them all away. No expense has been spared for this milestone birthday. No request will be denied for the woman he's still crazy about after eleven years of marriage. The memory of Drew walking down the aisle, the sunlight splashing through the chapel windows above, that adorable dimple flashing in her right cheek—it all comes rushing back to him.

She's his girl. And this weekend is all about her.

Now, if he can just refrain from screwing it up . . .

1

DREW

Everything Drew Starling knows about horse racing could easily fit into a mint julep cup—which is to say, precious little. Yet ever since she was a little girl, she's dreamed of attending the Kentucky Derby, as if it were a stylish pink hat beckoning her to try it on. *Come now,* it would say seductively. *You know you want to be part of the fun. Bet on a horse, cheer him on, and if you're lucky, maybe you'll win some money.*

The first weekend in May, her parents would throw a party, a smallish affair with a handful of friends gathered at the house. Guests would crowd around the television while sipping mint juleps (a mocktail, heavy on the maraschino cherries, for Drew) and place their petty-change bets. And the hats! So many outrageous colors and creative designs. Drew can still recall spying a hat that doubled as a miniature racetrack—tiny plastic horses parading around the woman's head—and thinking, *That. That's the hat I want if I ever go.*

Which is probably why, when Nate handed her a white envelope for her fortieth birthday back in February and she pulled out two tickets to clubhouse seats at Churchill Downs, she might have gone slightly berserk. "Are these for real?" she asked, swallowing hard, trying to tamp down the encroaching giddiness.

Nate nodded, grinning like a kid who'd just won MVP for his Little League team. "I wanted to give you plenty of time to plan your outfits—especially your hats. Happy birthday, honey." And Drew—who never liked surprises—was spectacularly, wonderfully surprised as she jumped up to hug him after extinguishing the single candle in her crème brûlée.

"What did you wish for?" Nate asked.

"Oh, you know, the usual: health, prosperity, infinite youth."

"Sounds like more than one wish to me," he teased.

Drew smirked. "Not if you say it fast enough in your head. Then it counts as only one."

That was back in February, before the golden shimmer of turning forty had quickly dimmed to something more like resignation, if not a kind of existential dread.

Because that number—*forty*—has sent Drew into an unexpected funk. Maybe it's because she still feels closer to thirty. Working with elementary school children as an occupational therapist demands a certain amount of energy and youthfulness, after all. On weekends, she likes to head out for a casual five-mile run. She's proficient with social media, and when the moment calls for it, she can toss back tequila shots with the best of them.

Forty feels like a misnomer, a description for someone else.

But she's noticed the crow's-feet spreading from the corners of her eyes; the parallel lines—like goalposts—between her brows. Features that once belonged to her mother.

Now that she and Nate have arrived, though—here in Louisville proper—Drew tells herself that she's done with wallowing in self-pity. Finished with grieving the end of her thirties. Because, honestly, how spoiled can she get? Her husband has pulled out all the stops to ensure that her Derby dreams come true this weekend.

Currently, they're sitting in the bar of the historic Brown Hotel while they wait for Leslie and Graham to join them. Both couples have left their sons behind in Boston under the watchful gaze of their respective grandparents. It's a weekend meant for adults only, a chance to have some fun, drink too many cocktails, and maybe bet a little money while wearing fancy hats. A weekend to confirm that age is just a number—and not, as Drew has been imagining, a hit man lurking around the corner to take her out.

That her husband has chosen perhaps the most expensive hotel in Louisville for their visit bodes well. Harry S. Truman, the Duke of Windsor, and Elizabeth Taylor have all been guests here over the years. And the more people they talk to, the more it seems that everyone south of the Mason-Dixon Line knows that the Brown Hotel, built in 1923, is *the* place to stay. It must be costing them a small fortune, but Drew's not about to ask. Not this weekend. This weekend she won't give a thought to how much money Nate lavishes on her, what ridiculous expenses they might incur. It's been a long three months since February.

She deserves a little fun. They both do.

On the table before her sits the signature Derby drink—a mint julep—which Nate ordered for them both. A fresh sprig of mint pokes out from the side. Drew helps herself to a minuscule sip, feels her eyes grow wide, and coughs. "Wow, they're not kidding around here."

Nate laughs. "No, they are not. Not with their bourbon, at least."

She lets her eyes sweep over the hotel's elegant lobby, lined with stately marble columns. To the right is a dining area, layered in lush burgundy carpet and dotted with elegant sofas and square tables. In the middle sits a grand piano, its keyboard open as if inviting guests to play. Overhead, a coffered ceiling unfurls in a honeycomb pattern while gilded chandeliers float down like candelabras from the sky. There's both a sense of intimacy and grandeur to the space, more reminiscent of a British tearoom than of a bar.

"Oh, look," says Drew. "Leslie and Graham." She waves in their direction, sending her silver bracelets jangling. "Over there, near the elevator."

Impossible to miss, Leslie appears stunning in a pale-pink dress with cap sleeves, dark squiggles across the middle, and a slit riding high up the thigh. Her wide-brim hat, the approximate size of a pizza tray, dances with feathers that are the pinkish hue of a flamingo. For a moment, Drew's mind flies to an image of her statuesque friend lifting a slender foot to her inner thigh in flamingo pose. Heads turn as Leslie and Graham—dressed in a pink linen suit, bow tie, and Tommy Bahama hat—make their way across the marbled lobby.

"Well, don't you both look fabulous?" Leslie exclaims, approaching their table in the corner. An errant feather flies free from her hat and flutters to the ground. Leaning in to kiss both of Drew's cheeks, she whispers, "You knocked it out of the park with that dress!" Then she takes a step back, her gaze lingering on Nate. "And you!" she cries, clapping her hands together. "The color pink really suits you, Nate." (Pink is the signature color for Oaks Day, and guests have been encouraged to dress accordingly.)

Nate says *thanks*, tips his hat as if it's no big deal, but Drew can tell that her husband is secretly pleased by the way a faint blush creeps up his neck. *It's true,* she thinks. *Nate* does *look handsome, all gussied up in his brand-new Vineyard Vines seersucker suit.*

"As do you," Drew adds, although there's really no need. Leslie knows she looks terrific because Leslie always looks terrific. She has the thick, golden hair of shampoo commercials, a megawatt smile, and a Pilates-toned body, all while heading up her own marketing team and raising a ten-year-old son. Complimenting her is like complimenting the Taj Mahal on having beautiful architecture: redundant.

"Thanks. It's Lalla Bee." Lalla Bee is Leslie's favorite Boston designer because, unlike Drew, Leslie can afford to have a favorite designer. That Drew and her friend inhabit such vastly different worlds when it comes to money is an unspoken undercurrent to their friendship, but not necessarily a bad one. Because Leslie is generous to a fault, and much of what she chooses to spend her money on—fashion, jewelry, fancy cars—doesn't interest Drew.

"Good morning, all." Graham slides easily into the seat next to Nate, his eyes quickly meeting Drew's. For an instant, her breath catches. "You look nice, Drew," he says, and the air knots between them . . . then unknots just as swiftly when he smiles.

"Thank you." She hasn't seen Graham since last Thursday (he and Leslie took an earlier flight down to Louisville yesterday), and Drew worried that the dynamic between them this weekend might be, well, awkward. That maybe they wouldn't be able to face each other without wanting to spin away. But it's clear that for all intents and purposes, last week's "incident," as she's come to think of it, will be swept under the rug. Which is just as well.

"And your hat!" Drew turns back to Leslie. "What are those? Flamingo feathers?"

Leslie shrugs and scoots in beside her. "I don't know if they're real. But if they are, there're a lot of naked flamingos running around Boston right now."

Drew laughs, smooths her dress over her legs. She's wearing a pink silk sundress, white lotus flowers scattered across the bodice. A minute ago, it looked sexy and sophisticated in the hotel mirror, but now, sitting next to Leslie, Drew's not so sure. She rented this dress—and a gorgeous kelly-green A-line for tomorrow—from Rent the Runway, her new favorite online store. For a small fee, Drew discovered she could borrow and return a set number of dresses and outfits each month. It was like borrowing a gown from your best friend's closet without the worry that she'd hate you if you wore it better.

As for her hat—which Drew is counting on to transform her into a stylish Southern lady for the day—it's crafted from pillowy organza and fronted by an enormous blush flower. *This is how they wear their hats in Louisville,* she explained when Nate asked if anyone had seen his wife "under there" while getting dressed this morning. *I mean, what's*

the point of going to the Derby if you don't allow yourself to be Derbified?
she insisted.

Even Nate had to concede that she had a point.

Yes, Drew Starling is fully embracing the mantra "Go big or go home." Because attending the Derby is a once-in-a-lifetime dream come true, one that had sparked a host of considerations while packing: How many outfits were too many? Were two hats enough? What kind of shoes were expected? Flats or boots? What if it rained? Were they allowed to bring an umbrella? The answer to that last question was a definite no. As it turns out, there are certain rules to abide by at the Derby, both spoken and—as Drew is beginning to learn—unspoken. The notion that the Derby is a one-day event, for instance, doesn't apply around here. At a minimum, it demands a two- to three-day celebration, which is why she and Nate flew in late last night, on Thursday.

Sitting in the hotel bar, Drew is tempted to ask Nate to pinch her, maybe give her a brisk slap across the face, if only to ensure that she's not dreaming. That, in fact, they're all here in Louisville (pronounced *Luh-uh-vul* by the locals), home to strong bourbon and fast horses. That starting this afternoon, they'll be watching the races in person. That today is Oaks Day, the precursor to tomorrow's Derby. That at this very moment, the four of them are sipping mint juleps, which taste like 98 percent whiskey and *maybe* 2 percent mint.

"I'm so glad you guys could join us," Drew says and means it sincerely. Now that she understands Graham has moved on from last week's kerfuffle, she can breathe easily. There will be no mention of it. Besides, the four of them have been friends since practically forever, since she and Nate first moved to Milton, a town about ten miles south of Boston. That was eight years ago. Leslie and Graham lived three doors down in a stunning colonial, a place they still call home.

Of course, Nate and Leslie were already friends. At Tufts, they'd been part of the same cohort, sharing a dorm their freshman year, smoking their first joint together behind Redbones, stealing the dining hall's secret stash of ice cream. The kind of silly, seemingly incidental events that forge a lifelong bond. Over the years, they'd continued to stay in touch.

Drew can still recall meeting Leslie for the first time at a Christmas party in Beacon Hill, the snow falling in big downy flakes beyond the window. She and Nate had been dating only a few months, and Leslie gushed about how wonderful it was to finally meet her. Drew decided on the spot that the two of them could never be friends. Leslie was too beautiful, too extroverted, too effervescent, too *everything*.

Afterward, Drew kept pressing Nate. *Are you sure you guys didn't date in college? Don't you think she's attractive?*

Questions that he dismissed as ridiculous. *No, we never dated. We both had serious relationships with other people in college.*

But would *you have dated if you weren't already in relationships?*

Nate shook his head. *You're not getting it. I don't see Leslie that way. I mean, yeah, she's cute, but she's like a sister to me.*

Every so often, they'd meet up with Leslie and Graham for dinner in the city, and eventually Drew found herself falling under Leslie's spell, too.

When their small condo in Somerville began to feel tight with a toddler running around, they started searching for a house farther afield, and as if by serendipity, a quaint Cape three houses down from Leslie and Graham went up for sale on Oak Drive. Leslie emailed them right away, insisting that they come check it out that weekend. She knew the owners, an older couple moving to Florida. If Drew and Nate wanted the house, Leslie was confident they could have it.

Did Drew hesitate? Maybe a little. Graham, a professor of literature, struck her as kind and funny, if a bit quirky. But she'd grown to appreciate Leslie's sense of humor, her practical approach to any problem, her generous nature (she was always gifting Drew small tokens—a silver bracelet studded with sea glass, a hand-spun pottery mug from a trip to Portugal). Would living on the same block, where it would be impossible to ignore each other, jeopardize their fledgling friendship?

Then Drew toured the charming yellow house with green trim—love at first sight. The fact that Leslie and Graham's son, Zach, was only a year younger than Owen helped cement their decision; they funneled most of their savings into a down payment. Over the years, their boys would dart back and forth between houses, sharing dinners and sleepovers, while the adults relaxed in the backyard, drinking in the languid summer nights. As far as Drew was concerned, it was the truest kind of friendship: a bond sealed in melted butter, skinned knees, barbecue sauce, and copious amounts of wine.

"Are you kidding?" Leslie responds now, nudging Drew back into the moment. "We wouldn't miss the Derby with you guys for the world."

Just then, their waitress—a young woman, maybe in her mid-twenties, with short, dark hair—materializes by their side. She's wearing a purple fascinator with peacock feathers, a nose ring, and a name tag that says MAYA. She's friendly in that Southern way, calling them *honey* and *dear*, even though they've probably got a solid fifteen years on her. Maya takes their order (four Hot Browns, the hotel's legendary turkey sandwich) and asks where they're from. When Nate mentions Boston, she shares that her cousin lives in Marblehead, then says she commutes from Jeffersonville, Indiana, every day, which requires crossing the John F. Kennedy Memorial Bridge (another Boston connection!) over the Ohio River.

When they act surprised by this, she assures them that the drive only takes fifteen minutes. "The rent is cheaper in Jeffersonville anyway," she explains. "And Louisville's too crowded for me." She gestures toward the packed room, as if she can't fathom putting down roots in a town so thoroughly steeped in tourism.

"So, wait . . . Let me get this straight," Nate says, playing the friendly tourist. "You live in Indiana, and you drive across the Ohio River so you can work in Kentucky? You're in three different states, all in one day?"

She laughs, rests a hand on her hip like she's older than she is. "Pretty much. I like to think of it as an ice-cream cone on the map. Kentucky is the base, Indiana and Ohio are the cone, and Michigan is the ice-cream scoop on top." She refills their water glasses while they ponder this.

"Huh," Leslie finally says. "I was never good at geography, but I always thought Kentucky was part of the South, not the Midwest."

"It depends on the day you're asking and *who* you're asking," replies Maya, hand back on her hip. "We consider ourselves ideologically aligned with the North—we were against slavery, you know—but our manners and pastimes are strictly Southern."

A beat of silence falls over them before Graham says, "That might be the best explanation of Kentucky culture I've heard so far. Thank you."

"You're very welcome." Maya offers a small bow before setting off for another table, seemingly pleased with herself.

"I don't know about you guys," Graham says, glancing over his shoulder, "but I think we've just been schooled." And they laugh.

When their Hot Browns arrive—turkey on Texas toast, drowning in cheesy Mornay sauce and topped with two strips of crispy bacon—Drew admits that she's been anticipating this moment almost as much as the Derby itself. The guidebooks are filled with mouthwatering descriptions of Louisville's well-known confection, and as soon as she takes a bite, she understands why: the Hot Brown is Kentucky's equivalent of a Wisconsin bratwurst, a Boston lobster, San Francisco's sourdough bread. In other words, insanely delicious.

"Okay, I'm only eating Hot Browns for the rest of the trip," Leslie declares.

"Me too." Drew talks with her mouth half-full. "Hot Browns and mint juleps . . . or maybe something not quite so strong."

"Oh, I'm in for the juleps all weekend," Nate says. "When in Louisville, do as the Louisvillians do." He pauses. "Or is it Louisvillans?"

Graham shrugs. "I have no idea. But after a few more of those"—he points to Nate's tin cup—"it won't matter."

"Right."

A handful of late risers is beginning to file into the bar for a last-minute cocktail before the buses depart for the racetrack. For more than a few, complete inebriation appears to be the day's main objective. Drew watches one woman at the far end of the bar empty a large pink cocktail into a thermos, no doubt to tide her over for the duration of the ride.

Along the back wall, a television tuned to the local news station flashes pictures of celebrities already in town for the preparties. Rumor has it that Aaron Rodgers and Patrick Mahomes will be here this year. As will Peyton Manning and local rapper Jack Harlow. Maya informs them, while refilling their water glasses, that celebrities flock to Louisville for the annual Barnstable Brown Gala, the star-studded event to attend if you want to shake hands with movie stars and sports icons.

Each year, she explains, twin sisters Patricia and Priscilla Barnstable Brown (best known for their starring roles as the "Doublemint Twins" in the 1970s ads) host the gala in their mansion on a hilltop. The event raises thousands of dollars for diabetes research every May, although Maya has no idea how a normal person would secure tickets. Drew laughs, says it's probably impossible with mere mortal dollars.

They're about to order another round of cocktails when the abrupt pinging of a spoon against a water glass travels through the room. The hotel concierge waits patiently for the guests to settle before speaking. "Ladies and gentlemen, thank you for your attention. We trust that you've been enjoying your late breakfast, or early lunch." A smattering of cheers goes up around the room.

"And I'm happy to report that our complimentary buses delivering you to the racetrack have arrived and await you out front. We'll be boarding in approximately ten minutes."

The announcement sets off a bustling of excitement, and Drew quickly shovels in her last bite of Hot Brown. If she's going to avoid getting carsick, a seat near the front of the bus will be crucial.

"Well, guys." Nate sets down his cup with a distinct bang. "I guess this is it: the real McCoy. When stuff starts to get serious. I love you all, but hey, may the best man—or woman—win at the races today."

"Hear, hear," chimes in Graham.

"Better watch out, Nate," Leslie says. "I'm a lucky woman."

"Is that right?" He cocks an eyebrow. "I have no problem with other people's good fortune, so long as it doesn't interfere with my own."

"Well, I'm here for the crazy outfits," says Drew. "Like that one." She points to a man wearing a loud madras jacket and green pants embroidered with tiny pink horses.

She refrains from mentioning the other reasons why she's here, such as to celebrate her birthday but forget her age, and to dress up like a fabulous Southern belle while ignoring the fact that, back home, her life is anything but a fairy tale.

Nate grins. "If that guy's not careful, his pants might run away without him."

Drew laughs along with everyone else at their table, but her mind is suddenly light-years away. When her eyes inadvertently dart to Graham, his gaze, like a spotlight, fastens on her.

2

GRAHAM

By the time the bus pulls away from the hotel for Churchill Downs, the passengers have struck up the kind of friendship that feels intimate in the moment but will, in all likelihood, Graham assumes, fade away like a sweet summer memory. Sitting kitty-corner from him are Betty and Joe from Tennessee, visiting Louisville for the third time. Behind them, Lisa and Derek, newlyweds here for the first time, are representing South Carolina.

And directly in front of Graham and Leslie sits a couple from Oklahoma—Benton and Trixie—who reveal that, incredibly, this weekend marks their *sixth* visit to the Derby. Graham eyes the Cartier watch circling Benton's wrist, the enormous diamond wedding ring flashing on Trixie's finger, and concludes that they're loaded. Oil money? Big Pharma? His suspicion is confirmed when Trixie, after complimenting Leslie's pink hat, recounts the lengths she went to in order to convince her milliner to create a "cotton-candy hat."

"I told him that, for the Oaks, I needed something pink, and what could be more festive than cotton candy, right?" she exclaims, leaning over her seat, the top of her hat brushing the underside of the overhead bin. Graham, who has never actually heard anyone use the word *milliner* in a sentence, nods amiably and has to agree that Trixie's milliner, whoever the poor bastard might be, outdid himself. Tufts of pink cotton rise like soft clouds above Trixie's frizzed blond hair. It's a masterpiece of ingenuity, one that manages to be festive and tacky all at once. In fact, Trixie's entire outfit—pink-and-white-striped dress, cotton-candy hat—suggests a style more in line with a candy striper than a fashion plate.

Like champagne bubbles, a general levity begins to rise in the air while the bus rumbles on toward the track. Beyond the window, however, Interstate 65 turns out to be a disappointing hodgepodge of billboards and fast-food restaurants. Graham doesn't know what he was expecting, exactly, but this wasn't it. Maybe rolling fields of bluegrass? Wild horses galloping in the distance? Instead, hovering above the treetops, a sign advertising the Expressway Church of Christ catches his eye.

"I wonder if the Expressway Church of Christ offers drive-by Communion for repentant sinners," he asks, nodding toward the window. His question prompts a laugh from Leslie, a good sign. For a moment, the idea that this trip might bring the two of them closer together seizes him.

"I'm pretty sure you mean drive-*through*," she corrects. "Drive-*bys* are for shootings."

"Oh, right. My mistake."

"Still," she says, "you have a point. Why would anyone go to an express church? It sounds like an oxymoron."

"Exactly." Graham folds his arms, vindicated. "You look nice, by the way," he says, suddenly concerned that he forgot to mention this detail back at the hotel.

"I do?" She half swivels in her seat, the brim of her hat brushing his right shoulder.

"Yes. But then, you always look nice."

A flicker of surprise darts across her face. "Thanks," she says. "I'm not sure about the hat, though. Too much?"

Graham tilts his head back and attempts an objective assessment. Maybe one too many feathers, but in general, it's a knockout, like everything else about his wife. Glamorous, hovering on ostentatious. But no, that's not the right word. *Insouciant.* That's the word he's searching for. A hat that exudes a breezy, come-what-may attitude.

It's this very quality that drew him to Leslie when he first spied her approaching the stands at the US Open fifteen years ago. Flushing Meadows, New York. The light shifting from the harshness of day to the softness of dusk. She was all legs, a physique meant for the gods, golden hair streaming down her back. Graham and his buddies couldn't believe their good luck when she and her friends made their way to the seats directly in front of them. A few drinks later, their conversation punctuated by the *thwack!* of tennis rackets, Graham learned that they both lived in Tribeca. Leslie worked in marketing, hailed from Boston, graduated from Tufts.

At the time, he was twenty-five, earning his master's in American literature at Columbia. And when he eventually landed an associate professorship at Northeastern in Boston, she offered to accompany him for the ride, as if a change of residence were as easy as switching out your shoes.

Three years later, on a mild June evening, Graham popped the question over buttery lobster. They laughed about how it took them a week of dating before either one admitted they couldn't play tennis. *And here I was worried that you'd want to volley every weekend,* Graham said. Leslie threw back her head and laughed. *Me? No way. Running is the only sport I was ever coordinated enough to do.*

A small smile plays across his lips at the memory. His life—*their lives*—seemed so flush with youth and promise then. Graham doesn't quite know how they got here, the two of them tiptoeing around each other like roommates who happen to now share a child. It's as if he's taken an exceedingly long nap and awakened to a world where everyone else has moved on. His love for Leslie used to run as deep and true as a taproot. But in the last few months (or is it years?), an iciness has edged its way into their marriage—and he's at a loss for how to fix it.

To be honest, Graham's presence in Louisville this weekend slightly mystifies him. He doesn't particularly care for horses and is averse to betting in general. Nothing good ever seems to come from wagering hard-earned money, other than losing heaps of cash. He considers horse betting a slight cut above playing the lottery at the corner store.

He's familiar with the famous Royal Ascot across the pond, held each June before the King and Queen of England, and knows about the Triple Crown, which requires that a horse win the big three American races: the Derby, the Preakness, and the Belmont. (Graham was surprised to learn that only thirteen horses have clinched the Triple Crown since the Derby's inception back in 1875.)

But he also understands that a darker side lurks beneath all the pomp and circumstance, that injuries are commonplace and that the sport can border on cruel. A couple of years ago, twelve injured horses were euthanized in connection with the Derby. *Twelve!* He's heard about the age-old practice of "bleeding" Thoroughbreds before a race, a practice that supposedly prevents the lungs from bursting when a horse runs at full speed. Nowadays, there's something called Lasix, an antibleeding drug to protect the lungs, but recently, the Derby and other Triple Crown tracks banned its use on race day. (Probably because Lasix can also encourage a horse to piss up to thirty pints of liquid, giving it an unfair advantage at the starting gate.)

And it's not unheard of for less reputable owners to run an injured horse with, say, a bruised leg, which can lead to a life-threatening injury. Yet despite the accusations of unfair treatment in the industry, the fanfare around the Kentucky Derby seems to intensify each year. Graham read somewhere that the only televised sporting event with more American viewers is the Super Bowl.

When Nate and Drew invited them back in February, Leslie instantly said yes, adding that she'd always wanted to go. Turning down the opportunity seemed rude—and perhaps shortsighted. The Derby was such a Southern institution, some might even say an *American* institution, that the professor in Graham—the inquisitive, curious side of him—found it hard to resist. The chance to watch unchecked capitalism on display at the track was nearly as tempting as a glass of hundred-proof bourbon, which, in and of itself, seemed to Graham good enough reason to go.

Of course, if he were being brutally honest with himself, Graham would admit that there's another reason why he's agreed to come along for this trip. Not to be polite, not for the "American" experience, and not for the whiskey.

A reason that's so verboten, he dare not voice it aloud.

And that motivation is none other than the woman sitting two feet away from him, so close that he could reach his hand across the aisle and touch her forearm. The woman who happens to also be Nate's wife, Leslie's dear friend. That Drew will be in close proximity to Graham for the next seventy-two hours makes him feel lightheaded and dizzy, as if he's misplaced his notes for an important lecture.

No one knows that, for months now, he's been harboring a secret crush, feeding it in small increments when the families share dinners at each other's houses one Sunday a month, as they've been doing for nearly a decade. Although those shared dinners have become even more frequent recently because Drew and Nate are renovating their kitchen, sending the entire family over to Graham and Leslie's once or twice a week.

I can't tell you how grateful we are, Drew has said on more than one occasion, usually when Graham is sliding a simple pork chop seasoned with herbs or a slice of homemade lasagna onto her plate. (One of Graham's few redeeming qualities is that he loves to cook.) *We owe you guys big-time. When our kitchen is finished, we'll have you over every night.* But all Graham could think was how lucky he was to lay eyes on Drew multiple times throughout the week.

Unlike Leslie, Drew is quiet, nurturing, armed with a gentle wit. Her entire aura radiates serenity. His wife, on the other hand, lives for the spotlight. Only when their son is involved does Leslie willingly step aside.

But Drew, he thinks. *Drew is different.* Drew will comfortably stand backstage, gladly handing out missed cues from the wings. Whenever she goes to brush her son's bangs off his forehead or bends down to talk to him so that they're eye level, Graham's heart skips out of the room. As far as he's concerned, his friend's wife plays the unsung hero in a world inhabited by far too few. Drew works with children who have special needs at their local elementary school, where she helps them wrap their fingers around pencils, teaches them how to pump their legs on a swing. That she spends her day at that job, then comes home to care for her own son, speaks to deep pools of patience, pools that Graham somedays wishes he could dive into.

A harmless crush, he tells himself. And yet, apparently powerful enough to make him shell out thousands of dollars for one precious weekend in Louisville. *Is this what having a midlife crisis is like?* he wonders. He's only forty-one, but buying a sports car or flying to Europe holds zero appeal for him. All he wants is to be in Drew's lovely, calming orbit for as long as possible.

Sometimes he swears he catches her watching him, telegraphing a hooded glance across the table or along the sidelines at the kids' various sporting events. There have been gazes held, small smiles exchanged at something either Leslie or Nate says, usually a self-aggrandizing remark. Leslie and Nate are the *doers* in their group, the list cross-off-ers, the ones who crave structure and feedback and constant admiration. And while his wife's ambition used to be one of the traits Graham admired most (she heads up the marketing department of a large cosmetic company based in Boston), these days, it more often exhausts him.

Midlife crisis or not, Graham finds himself grasping for something more. How is it, he sometimes wonders, that he and Leslie ended up together—and Nate with Drew—when really, it seems that, in a perfect universe, the reverse would be true?

Is there such a thing as the twelve-year itch? The seven-year itch, he always assumed, was about the big stuff: finances, kids, achieving a balanced share of labor in the household. But a twelve-year itch would seem to derive more from those marital misdemeanors that begin to grate on a person. For instance, Graham enjoys reading in bed with his clip-on booklight, while next to him, Leslie tosses and turns, harrumphing that she can't possibly fall asleep until it's completely dark. Or that Leslie recently remarked on how Graham consistently fails to push in his chair at the dinner table, and Graham thought, *Really? After twelve years, this is what bothers you? Why now? You'd think it would've come up sooner.*

The other day she grew upset when he returned home from a grocery run with mint chocolate chip ice cream instead of her favorite: chocolate chip. *You know I can't stand mint,* she complained. Graham could only shrug. It was an innocent-enough mistake; he'd been in a hurry and had forgotten his reading glasses. Leslie insisted that if he really cared, he'd have taken the time to double-check. It's quite possible that Graham rolled his eyes before grabbing a spoon from the cutlery drawer and shuffling off to the living room, where he enjoyed the evening news and his pint of mint ice cream alone.

I say tomayto; you say tomahto. Small, forgivable offenses in a marriage, perhaps, but after twelve years, they seem to have escalated into a never-ending tug-of-war. While his wife sits silently beside him and gazes out the Greyhound's window, Graham has the sinking feeling that the dynamic of their marriage, rather than improving, has shifted even further south. Somedays he wants to shake Leslie by the shoulders and shout, *Don't you feel it? The ship is sinking! The ship is sinking!*

Even worse is the thought that she *does* feel it . . . and doesn't give a damn.

Nate leans across Drew's lap to offer Graham his flask, which he gratefully accepts, doing his level best to avoid eye contact with Drew. He unscrews the metal top and sips, the whiskey burning a sharp path down his throat. Does his pal have any suspicion of Graham's crush?

Slim chance, but then again, Nate has been so consumed with work these past few months, he probably wouldn't notice if a golf club struck him in the head.

Of all Graham's friends, Nate is the only one to have reaped financial benefits from the pandemic: sales for a particular brand of indoor bike that he promoted—a knockoff for half the price of a Peloton—skyrocketed. But now everyone was rejoining their gyms and dragging their exercise equipment out to the curb (or selling it for a couple of bucks on eBay). With layoffs already making their way around his company, Nate worries that he could be next.

Graham understands that his friend is under a lot of pressure and has no intention of rocking Nate's marital boat. But his encounter with Drew last week has rocked him. Because he's pretty sure his secret crush no longer remains a secret to her. Well, that was silly of us! she texted later that evening. No more chocolate cake for you! Let's put it behind us, okay?

Silly? Graham thought. As if one of them had tripped accidentally or forgotten to put away the ice cream. As if they could simply pretend nothing happened. Graham didn't reply for twenty-four hours, uncertain how he felt, unclear about how best to proceed. Finally, he typed back, Okay.

Now he offers the flask to Leslie, who shakes her head. "That stuff is deadly when it's mixed with something else. No way can I sip it by itself."

"Fair enough." He indulges in one more sip, then another and another, until the singing that has started up on the bus—a rendition of "My Old Kentucky Home"—seems to improve exponentially with every mile they cover.

After a few more passes of the whiskey flask, they pull off the highway for their exit. Trixie's husband, Benton, twists around in his seat to share that they'll be sitting in Millionaires Row. "What section are you folks in?" he asks, and for a protracted beat, no one in their group answers, because what's the appropriate response? *Not Millionaires Row?*

As its esteemed name suggests, Millionaires Row houses the stadium's premier seats, situated directly above the finish line. But before Graham can begin to formulate an answer, his wife swiftly replies, "Oh, we're in Section 13. You know, the fancy-*adjacent* seats." And there it is: Leslie's enviable talent for snagging the perfect tagline from the air, the perks of her impeccably honed marketing skills. Either Benton isn't self-aware enough to know when he's being teased, or he's pretending not to understand the joke's on him.

"Section 13," Trixie says thoughtfully, her head popping up above her chair. "Isn't that right below us, honey?" Graham and Leslie briefly lock eyes, as only a married couple can, and silently parse the condescension layered into that comment. *Yes,* he thinks. *At least, figuratively speaking.*

"Not sure," offers Benton. "But I bet we'll bump into you guys at the snack bar or in the drinks line. Be sure to check out the chocolate-covered cheesecake on a stick."

"Cheesecake on a stick?" This gets Nate's attention from across the aisle. "Is that a real thing?"

"Most delicious snack at the racetrack, in my opinion," Benton confirms. "Well, aside from the mint julep, of course."

"Oh, phooey! I can't stand those juleps," Trixie protests with a dismissive wave. "Kentucky whiskey knocks me flat on my ass. No, thank you. I much prefer the Lily."

They stare back at her blankly.

"What? You guys haven't heard of the Lily?"

Graham shakes his head.

"Well, you're going to thank me later! Not a hair of whiskey in it. Just cranberry juice, vodka, a splash of triple sec, and lime. It's the specialty cocktail for Oaks Day because, you know, the winning horse's garland is woven out of Stargazer *lilies*. Lilies for the fillies. Anyway, I'm sure you'll see it everywhere once you set foot in Churchill Downs. It's mostly for the ladies." She shoots Graham a wink. "Although I'm sure men can have one, too."

"I might have to call it by another name, though," Graham jokes. "Something more masculine." He hesitates, considering. "Maybe the Manly?"

"I like that!" Trixie claps her hands together, as if it's decided. "The Manly it is!" She plops down in her seat, her hat inadvertently catching on the headrest, leaving behind a tuft of pink cotton. Graham watches the cotton flutter in the cool air blowing from the vent above and wonders if he's just tagged himself as an asshole for everyone else on the bus. Who declares a drink "the Manly" in an era when it seems nearly half his students identify as "they"?

Eventually, the bus begins to roll through a stretch of local neighborhoods in a manner that feels slightly illicit, as if they might be sneaking into Churchill Downs the back way. *Then again,* Graham thinks, *that's what we're paying for with our all-inclusive package, isn't it?* Priority access. The white-glove treatment. The chance to pretend they're rich for a few days and bypass the crowds. On the front lawns of the low-slung houses, small parties are beginning to form. A handful of revelers waves at them, pointing to homemade signs for all-day parking on their grass for fifty bucks. Graham waves back but then remembers that the bus's windows are tinted. *If a person waves behind a window but nobody sees him, does he really wave?* he thinks, invoking the old "If a tree falls in the forest . . ." adage. It's the kind of existential question that he and Drew could discuss for hours.

When the bus rounds the final corner, an enormous billboard made of red roses welcomes them to Churchill Downs. An assortment of Greyhound buses—sleek, silver bullets sweating in the Kentucky sun—is already lined up at one end of the expansive parking lot. Graham can make out the track's iconic Twin Spires in the distance, two pointy gray hats sitting on top. Seeing the Spires in person sends an unexpected thrill through him. It's like stepping into a replica of a postcard he's viewed a hundred times.

"Wow," Leslie says. "It looks exactly like it does in the pictures."

Graham shifts forward in his seat to better peek around her shoulder. "Disney World for adults."

"Ha! You're right."

And once again, he feels as if he's scored a small victory. Maybe all they've needed is a change of scenery to stoke the dwindling flames of their marriage.

As soon as their bus driver, a nice elderly man with a handlebar mustache and cowboy boots, throws the bus into Park, their fearless leader, Marcus—or, as Graham has come to think of him, their cruise director—hops up front, clipboard in hand. Dressed in a pair of bright-pink chinos, a short-sleeved white oxford, and a madras bow tie, Marcus embraces Derby fashion in a *Miami-Vice*-meets-*Love-Boat* kind of way.

"Alrighty, folks. We are officially *here*," he announces. "Welcome to Churchill Downs! A few quick things to review before you leave." And he goes on to enumerate their parking-lot number and what time the bus will be leaving later today, as well as cautions them not to lose their lanyard—their ticket in and out of the racetrack. When he wraps up, he reminds everyone to stay hydrated and discourages them from betting "the whole farm" today: "Don't forget! You've still got tomorrow to win millions." They laugh as they gather up their belongings.

Graham stands, stretches his legs, flips his hat back onto his head.

Across the aisle, Drew does the same. "I can't believe we're actually here," she tells him, her voice breathy with excitement. Beneath her enormous pink hat, her cheeks glow, as if she's just returned from a long run, and Graham can't recall her ever looking quite so lovely.

"Well, come on," she says in a faux Southern lilt, her eyes flying to his. "What are you waiting for? Let's get this show on the road."

And Graham, who moments ago was reminding himself not to be an idiot, follows behind his wife's best friend like an obedient puppy, forgetting to even ask Leslie if she has her pocketbook, her hat, herself.

3

LESLIE

As soon as they step off the bus, the Louisville heat descends like a sledgehammer. It's only 12:30 in the afternoon. *No wonder they hold the Derby in early May,* Leslie thinks. *It'd be too darn hot in June or July.* Immediately, she's grateful for her sun hat and summer dress, unlike the men who'll have to suffer through wearing long pants and jackets all day. Their group hovers near the bus for a few minutes while getting their bearings, and Graham snatches a couple of water bottles from a cooler that Marcus has thoughtfully provided. She watches while he stuffs one into each of his jacket pockets.

"Whoever said that Kentucky doesn't get hot until June lied." Nate is fanning himself with his Panama hat.

"Aww, you're getting soft, Nate. Remember all those August football practices in college?" Leslie says. "You guys were passing out from the heat."

"That's because we were running two miles on the track, followed by a hundred push-ups and sit-ups all in our pads."

"I don't know. I don't think it's so bad," Graham offers affably. "Although, why do I suddenly feel like I've stepped onto the set of the *Barbie* movie?"

Leslie scans the crowd and laughs. He isn't too far off. From every direction, a wave of pink humanity rolls toward the entrance gates.

"I love it!" Drew exclaims, clapping her hands together. "It's exactly how I imagined it would be."

"And remind me why pink is the official color for today?" Nate somersaults his hat back onto his head. "Is it because only the fillies race?"

"Not exactly," Drew corrects him. "Pink is the color of the Stargazer lily, which is the official flower of the Kentucky Oaks, just like the red rose is for the Derby." She pauses, clearly pleased to be the only one in their group to have done her homework. "And it's also meant to raise breast cancer awareness. There'll be a parade later for breast cancer survivors."

"Oh, right," Nate says, sounding only mildly interested. "Hey, check it out." He points to a stocky man, dressed in a white muscle shirt and red shorts, who's selling flip-flops in the middle of the parking lot. "Now *that's* a clever business idea."

"It explains how all these women can wear high heels to the track," remarks Drew. It's the first time that Leslie notices her friend's footwear—sensible platform sandals. "I was wondering how they were going to survive all day in stilettos. It's because they can swap them out later for flip-flops."

"Guess it's not their first rodeo," Leslie jokes.

All around them the jingle of laughter mixes with the scents of perfume, cologne, sweat, and—Leslie thinks—a hint of weed. She and Drew lock hands so as not to lose each other in the crowd, and Drew latches on to the back of Nate's jacket. Somewhere behind them, Graham follows their jumbled, makeshift conga line.

As they weave their way toward the entrance, Leslie spots a woman whose hat is topped by a mint julep cup, complete with a mint sprig and faux ice cubes. "How fantastic is that?" she asks, directing Drew's attention.

"If only it were real," Drew moans. "And why do I suddenly feel underdressed and out-hatted?"

"Yeah," Leslie, who's been thinking the same thing, agrees. "I know what you mean."

Both she and Drew spent weeks deciding on their outfits for Derby Week, and while the two of them look perfectly presentable, they may have underestimated just how seriously this crowd takes their fashion. The women, wearing mostly formfitting dresses, have put their cleavage on full display, and their hats are a cornucopia of fruits and flowers. "Do you think it's the South, or the Derby in particular?"

"I'm not sure, but everyone looks so fancy. And *tan*. How can everyone be so tan in May?" Drew demands.

Leslie shrugs. "The sun is hotter down here."

"I'd venture to say a lot of things are hotter down here," Nate jokes as they finally near the turnstiles at the entrance. Drew swats him for being fresh, but Leslie agrees. Everything *is* bigger—and somehow better. When Drew hands over her pocketbook to security, the rest of them follow along, holding up their lanyards for scanning, then collecting their belongings once they're safely through the gate.

On the other side, Leslie admires the towering white arches dripping with roses, the vibrant murals of horses, and the enormous white tents that house food vendors and stores. It's sensory overload to the nth degree. When a young man armed with a tray of cocktails passes by, Leslie stops him and helps herself to an ice-cold Lily. It tastes exactly like pink lemonade with a kick, and she quickly decides to gulp it down as if it *is* lemonade. "Trixie was right," she admits. "Definitely superior to the julep."

They begin wandering toward the tents when Graham stops abruptly. "What on God's green earth is that *smell*?"

Nate, grinning, points to a sign with a blue arrow and the word PADDOCK printed on it. "That, my friend, is the loamy scent of horses." He claps Graham on the shoulder. "Welcome to the Derby."

"Oh, Graham, don't be such a killjoy." Drew lightly punches him on the arm. "*We're* the guests here. Of course it smells like horses. What did you expect?" It's no secret that Graham was less than thrilled to dish out thousands of dollars to watch horse racing in Louisville. Leslie's husband is not a betting man, nor does he share a particular interest in animals. A city boy who grew up navigating Manhattan's street grid, he's as easily spooked by a dormouse as a bull. But Leslie practically begged him, arguing that maybe this trip was the very thing they needed to break them out of their rut (even though she secretly believes they're stuck in their own individual ruts).

Honestly, Leslie doesn't know how much longer she can sustain the manner in which they've been living. She spends sixty hours a week working while simultaneously raising a ten-year-old boy (with little to no help from Graham). Graham, meanwhile, seems to think she can balance all her responsibilities and also keep their marriage as fresh and affectionate as it was twelve years ago. *But things change,* she tries to explain. *Life changes.* Sometimes she feels as if she's on a runway, waving those orange air-traffic batons, signaling for him to take a hard right before they collide . . . and Leslie explodes.

She will tell him later. *Not now,* she thinks. *Of course not now.*

They fall in line behind Nate, who, like the right tackle he played in college, cuts a path to the escalators. Their lanyards get scanned a second time before they're allowed up to the next level, where their seats are. Stepping off the escalator, Graham instantly gestures to a nearby bar with bottles of golden whiskey lining the shelves.

"So." His tongue makes a clicking noise. "This is how the other half lives. I've always wondered."

"Buddy," Nate says. "This weekend we *are* the other half." And they share a laugh.

Their group passes through a large room that could double as a banquet hall, Leslie's heels making sucking sounds against the already sticky floor. Around the corner, a long line snakes from the betting window, and Nate holds his phone aloft with a triumphant grin. Earlier this morning, he helped them all download the electronic betting app TwinSpires. *This is gonna save us light-years of time,* he explained. *It's the easiest way to place bets. No standing in line at the window.*

It all sounded perfectly innocent and efficient at the time, but now Leslie hopes for Drew's sake that it's not *too* efficient. They haven't discussed Nate's gambling "problem" of late, but Leslie senses an undercurrent of tension already. Drew's husband clearly has his sights set on winning big this weekend.

As soon as they set foot in the stands, the air hums with excitement. Leslie has heard that the worst behavior happens on the infield (where tickets are significantly cheaper), but there seems to be no shortage of bad behavior up here. More than a few spectators appear plenty sloshed already. One guy whistles at her, then sees she's with Graham and apologizes profusely. *Oh. Sorry, man. No offense. I didn't know you two were together.* Graham brushes him off like a pesky fly.

Catcalls may be par for the course, but Leslie doesn't imagine anyone will be running naked across the tops of the Porta Potties in the club-seating section. That special trick is reserved for the infield, or so she's heard. Nate presses on while the rest of them follow and dodge spilled-drink puddles as best they can.

At last, Nate comes to a complete stop. "Here we are."

He gestures expansively, as if he's offering up the entire racetrack to them, which he kind of is. Their section, well above the bleacher seats, sits maybe twenty to thirty rows up. And in a stroke of good luck (or more likely, excellent planning by Nate), they're situated right before the first turn. Short of the finish line, it may well be the best view in the arena.

"Wow," Drew says, echoing everyone's thoughts. "This is amazing, honey."

Below them, the infield unfurls like a bright-green blanket, and the sky above is a brilliant slate of blue. A tractor works to smooth the dirt along the front stretch of the track for the next race. Down near the starting gate sits the bugler's pagoda, a white tower that shoots up like a slender finger. A curved walkway, shaped like a horseshoe, fronts the tower along with a lush garden of red roses. In the background, Leslie can just make out the outline of the University of Kentucky's football stadium.

Drew leans over to peck Nate on the cheek. "Well done."

"Glad you approve, Birthday Girl."

"Yeah, fantastic view. Not bad at all for 'fancy-adjacent' seats," Graham chimes in. "I wonder if we can wave to Trixie and Benton in Millionaires Row from here?" But when they swivel around to stare upward, it's evident that the truly expensive seats reside in a world of their own, a sheet of glass separating them from the rest of the grandstand.

As for their own "box," it's not so much a box as a raised cement block with six green folding chairs. A waist-high green bar delineates each box's perimeter. Although their seats aren't protected by a canopy per se, the shadow cast by the canopy behind them offers a sliver of shade. Specifically, over the last two chairs in their box, where a couple of plump, older women—complete strangers—already sit.

"Hello, there!" The younger one with a mop of dark, curly hair holds out her hand, and Graham, ever the gentleman, rushes to shake it. "I'm Betsy, and this is my mother, Della. We're from Minnesota. The Derby has been on my mom's bucket list for years, so here we are," she rambles on, as if in a rush to hand over all their pertinent information.

"Well, isn't that wonderful?" replies Graham before adding, "We four are from Boston," then proceeds to make introductions.

Both mother and daughter are wearing wide-brim hats, pink satin bows woven around the crown. "Hope you don't mind that we took the two shady seats. I'm eighty-two and sensitive to the heat," says the woman introduced as Della.

"Not at all," Drew replies magnanimously. "You're exactly where you should be."

Betsy quickly informs their group that she's also a breast cancer survivor, and although she wasn't chosen to march in the Survivors Parade today, she wanted to come watch. "Did you know that the number of women who march matches the number of the Derby year?"

"I did not," Graham acknowledges.

"So that means there'll be one hundred and fifty-one survivors on the field today."

"Outstanding."

Somewhere around this point, Leslie begins to tune out their conversation. Not because she doesn't support breast cancer awareness or its survivors, but because she doesn't feel like engaging in small talk with strangers. She came to the Derby to be with *her* people, not to make new friends. *And where is the drinks guy, anyway?* She plops down in the chair beside Nate.

"This is really fantastic, Nate. You've outdone yourself."

"Thanks. I wanted it to be, you know, special for Drew."

"Aww . . . You really are a softy, aren't you? All that tough-guy bravado in college was only a front."

He grins. "Don't tell anyone." There's a beat of silence before he asks, "So, which horse are you betting on for the Oaks?"

Leslie opens her program with fanfare and peruses the roster. "Let's see." There's a total of thirteen different races today. They've already missed the first few, but the big one, the Oaks, isn't for another few hours. Her thumb travels down the list of names and stops on a horse called Amendment Nineteen.

"There she is," Leslie says. "Amendment Nineteen. That's my girl."

"You sure about that?" Nate presses, scanning the program. "Thirty-to-one odds?"

"Yup. It's all about the name. It has to speak to me." She shoots him her best appraising look. "I bet you don't even remember what the Nineteenth Amendment was for."

"And you do?" he teases.

"Of course I do! The Nineteenth Amendment gave women the right to vote. Some of us went to class, you know." She will never tire of giving Nate a hard time about the fact that he barely passed his courses, while she graduated summa cum laude. How many times had he asked Leslie for her notes before finals? How many times had she bailed him out on a paper? *You know, Stephanie should really be helping you with this,* she'd tell him, referring to his girlfriend at the time. *I don't know why I'm the one you always bug.*

And Nate would shoot her one of those smug grins and say, *Because you're the smartest girl I know. And you get a case of beer for all your hard work.*

Now she pulls up the app on her phone, places her bet while Nate looks on.

"Fifty bucks? That's all you're willing to bet on women's rights?"

"Don't get carried away," she fires back. "It's just a horse."

Nate shrugs. "Suit yourself."

"What about you? When are you planning on telling us your pick?"

"In due time."

"Why so secretive, Nate? Do you know something the rest of us don't?" She's goading him on.

But he doesn't bite, only lifts his shoulders noncommittally. "Oh, look. There's a guy with an entire tray of Lilies. You wanted another one, right?"

"Yeah. How did you know?"

"Easy. Because you tossed your cup out a few minutes ago."

Leslie smiles. "So you *are* smart about a few things."

Nate calls the vendor over. "I live to surprise you."

For all Leslie knows, Graham hasn't even noticed that she's sitting directly in front of him, he's been so busy talking with Drew and their new friends. It's nice to have Nate looking out for her; it feels comfortable, familiar. She thinks of all the times he helped her back to their dorm after they'd gotten plastered at some party. How he told her he felt like her big brother, and how safe that made her feel. Protected.

Behind them, there's a loud, booming laugh. Graham.

Leslie sighs. *I will tell him later,* she thinks. *Not now. Later.*

AGAINST ALL ODDS

4

DREW

Drew has been studying the playbook, if that's what you can call the spread in the program. She figures she might as well learn *something* about betting and horses while she's here. So far, she's lost three bets and won one. Not exactly an enviable record, but she feels as if she might be closing in on some markers for what makes a great horse—or more specifically, what makes for a good race. The official program suggests reviewing the highest average speed for any horse against the highest average speed of the other horses racing. Supposedly, the horse with the highest average should win. There's also something called a "prime power," which factors in multiple features (speed, distance, form, etc.). The highest prime power can also predict a winner.

But unless Drew's calculations are off—which, she admits, is entirely possible, given that she's forgotten how many Lilies she's consumed now that it's 3:30 in the afternoon—there seem to be other, more loosey-goosey variables. For instance, if the horse has been racing frequently in the past few months, it might not be fully rested. If the horse has traveled from afar, it might be jet-lagged. (She was surprised to learn that horses get jet-lagged, too.)

And then there was the matter of being hungry enough to *want* to win. If a horse had only *placed* but hadn't actually won a race before, did that translate into its wanting victory more badly than the others? And what about the jockey? Drew used to assume that selecting a jockey was a matter of picking one with the appropriate experience and weigh-in requirements. But she's beginning to discern a certain pattern in horses run by particular jockeys. (Again, she was surprised to learn that jockeys often race multiple horses throughout the course of a day.)

Horse betting, it turns out, is a strange alchemy, which if stirred just right could result in a winner. For instance, she's noticed that Guillermo Vázquez has consistently placed in his races, even when riding horses who weren't supposed to place. In fact, the top horses with the highest prime power rarely seem to be winning; only in one race, so far, has the horse with the highest number won. More often than not, it's the filly with the second-best prime power—and a handful of times, a horse that hasn't even been mentioned—that wins. It's those horses, the long shots, with 15–1 odds, or even 30–1, that interest her the most, especially if a jockey whose name Drew has learned to recognize is riding them.

"This one," she says, pointing to a name in the program: Handmaid's Tail. After various snacks and bathroom runs, she and Leslie have traded seats so that they're now sitting next to their respective spouses. Drew has taken over the other front-row seat in their box. "This is the one I want for the Oaks," she reveals. "She's going to win big."

"Oh, yeah?" Nate says around his cigar. "Spoken with the confidence of someone who's had a few cocktails." Drew laughs. "Seriously, what makes you think that?" he asks. His lips push out round, smoky O's, sending them drifting lazily through the air.

She appreciates that he's considerate enough to blow smoke in the opposite direction, away from her, and most especially, away from the grandmother, Della. Nate isn't typically a cigar smoker, but when offered one (as he was by a complete stranger today), he'll happily oblige.

"She's placed second in every race except one, and she's hasn't raced in two months, which means she should be fully rested."

"Also might mean she's coming off an injury."

"I don't think so." Drew shakes her head as if she knows what she's talking about. "I think it means she's well rested and ready for blood."

He laughs easily. "Okay, then."

"Hey, I got it right once before." She rubs her thumb against two fingers to indicate the forty bucks she collected a few races ago. "I think I'm getting the hang of this betting stuff. And I like the name. It's clever—just like the book."

"Well, I, for one, like how much you're enjoying your birthday trip." He scans the odds. "Twenty to one, huh?"

"Another reason I like her," Drew explains. "Always root for the underdog; sometimes they surprise you, and when they do, the victory is even sweeter."

"Kind of how you got me, huh? The underdog?"

"Oh, honey, no," Drew says, instinctively grabbing his hand. "You've always been a catch." She hesitates for a second. Should she say more? Like how he's always been handsome and athletic, but lately his obsession with work has made him a bear to live with? How she feels like she never sees him anymore? He's either at work or off to the casino. That she's pretty sure Owen's acting up at school lately has to do with the fact that he's been missing his dad? They used to play catch all the time, go to the batting cages in the winter, watch funny movies together. Drew sees their son playing video games by himself, the seat next to him on the couch empty. Her husband is under incredible pressure; she understands that. But what's the point of driving himself crazy at work if he can't even reap the benefits of spending time with his family?

At that moment, the starting gates blast open, causing them both to jump. It's a smaller race, the stakes not as high as the Oaks. Drew has already picked Haley's Comet for the win, although she didn't put any money down. In her mind, it's a test run. A chance to see if she can actually tag the winner. The announcer's voice booms over the loudspeaker as the horses round the first turn, then thunder down the backstretch. By the time they hit the final turn, Haley's

Comet has moved up to third. Drew jumps to her feet, cheering, "Go, Haley! Run!"

The horse pulls into second, and Nate joins her on his feet. For a split second, it seems as if Haley's Comet might actually win, fighting to close the distance between herself and the filly in first, Morning Dove. But in the last gasp toward the finish line, the other horse digs deep, leaving Haley's Comet behind by a length.

Second place. Drew drops into her chair.

"Wow, I really thought you had that one," Nate says. "Did you bet on her? I don't remember."

"No. I was testing my theory. All the predictors I look for said she'd win."

Nate flashes a grin.

"What?"

"Nothing. Just that my wife is becoming an expert at horse racing."

"Not an expert. But I am learning a lot. Anyway," she says and pulls out her phone, "I'm still putting my money on Handmaid's Tail for the Oaks." She taps a few buttons before proclaiming, "There. Done."

"How does the old adage go?" Nate asks. "'The more you think you know, the less you really do?' Something like that."

"Yeah. I should probably just stick to my hunches. When you come down to it, it's all about luck, right?"

He reaches out and winds a strand of hair behind her ear—difficult to do, given her enormous hat, but he manages somehow. "It's always about luck, sweetie. And you," Nate says softly, "are my lucky charm."

It may be the nicest thing he's said to her all week, and Drew, unsure if the sentiment is true or if the cocktails are responsible, feels a rush of warmth ride up over her chest because she so wants to believe him.

~

When her stomach starts to rumble, she decides to go in search of the legendary cheesecake on a stick. Doing so requires sidestepping any number of people who are, to put it kindly, less than sober. It's not that everyone is drunk at the Oaks, but those who are stand out the most. Such as the gentleman who's trying to walk a straight line with a drink cup on his head (he makes it about two feet). Or the young woman who's clutching her girlfriend's arm, saying she needs to find a bathroom *pronto*.

Drew is almost to the dessert booth when she notices that the lines for the betting windows have shrunk to a handful of people. It occurs to her that an old-fashioned paper ticket would be a nice souvenir, and this might be her best chance. Why not place her bet for tomorrow's Derby race right now?

She joins the line behind two older men who reek of cigar smoke. In fact, most of the people in line appear to be men, making her wonder if the betting window represents the last bastion of sexism at the races. Are women too afraid, too uninformed, to make their own bets?

But no, she realizes that there are plenty of other threads of sexism woven throughout the sport. Such as the jockeys who are predominantly men, as well as the owners and the trainers. A quick search on her phone reveals that the first woman to ride in the Kentucky Derby, Diane Crump, had to sue to do so, and that was in 1970. To date, only six women have been riders in the Kentucky Derby's 150-plus years. In 2023, Jena Antonucci was the first female trainer to win the Belmont Stakes race (or any Triple Crown race, for that matter). Drew reads about another woman, Ferrin Peterson, an accomplished jockey and veterinarian, who hopes to soon boost that dismal number to seven female jockeys who've raced in the Derby.

"Can I help you?"

Drew startles, her focus shifting from the *Lexington Herald-Leader* article she's been reading. "Oh, sorry. Yes, um, I hope I'm doing this right." The woman on the other side of the window smiles at her encouragingly. "I'd like to bet on Race 12 for tomorrow, one hundred dollars to win on Number 9. Please. That's the Derby, right?"

"Yes, it is." The teller taps it in, and a short white slip of paper spits out of the machine. She hands it to Drew. "Good luck."

"Thank you." Drew double-checks the numbers, then slips the ticket in between the pages of her program as a bookmark and experiences a slight thrill. Is this how Nate feels whenever he spends those late nights out at the casino on the weekends, sometimes not turning in to bed until two or three in the morning? A flicker in her—but just a flicker—hints at the allure of gambling, how intoxicating it must be, if every time you purchased a ticket, you thought yours was the Wonka Bar hiding the prize inside.

"Sure thing. Next?" The teller has already moved on to the gentleman behind her.

Making her way back to their section, Drew realizes halfway there that she's completely forgotten about the cheesecake skewers. And Nate specifically asked for one. She owes him at least that much after all the work he's put into planning this trip. And while she's been worried that the Derby might spell disaster for his gambling predilection, nothing so far has set off her radar. His bets have been modest, conservative, almost as if he knows she's keeping an eye on him.

Don't do anything too crazy, okay? she instructed on the ride over to the track, trying to tread the line between a stern warning and a flirtatious suggestion.

At the track, or with you? he replied, prompting her to grin.

You know what I mean. Let's not bet our entire life savings at the Derby. I'd like Owen to go to college someday, she joked.

Not to worry. Besides, I already spent our life savings on our seats.

She rolled her eyes. *Oh, that's comforting.*

Nate reached over and squeezed her hand. *Honey, don't worry so much. This is your birthday weekend, remember?*

She did remember. Which was why it was so critical that he didn't do something stupid and ruin the entire trip.

His weekend outings to the casino, she understands, are as much a chance for him to unwind and blow off steam as they are to win some extra cash. That he loves the ambience—the bravado, the smoky spaces, the pinging of slot machines, the rumble of dice hitting the roulette table—as much as she enjoys going to the movies for the popcorn and licorice makes sense. Plus, Nate has always been good at reining himself in, stopping before he loses too much.

But a few weeks ago, a stack of vinyl records appeared on the kitchen counter, and when she asked about them, he quickly explained them away.

These old things? They're not worth much. Just trying to make some space in our home office. Selling a few on eBay.

His albums, all carefully preserved in their jackets, occupied five solid shelves in the smallish corner room, but they were his keepsakes, each one tagged with a specific memory. *I listened to this song about a million times after my first girlfriend dumped me,* he said of Jimi Hendrix's "The Wind Cries Mary." Well-known bands—U2, Pearl Jam, the Beastie Boys, and Pink Floyd—sat next to lesser-known albums by Sloan (*Twice Removed*) and Screaming Trees. Nate's taste in music was varied and eclectic. Once, he confided that his Miles Davis album *Kind of Blue* was probably worth a thousand bucks.

Someday, Nate told Owen, *these will all be yours. You'll have to take very good care of them because they'll probably be worth a lot of money.* And Owen had nodded his head very seriously, as if his father were entrusting him with national security secrets.

Back in the kitchen later that afternoon, she put the question to Nate when they were alone: *Is everything okay?*

What? With us?

Yeah, I guess. I mean, we're okay moneywise? They kept separate checking accounts, but Nate's account was where the bulk of their money went—his salary, their tax refunds, any generous gifts from his parents—and from where the bulk of their expenses got paid electronically. Drew's paycheck deposited directly into her own account, but once groceries and any Owen-related expenses (clothing, sports equipment, dentist's and doctors' appointments, birthday parties, etc.) were accounted for, it ended up essentially being a draw.

Nate came up behind her and wrapped his arms around her waist. *Of course we're okay. We're going to the Derby in three weeks. How can we not be okay?*

He has a point, she thought. Nevertheless, she checked the balance on their savings account, which they shared, to be certain. There was roughly five grand, the same as last time she'd looked. Enough to cover any small emergencies. And who was she to tell her husband not to gamble? She wasn't his mother. So long as he played smart, everything would be fine.

And Nate is *being smart about it,* she tells herself now, pushing her way through the crowd and calculating how many cheesecake skewers she can carry at once. Four? Six? She hopes they're as delicious as Benton advertised. But by the time she finally reaches the booth, all the skewers are sold out, and rather than wait for another, surely inferior, dessert, she decides to head back to her seat, empty-handed, her stomach still growling.

5

LESLIE AND GRAHAM

Southerners are unfailingly polite, Leslie thinks as she waits in line for a pretzel; she could give them that. A lot of *sir*s and *ma'am*s and *honey*s flying around at the Derby. But beneath the sweetness, she detects a subtle vein of judgment, a feeling that the locals are masking their true thoughts, just as they disguise their iced tea's bitterness with sugar. Leslie is accustomed to Bostonians calling out jaywalkers and blasting their horns at slow drivers. But at least Bostonians were transparent— some might say rude—with their criticism. The Southern way, she thinks, muddies the waters, demands puzzling out whether you're being complimented or insulted.

It puts an outsider on edge.

While she waits for food (ten minutes so far), a man a few people ahead sneezes loudly, and the line physically recoils, reshaping itself. Someone says, "Gesundheit," and someone else offers, "God bless you." Both sound sincere, although she's been warned that around here, "Bless your heart" most often means *You poor thing,* or *Aren't you dumb as a post?* As in, an insult, not a blessing. *Is* God bless you *the same?* she wonders. She sighs. A dictionary complete with translations of Southern idioms would be useful right about now. That's when she notices the young man behind her, probably late twenties, smiling at her.

"Let me guess: You're not from around here, right?"

Leslie hesitates before responding but can't summon a good reason not to. "Yeah. Is it that obvious? I was kind of hoping I fit in with everyone else."

"Oh, no worries. You do. Absolutely. But I heard you talking with the woman ahead of you earlier, and I definitely detected an accent."

"Ah." She smiles. "Got me. I'm from Boston—or the Boston area, I should say."

"Uh-oh," he replies, and Leslie feels her brow crease with confusion. "Uh-oh?"

"That means you're a Red Sox fan."

"Oh, no, not really. Well, my husband is, I guess, but I'm not really into sports." Is it her imagination, or did the guy's face fall just a smidge at the mention of a husband?

"Phew," he says. "I guess that means we aren't mortal enemies after all."

Leslie laughs. "What about you? Where are you from? You're local, I presume?"

He shrugs, hands in his pockets. "Is it that obvious?"

"You've got an accent yourself."

"Yeah, grew up in Louisville, went to the U of Louisville, and now I'm a lawyer, the profession everyone loves to hate."

"Well, then, I guess we can't be friends after all."

"I knew it. You hate lawyers."

"Not necessarily," Leslie says, wondering why men in general feel compelled to reveal their occupation in the first few minutes of meeting someone.

He frowns. "Is it because I live too far away from Boston, then? I can always move, you know." Which summons a laugh from her. Is this boy, who's probably ten to fifteen years her junior, hitting on her?

"Some lawyers actually do good in the world. Are you one of those?" She hooks a skeptical eyebrow, wondering if he'll admit to selling out to the corporate world or tell her about the one time he argued a pro bono case.

"I wish I could tell you I do good. I work in estates, drawing up wills, that kind of thing. Not very interesting, I'm afraid." His eyes are the most gorgeous brilliant blue, and she finds it difficult to stop staring.

"That counts as helpful, at least. I mean, everyone needs a will, right?"

"Exactly." When he smiles, his teeth are staggeringly white.

It's been so long since she's flirted that she almost doesn't recognize the feeling when her heart rate speeds up. If she doesn't get some real food in her stomach soon, she'll be in danger of passing out. *Do pretzels count?* she wonders. *Yes, yes, they most definitely do.* Unfortunately, the exact number of cocktails she's procured so far today remains hazy. Three? Four? Five?? How many pretzels would it take to counteract all that alcohol? She decides she doesn't know and doesn't care.

They've nearly reached the front of the line when Lawyer Boy says, "So, where are you sitting?" A bold, bordering on brazen, question.

"Oh, you know, somewhere over there." Leslie gestures vaguely, noncommittally.

"Okay?" It's obvious he's trying to read her, but she honestly doesn't know how she wants to be read. As an open book? A closed book? A partially open book? She's flattered by the attention, naturally, but she didn't come to the Derby to meet someone. Still, the thought of revealing exactly where her seat is so that Lawyer Boy can drop by and make Graham jealous is appealing.

The guy shrugs as if it's no loss to him. "Well, it was nice talking to you . . ." His voice trails off, waiting for her to fill in a name.

"Leslie," she supplies.

"Leslie," he says, his face suddenly brightening. "That's my little sister's name."

At the mention of a "little" sister, she feels herself aging twenty years in front of him. Exactly how old *is* he?

Then he adds, "Well, not so little anymore, I guess. She's twenty-three. I'm Jackson, by the way."

"Nice to meet you, Jackson." Leslie's trying to calculate how old that would make him—at least twenty-five or twenty-six? His parents probably waited a few years before having another. But before she can inquire, a girl behind the counter wearing a cherry-striped hat asks if Leslie prefers a salted or unsalted pretzel, and would she like mustard?

"Salted, please, and yes to mustard." The pretzel is still warm in the wax paper when the girl hands it over. "You're up," she tells Jackson, turning to go. He offers a small wave, which probably means nothing. And yet . . .

As she wanders back to her seat, replaying the interaction in her head, Leslie does a double take near the bar area. Off to one corner, she spies a familiar pink seersucker suit and a Panama straw hat. She's about to go over and instruct Nate to grab her another cocktail while he's in line but then stops abruptly. Because Nate is talking to a stunning woman—straight, dark hair; deeply tanned; a *very* fitted pink dress; and an enormous hat that's sprouting what appear to be giant swan feathers. A true Southern belle. Is Nate *flirting* with her?

But then she chides herself. *I was doing the same thing myself a minute ago. Probably just a friendly conversation.* The woman lifts her phone so that Nate can see it better, and Leslie watches him tap something into his own cell. Perhaps a dinner recommendation for tomorrow night? A popular place to go dancing later? She decides not to interrupt their little exchange. It'll be easy enough to get the details later. Because no way would Nate have the audacity to hit on someone—a complete stranger, no less—on Derby weekend, a weekend that's a birthday gift to his wife.

As she pilots herself to their section, an older woman bumps into Leslie with a sharp, bony elbow—hard. An accusing look flies from Leslie's eyes; she's pretty certain the jab was intentional. It's so crowded, though, it's difficult to be certain. Before she can say anything, the woman smiles disarmingly and remarks, "Oh, bless your heart. Don't you look pretty?" And the vicious words Leslie was about to mutter a second ago tumble back down her throat, where she swallows them like a fork.

Compliment or insult? She'll never know.

~

Behind the bar are shelves lined with golden bottles. There's Maker's Mark, Jim Beam, Wild Turkey, Woodford Reserve, Evan Williams, and something called Knob Creek. When Graham inquires how much a bottle goes for, the bartender, whose name tag reads STU, replies anywhere from $100 to $500, causing Graham to gulp so deeply he's convinced Stu can make out his Adam's apple.

"Might sound like a lot, but Kentucky bourbon is hands down the best. You'll see."

Graham observes while Stu begins mixing a mint julep and thinks to himself, *Highway robbery!* But today's whiskey is free, at least in the sense that their "Derby package" already covers it.

"It's the limestone," Stu explains, leaning in as if he might be divulging a well-guarded local secret. "Kentucky water runs across limestone, and the limestone absorbs the iron. Otherwise, the iron in the water can give the bourbon a bitter taste. Limestone's calcium and magnesium get diffused in the distillery water, too. It's what gives Kentucky bourbon its smooth, rich flavor. Trust me, it's the best."

"You've convinced me," Graham says simply.

There's a certain flair to Stu's motions as he works at his craft, muddling the mint in the bottom of a large metal cup, straining out the leaves. "So you don't get any green stuff stuck in your teeth," he explains. Next comes the simple syrup and then the bourbon, followed by copious amounts of crushed ice in a copper cup. Stu stirs the julep with a swizzle stick, "to help the bourbon breathe," before topping it off with more ice and a fresh sprig of mint.

He sets it before Graham, who slides a few bucks into his tip cup. "Thank you, sir."

"Well?" Stu stares at him. "Aren't you going to taste it?"

"Oh, right. Sure thing." Graham takes a generous sip and swallows the tickling sensation at the back of his throat as the whiskey travels down.

"That'll put some hair on your chest, huh?"

"You bet. I'll be a gorilla by the time I'm done with this." He thanks Stu again and grabs a seat farther down the bar. He's not quite ready to head back to the stands—needs a moment to clear his head, figure out what, exactly, is the situation between Drew and himself.

He was watching them together, Drew and Nate, just before he stepped away for a drink. From behind, Graham noticed the way Drew's body leaned in toward Nate's. The way they laughed together when Nate casually threw an arm around her after stubbing out his cigar in an empty cup. The way Drew's face lit up whenever she spoke to him. There was a lightness there that had been missing the night she showed up at his front door a few months ago. A night when she needed someone to talk to, and only Graham was available. The disappointment on her face when he, not Leslie, answered the door was evident, but he won Drew over, ushering her into the living room, opening the bottle of wine she'd brought, and pouring them each a glass. He could tell she'd had a hell of a day—or, at least, that something was off.

While he sat across from her in the living room, the dusk light spilling through the window, he'd been struck by her loveliness . . . and by how fragile she seemed. Usually, whenever the four of them were together, Drew and Leslie would talk like sisters, their voices rising and falling, cackling, teasing, whispering. But his simple question to Drew that night—*What's new?*—unleashed a torrent of tears, a stream of words that didn't make much sense. He caught a mention of her birthday, about how she'd been feeling down, and Nate was stressed about work, so she couldn't unload on him. She kept apologizing.

"I'm so sorry to be a basket case, especially on your night alone, your one chance to read your book in peace and quiet."

"Nonsense," he said and got up to fetch a glass of water, then gently pushed her wine goblet aside. Got her to slow her breathing and handed her a box of tissues. "Did something in particular happen?" he asked.

She shook her head. *No.* "I've just been feeling so blah lately. I don't know why, exactly. But I'm worried about Nate. He's been going out a lot with the guys to the casino. And Owen misses him. I'm pretty sure it's why he's been acting up at school. It's just . . . a lot."

Graham nodded, dragged his chair across the Oriental rug, closer to hers. He distinctly remembered a time when Leslie would come to him with her problems. Was Zach developing the way he should be? Why were her clients always so demanding and oftentimes rude? When would she lose the baby weight? Why was the world so messed up? They would talk for hours after Zach crawled into bed, and usually, by the end, both of them were in a better space. Once upon a time, they'd propped each other up.

That night, he understood that Drew wasn't seeking *him*, per se, but someone to listen. Graham just happened to be in the right place at the right time.

After maybe an hour, she stood, blew her nose, and announced that she was feeling much better. "Thank you for listening, Graham. You're a good friend."

And he walked her to the door while saying, "Sure, yes, of course. Anytime."

He didn't mention it to Leslie, felt as if it would be a betrayal of Drew's trust. Figured if she wanted to open up to Leslie herself, she would. But as February gave way to March and March to April, Graham came to look forward to the Sunday-night dinners when Nate and Drew and Owen would come over, or vice versa. Invariably, the boys would retreat to the basement to play knee hockey or video games, and Leslie and Nate would bow out, saying they had to get up early for work. It left Graham and Drew alone, usually with a half-finished bottle of wine sitting between them.

Sometimes they'd talk about their boys, other times about how emotionally taxing Drew's job could be. Graham might entertain her with a story about something foolish one of his students did, such as writing an entire paper about Ernest Hemingway's *The Sun Also Rises* while citing the author throughout as William Faulkner. She mentioned that Nate was still ducking out to the casino but that anytime she confronted him about it, he'd blow her off . . . or grow angry. How Graham longed to tell her that he and Leslie were having problems, too! That when he climbed into bed at night, she rolled away from him. That they were amicable enough, especially around Zach, but their relationship felt more like a neighborly arrangement these days, one that could shift at any moment. Maybe the fact that he was loyal to a fault kept him from saying anything. Or maybe it was because he assumed Drew already knew—that Leslie had confided in her—and his complaints would come across as a husband's sour grapes.

Was it on those evenings while they talked that his crush first took root? He'd always thought of Drew as attractive, but not in *that* way. She was his wife's friend! But the more they talked, the more their similar personalities, their alike dispositions, became apparent. Drew was thoughtful, kind, a good listener. And clever. Oh, so clever! There were glimpses of it when the four of them got together, naturally, but Nate's presence somehow always seemed to dwarf Drew's (probably much in the same manner that Leslie's dwarfed Graham's). Being married to someone larger than life often meant being diminished by their light.

Gradually, their talks became more frequent, extending to the occasional weeknight. Drew would appear at his door, sometimes with Owen by her side, and ask if they might come in for a few minutes. The last few weeks, Leslie had been managing an important account at work, rarely arriving home before nine or ten o'clock. Graham was glad for Drew's company. It wasn't as if they were doing anything illicit—the kids were downstairs!

A few times, Leslie came through the front door when Drew was still there. She'd raise an eyebrow at the wine uncorked, their glasses full.

Is there a party that you two forgot to tell me about? she would tease. And although the whole exchange was perfectly innocent, his wife's presence threw a certain shade over the room. One night after Drew and Owen had gone home, Leslie asked, *You're not trying to steal my friend, are you?*

And Graham laughed. *Of course not.*

But later he wondered if that was precisely what he was doing.

As he makes his way back to his seat, he thinks of Nate and Drew together earlier today, how happy and content Drew seemed by Nate's side. Is it possible that Graham has been projecting his own unhappiness onto Drew's marriage? That he's taken her words, her confidences, and spun them into a much larger, nonexistent problem?

~

"Oh, good. You're back just in time," Betsy says when he returns to his seat. "The Survivors Parade is about to start." Graham has to look twice because she's holding an honest-to-goodness Kodak Printomatic Instant Print Camera, ready to capture the moment. He's always assumed that, with the advent of cell phones, such gadgets had gone the way of the dinosaurs. Apparently not.

"I'm glad." He refrains from commenting on the camera. "I didn't want to miss it. Especially when we have the honor of sharing our box seats with a survivor herself."

"Thank you, Graham. I appreciate your saying that." In the last few hours, he and Betsy have grown surprisingly close while discussing a wide range of topics, including cancer treatment; pickleball; *The Grapes of Wrath*; and the Mall of America, one of the highlights—if not the only—in Bloomington, Minnesota, in Graham's humble opinion. (He visited several years ago for a friend's bachelor party, and it ended with the groomsmen and groom jumping into the wishing fountain before the mall police booted them out.)

"My mom was there with me every step of the way," says Betsy, and Della, tough cookie that she appears to be, rolls her eyes underneath her tufted pink hat. "I know you hate to admit it, Ma, but you were," Betsy insists. "You were there for me through all the awful chemo and trips to radiation. You were my rock."

And much to Graham's surprise—and delight—the formidable Della suddenly begins to melt before them, dotting the corners of her eyes with a napkin. "Okay, okay. That's enough. It was a difficult time; you're right. But it's behind us now, honey." She reaches over to squeeze her daughter's hand.

"She's really a softy on the inside," Betsy whispers, patting her mother's powder-white hand. "Even if she likes to pretend that she's a tough old broad."

"Stop," Della scolds, but it's obvious that her daughter's character assessment pleases her.

"Hey, look! The parade's starting."

Graham turns his attention to a group of women gathered down on the infield near the bugler's pagoda. "My goodness, that's a lot of pink, isn't it?" he says, not meaning to sound judgmental but never having witnessed anything quite like it before.

The marchers have organized themselves into two lines, each one fronted by a banner that reads 2025. As they begin to march forward, they wave their lilies in the air and hoist signs declaring their number of cancer-free years. Beside each survivor, the announcer explains, walks a sponsor, the person who helped them through their journey. A few warriors, still weak from treatment perhaps, grip their sponsors' arms as they make their way down the field.

It's a touching ceremony, impossible not to be moved by the valiant show of courage and strength on this gorgeous, albeit hot, spring day. For a brief window of time, horse racing, betting, and fashion all take a back seat at Churchill Downs, and the crowd breaks into applause, then a standing ovation. Across the wide digital screen on the field, known as the Big Board, the marchers' faces, beaming and defiant, flash back at the grandstand. If Graham didn't fully understand this morning why wearing pink on Oaks Day was such a heralded tradition, he does now.

He turns to offer Betsy his personal congratulations, but her gaze remains locked on the screen. Staring back at Graham with deep, soulful brown eyes, however, is Della, who nods, as if to say, *Yes, now you see. There's more to this day than you think. So stop with your judging.*

RIDERS UP!

6

NATE

Nate is trying to play it cool, but *cool* is an oxymoron when he's got a boatload of money riding on Glory Days. The truth is, he's sweating it out, to the point where his jacket hangs on his chair and he tries to discreetly unstick his cotton shirt from his back. About thirty minutes to go. They've refreshed their drinks, filled their stomachs with chicken, pizza, french fries—you name it. Now it all comes down to a horse and a jockey, and the untold hours of training that have led up to today.

He has some idea of the dedication demanded in this business: The early-morning workouts at the track under the hush of darkness. The carefully monitored diets (some trainers are superstitious about what their horses eat). The endless evaluation of a horse's health and necessary treatments, liniments, and heat therapy applied to sore, tired muscles. The complicated arrangements necessary to cart the horses to Louisville (and to all the qualifying races before that). Not to mention the countless hours spent strategizing, getting a feel for a horse's personality, trying to decide how she'll race best. Only the best of the best competes at the Oaks and the Derby. It's the Olympics of horse racing.

And they're here to watch it. Up close and personal.

He remembers reading about Seabiscuit, the horse everyone had written off until genius trainer Tom Smith came along and saw a spark in the animal. Seabiscuit was too old to qualify for the Derby in the late 1930s, but he went on to break records in the biggest races, racking up more winnings than any of his competitors. He also happened to have a posse of emotional support animals, including a horse named Pumpkin, a rescue dog, and a monkey, all of whom shared Seabiscuit's stable.

Nate thinks he could use his own emotional support animal right about now. He's got a solid grand riding on the Oaks.

Thank goodness he has Phil to give him a heads-up on sleeper horses like Glory Days, the horses with the potential to win big. Without Phil, Nate wouldn't stand a chance at recouping the cash he lost at the roulette table over the last three weekends. This little birthday vacation for Drew has maxed out their credit cards, too, but he's confident he'll be able to turn things around this weekend.

When he approached Leslie two weeks ago, asking for a loan so he could pay off some debts—namely last month's mortgage and a loan from a gambling buddy who was starting to get hotheaded—she acted concerned. "What's going on, Nate? Why do you need so much money?"

He was surprised, even angry, that she fired so many questions at him. "C'mon, Les. Are you really going to make me grovel for it?"

She marched out of the kitchen and into the study, returning with her checkbook. "You're not in some kind of trouble, are you?" She sat down at the table and wrote out the number in big, bold strokes.

"Look, if I told you, I'd probably have to kill you," he kidded.

"Don't joke about stuff like that. I'm serious, Nate." She ripped the check free, and he resisted the urge to lunge for it. "You know I'd do anything for you guys, but I don't want this money to get you into deeper trouble. Do you understand what I'm saying?"

"Yeah, yeah. I get it." He reached for the check, but Leslie pulled back her hand.

"I mean it. This is not your money to throw away on gambling. It's to pay off your current bills."

He nodded, all serious. Leslie could act high and mighty sometimes, but they both knew she had enough money to bail Nate out a dozen times over. Her annual salary probably came close to half a million, counting bonuses. *Guess all that studying in college really paid off,* she liked to tease. It wasn't the first loan Nate has asked for over the years, but it certainly counted as the most generous. As long as he paid her back by the end of the year, though, they'd be square. "Just one more thing," he said.

"Oh?" she said. "Now you're giving *me* orders?"

"Please don't tell Drew," he implored. "I don't want to stress her out."

Leslie stared at him for a long while before saying, "It'll be our little secret. But if I don't see my money by the end of the year, I'm free to tell her. Deal?"

Of course he agreed. What else could he say?

Drew grabs his hand now while they wait for the walkover to the paddock to begin. He has no idea what she's thinking. Is she as nervous as he is? Excited? Too buzzed to care?

As soon as the first horse steps onto the track, the crowd starts to holler and cheer. Nate, Drew, and the rest of their crew watch while the fillies, some already sheathed in a visible coat of sweat, follow alongside their trainers, owners, and what appear to be the owners' families. The "parade" turns out to be more of a brisk walk from the barns to the paddock on the other side of the track, where the horses get saddled. It's obvious who the trainers are—they're the serious ones walking alongside the horses, patting their sides, talking to them, keeping them calm. The horse whisperers.

Drew points to a muscled bay, an emerald-green blanket tossed over her back. Handmaid's Tail. "Looks like a winner to me," she says, and Nate affably agrees. The horse appears plenty powerful, and slightly feisty, swinging her head back and forth.

Immediately behind her comes Glory Days, a chestnut beauty emblazoned in green and pink silks, her ears pointing forward—a good sign. It means she's focused, ready to race. Passing by, the owners and families wave up at the stands, garnering whistles from the crowd. Nate can't imagine what it must feel like to be down on the track, a hundred thousand people cheering for you.

"You okay?" Drew turns to him. He notices that her hand is resting on his left knee. "Your leg is bouncing like crazy."

"Oh, yeah. Prerace jitters, I guess."

"Relax. What difference does it make if you win or lose? Isn't that what you always tell me? Even if you lose a couple hundred bucks, you've still had a fun night out."

"Right. Thanks for the reminder."

A couple of rows down, a group of twentysomethings starts singing the Bruce Springsteen song "Glory Days."

"Looks like someone else has their money on your horse," says Drew.

"Smart kids."

He nods toward the bugler's pagoda, where a man, like a cuckoo bird in a clock, emerges from behind the white door. He's dressed in a pink jacket, black hat, black boots, and dungarees. A hush settles over the crowd while he waits a beat, then lifts his horn and begins to play. An almost surreal feeling drops over Nate. He can't quite believe they're here. When the final note rings out, the fans explode with applause. Soon, the fillies begin to make their way from the paddock to the starting gates.

Nate holds his breath, watches Glory Days walk to her slot, Number 9. They're moments away from the start. Drew squeezes his hand. The last horse gets gated, and before he can wish Drew good luck, the doors swing open. "And they're off!" cries announcer Travis Stone.

A thunderous boom explodes as sixty-eight hooves and roughly seventeen thousand pounds of horse break free of the gates. It's a clean start, and as expected, Glory Days hangs back a few lengths going into the first turn. *That's right,* Nate coaches silently. *Take your time. Don't rush it.* Graham's horses—Rachel's Rebuttal and Nobody's Business— have already grabbed the first and second spots on the track.

After the horses round the first full turn, Glory Days starts to pick up speed, slicing through a space to move up to the middle. Nate remembers a jockey once comparing horse racing with threading a needle. *You have to look for the smallest opening that a horse can squeeze through without throwing the other horses off-balance,* he explained. A few horses have already dropped back, but Glory Days' taut, muscular body is a long dark wave, rolling down the backstretch. A couple more seconds, and she's pulled past sixth and fifth. Incredibly, Drew's horse, the underdog, runs in third place. Drew's nails dig into his hand, but Nate barely notices.

Glory Days chases a horse called Summer Day. *Don't let them underestimate you,* Nate thinks, as if he and the horse share telepathic powers. *I've been watching you. I know your true worth.*

His buddy Phil has been texting him all week, studying the horses at the track. You should probably put some money down on Spitting Image for the Derby, Phil texted earlier, because everyone thinks he's gonna win and he looks promising. But if you want to win big—as in huge—Glory Days is your horse for the Oaks. No one's talking about her yet, but they should be.

When the horses lean into the turn off the backstretch, Glory Days' green and pink silks sail past those of Summer Day. And then she's practically running even with Handmaid's Tail, still in third. Amendment Nineteen, Leslie's horse, has fallen all the way to the back. Rachel's Rebuttal takes the lead, rounding the corner into the homestretch, Nobody's Business chasing at her heels. Graham bellows like a man who's had five or six mint juleps.

But then, seemingly within seconds, Glory Days pulls ahead of Handmaid's Tail, the jockey laying on the whip and sending dust flying everywhere. The filly's legs are turning so fast that they're blurry, indistinct from the stands. *Come on, girl,* Nate urges. *You can do it.*

Halfway down the final stretch, Nobody's Business starts to fall back, as does Rachel's Rebuttal, as if she's confused, waiting for the other filly to catch up. Meanwhile, Handmaid's Tail has snuck up again and is back running even with Glory Days.

Or maybe Glory Days and Handmaid's Tail have turned up the heat? It's hard to gauge relative speeds from the stands, but before Nate can say *Kentucky Derby*, Rachel's Rebuttal and Nobody's Business have fallen a full two lengths back. Both Nate and Drew, on their feet, scream like maniacs, because now it's Glory Days versus Handmaid's Tail.

"Run!" Nate's yelling himself hoarse, jumping up and down.

"Come on! Push it!" screams Drew. "You've got this!" They both lean in as their horses dart across the finish line, seemingly in one even stroke.

An eerie hush drops over the stadium. "Wait. What just happened?" Drew spins around. "Who won?"

But it's a dead heat. Impossible to tell with the naked eye which horse placed first. A moment later, the words PHOTO REVIEW splash up on the Big Board, and the crowd hums with anticipation. Drew presses her face into his shoulder. "I can't look."

"I was positive Rachel's Rebuttal was going to win," Graham says dejectedly.

"Yeah, what was all that shouting about?" Leslie demands. "For someone who pretends not to care for horse racing, you sure seemed to be enjoying it."

"What can I say? The bug finally bit me."

Nate's not a religious man, but he offers up a small prayer for the win. He's either just lost $1,000 he doesn't have or raked in fifteen grand. If Drew's horse wins, she'll pocket a whopping $400. A low murmur ripples through the stands while the fans continue to wait.

It feels like the longest two minutes of Nate's life.

At last, the Big Board declares a winner. When the name flashes on the screen, he fist-pumps the air. *Glory Days.*

"Yes!" he shouts. He can't believe it. Drew's horse, Handmaid's Tail, is the runner-up. Second place. There's a piece of him that's waiting for the announcer to come back and say, *Hold on a minute, folks. Sorry, there's been a mistake. It's actually the other way around. Glory Days, second place. Handmaid's Tail is our winner.* But the announcer never does.

A couple of college kids in the bleacher seats start screaming and hugging, chanting, "Glory Days! Glory Days!" The sounds of cheering and champagne-popping pepper the stands, and the camera swings to the horse's owners, who hug and kiss as if they might be long-lost relatives.

"Well, I guess congratulations are in order." Drew offers a sly grin, but Nate's still in shock. "Please tell me that you bet more than my $20 and that you made more than the $400 I was supposed to win."

Graham and Leslie high-five him. "Way to go! You did it!" Their faces beam back amazement. "Even with crappy odds," Graham adds. And ever so slowly, the news begins to sink in. Nate tosses his hat, rakes his fingers through his hair. Only then does he notice that his hands are trembling.

"C'mon, honey. Tell us how much. How much did you win?" Drew presses.

But Nate's afraid of jinxing it, doesn't want to say how much just yet.

"Enough." He grins and presses his lips against hers. "We won enough." His phone starts buzzing, a text from Phil. Glory Days wins! HUGE congrats.

With shaky fingers, Nate types back, Thanks to you. CAN'T BELIEVE IT!

The loudspeaker blasts the Boss singing "Glory Days," and Nate does his level best to take in the whole moment, to appreciate what's just happened here. He's not going to let his glory days pass him by. Not a chance. He's making things happen. When he gets home, he'll start to pay off his remaining debts, including the loan from Leslie. Relief floods his veins. Relief and adrenaline. He assumed everything would work out, but it's nice to have the universe confirming it for once.

"Seriously, tell us," Graham presses. The four of them have wandered back into the clubhouse in search of a celebratory cocktail. "How much did you rake in?"

"Enough to buy you all dinner tonight," Nate jokes. "I'll tell you this much: I bet a thousand bucks."

"A thousand dollars!" Drew exclaims.

If he didn't know better, Nate might think she's upset, but it must be her incredulity. Because he just *won*. She's only beginning to connect the dots of what happened.

Instead, she says, "You did *not* bet that much money on a horse."

"But, babe, we won."

"Yeah, but what if you didn't?"

Nate looks to Graham and Leslie for help. "Um, we would have lost some money? Listen, it's peanuts compared to what most people bet around here."

"But we're not those people, are we?" she sputters. "That could have gone toward paying off our kitchen renovation."

Nate's gaze quickly meets Leslie's. *Please don't say it,* he thinks. *Please don't tell.* His wife has no idea of the depths of his misfortune, the financial hole he's so handily dug for them. The few thousand they still owe on the kitchen pales in comparison with what he owes Leslie and his gambling buddies.

"Trust me," he says finally. "It's all good."

"That's what I thought I was doing," Drew says flippantly. "Trusting you."

Graham steps in. "You're right, Drew, that *is* a lot of money to bet."

"Oh, don't be so condescending, Graham," quips Leslie. "I think Drew knows perfectly well what constitutes *a lot* of money."

He holds up his hands in self-defense. "Sorry. It's just that Nate took a big gamble, which means he won big." He lowers his voice and addresses Drew directly. "As in fifteen grand, if my math is correct."

Nate nods. "It is."

"Wait. Fifteen *thousand* dollars?" Drew's eyes dance back and forth between Graham and Nate. "Isn't that, I don't know, impossible unless you own a horse?"

Graham shrugs. "Apparently not."

She spins back to confront Nate. "You're telling me that you won *real* money. Not that Bitcoin stuff?"

Nate laughs, says, "Yes, real money. It's already in my account. I checked."

"Oh my God," she mumbles. "That's a ton of cash."

"Yes. Yes, it is."

"But how did you know? How did you know Glory Days was going to win?"

Nate shrugs, grins his *Who, me?* smile. "I didn't. That's why they call it gambling."

HOLD YOUR HORSES

7

LESLIE

As soon as they get back to the hotel, Leslie blasts the air conditioner. "I don't think I've ever felt this gross and sweaty. I'm hopping in the shower before dinner."

"Good idea."

The bus ride has put some much-needed distance between her and her new favorite cocktail, the Lily. From the TV console, she grabs a water bottle and imagines her crinkled, depleted cells plumping up like rotund balloons while she drinks. By the time she steps into the shower, her body has started to feel vaguely human again.

At the moment, she understands that she's in a dangerous place, one where she might say something regrettable to her husband. The hazy fog that descends from having too much to drink, edged by a certain irritation when the buzz begins to wear off. She might ask Graham, for instance: *Did you forget that your wife was sitting beside you for the entire day?* Most of the afternoon, he'd spent ingratiating himself with the mother-and-daughter pair sitting behind them, discussing everything from the Minnesota Twins to why hamsters make excellent pets. He was adept that way, her husband, setting complete strangers at ease. Leslie's response to his neglect, however, had been to shift her focus completely to the races.

And to keep the Lilies coming.

She knew it was silly, growing jealous of two older women from Minnesota. Graham wasn't trying to woo them, after all, and given her frustration with her husband over the last several months, her jealousy seemed spectacularly out of place. But he was still her husband, and they talked about this weekend maybe giving them a fresh perspective, a new start. At the very least, Graham could *try* to make a concerted effort. It's as if he's given up before the weekend even gets going.

Now she wills herself to stay on neutral ground. Swaddled in the hotel's signature robe, she exits the bathroom, her wet hair spun up in a turban, a style that inexplicably used to drive Graham crazy. Sadly, its effect appears to have waned over the years.

"Hey, did Nate happen to mention that he bumped into someone he knows at the track? Outside of our group?"

Graham lies on the bed, tossing back a bag of FRITOS while watching the news on TV. "Huh? What? Nate has another friend here?"

"No, I'm asking you. Do you know if he does? As in, a woman friend?"

This gets him to stop munching. His brows creep up on his forehead. "What are you asking, exactly? You think he brought Drew here for her birthday while secretly planning to see his mistress on the side?"

Leslie laughs despite herself. "No, of course not. It's just that I caught him talking to another woman—a very attractive woman—in one of the lines. She was holding up her phone for him like she was showing him a photo."

"Huh." Her husband resumes chewing. "Did you ask him about it?"

"No, I didn't want to mention it in front of Drew."

"Well, he didn't say anything about it to me. Maybe it was someone from high school."

"Maybe." Leslie unwinds the towel, thinking. "Or maybe it was a local, recommending a restaurant. Something like that."

"Could be." Graham's lack of concern—or interest—is maddening. She combs through her hair, tugging out the snarls. Leslie has always assumed that keeping her long, thick hair would be one of the few perks of middle age. An assumption that struck her as fair and true because, well, women had *so much else* to bear.

The periods and cramps of adolescence, the pain of childbirth, the feeding and caring of said children. Boiled down to its pure physicality, motherhood was a strenuous undertaking. It was a wonder, really, that anyone survived it. And that was without taking into account the hormones and the emotional shifts. Or later, menopause and its stepsister, perimenopause.

Now that she's forty-one, Leslie has come to think of "Perry Menopause" as one of the mean girls at school, the one she tries to avoid in the hallway, the one she prays she doesn't get paired with in gym class. Already, a few of Menopause's best friends have introduced themselves, namely Night Sweats and Insomnia. That her hair also appears to be thinning feels like a cruel joke. As if Hair Loss has longed for years to become part of the gang and only recently joined the cool crowd. (Leslie imagines Hair Loss slapping high fives with the other BFs.) She pulls the loose strands from her comb, tosses them into the miniature trash can beneath the console.

"So, pretty cool that Nate won fifteen grand, huh?" Graham says. "That guy must have a lucky rabbit's foot in his pocket."

"It's remarkable, actually."

"Drew must be happy."

"I would think so," she says. "Or maybe she's still pissed that he bet a thousand bucks on one race. I haven't talked to her about it yet."

"Why would she be angry? Fifteen thousand is a windfall!"

"Yeah, but Nate could just as easily have lost that money. And," she adds, "I get the sense that they're hardly in a position to be losing right now."

Graham removes his hand from the FRITOS bag. "Huh, it's funny you should say that."

"Why?"

"I noticed the other day that there was a check for ten grand debited from our account, and I couldn't for the life of me recall what it was for."

She feels the blood draining from her face while he continues to talk.

"And you know what I discovered when I called the bank? I think you probably do because it was signed by you. And made out to Nate Starling."

She turns toward him, away from the mirror. "Honey, I was going to tell you, but work has been so crazy and I forgot."

He tilts his head. "Really?"

"Yes, really. Nate needed a loan, said he had some debts to pay off. I made him swear he wouldn't use it on gambling. He'll pay me back by the end of the year. Oh, and Drew can't know."

"Huh." More than anything else in their marriage, her husband's silent treatment gets under her skin.

"That's all you have to say? *Huh*?"

"Well . . ." Graham hesitates, thinking. "So you didn't tell *your* husband, and we can't tell Drew what *her* husband is up to. It all feels a little, I don't know . . . sketchy."

"Trust me, the only part that's sketchy is you not trusting me with my own money."

Graham's face darkens. "Don't play that card. Not now."

"What card, honey? Don't be silly. We both know that the majority of the money in that account is from my salary. If we had only *your* money, I would have given Nate a buck." Graham visibly flinches at this comment. "I happen to think, though, that when our friends ask for help, it's important to give it, if we can."

"That's a lovely philosophy," he snaps. "Thank you for sharing it with me."

"Honestly, Graham, who cares where the money comes from so long as we have it?" She turns back to the mirror.

"It matters because you seem to enjoy bringing it up, the fact that your company pays you roughly four times what I make in academia."

"You brought it up first."

"Did not," he says, and if their disagreement weren't rooted in such longtime bickering, Leslie would laugh. They sound like a couple of four-year-olds arguing over a Tonka truck in the sandbox.

"Did too," she says. "You're the one who mentioned the check."

"Exactly. Because you never told me, Les. What am I supposed to think? That it's some kind of payoff?"

"Don't be ridiculous." She stands behind the closet door and drops her robe to get dressed. She's certainly not going to give him the satisfaction of seeing her naked. Not now. "Nate is one of my best friends."

"Well, maybe he'd be better served by your not caving every time he asks you for money."

"Oh, really? That's rich. And how many times is that? Do you even know? And do you know how often Nate helped *me*, the scholarship kid, back in college?" She steps into her underwear, snaps on her bra, and slips into a sundress.

"Whatever you say, honey."

Her head pokes out from behind the closet door. "Don't give up like you don't care."

"Oh, I care." His eyes are trained back on the TV.

"Personally, I think you might have done a better job of keeping an eye on Nate today," she says coolly.

"And how was I supposed to do that?"

From her cosmetic bag, she pulls out a tube of blush and draws two wide swipes across her cheekbones before rubbing it in. "By making sure he didn't bet a thousand dollars!"

"But he made fifteen times that, so what's the problem?"

"Never mind. I can't make you understand that Nate has a gambling problem."

"Is that really what you're upset about? Nate's gambling?"

"Yes."

"All right, then. I'll do my best to keep an eye on him tomorrow. How about that?"

"I'd appreciate it." But she doesn't believe him.

"Maybe," he says, "I should be keeping an eye on someone else, too."

"Like who?" The mascara brush accidently connects with the top of her brow, and she wipes it away with her thumb. "You certainly paid enough attention to those two old ladies in our box today."

When he sits up on the bed, his face comes into view in the full-length mirror. "Like you."

"Me?" Her voice softens. Maybe he's finally realizing that he ignored her for most of the day.

"Yes, you. As in, I should've cut you off after three Lilies. We both know you can't handle more than three cocktails at a time."

The statement lands like a punch. "I'm sorry, but I was enjoying my day at Churchill Downs, where drinking is acceptable, if not encouraged." She crams the mascara brush back into the tube.

"Sure, but not drinking yourself silly until you're slurring your words."

"I was not."

His eyebrows arch at her in the mirror.

Hurriedly, she searches for her silver hoop earrings. "Since when did you become such a buzzkill?"

"That's funny. Drew called me something similar today."

Leslie loops an earring through her right lobe, then the left. "Well, maybe you should listen to her."

"I will." Suddenly, he jumps up and breezes past her to the bathroom, where the FRITOS bag gets tossed into the trash. "As soon as I'm showered, I'm heading down to the lobby. I told Drew we'd meet them at seven thirty before going to the restaurant."

"Fine. I'll see you there." The bathroom door swings shut with a bang.

Leslie pulls her damp hair into a loose bun and slips on her flats. Grabs her pocketbook. *Maybe,* she thinks, *my fury will have dulled to a quiet storm by then. But only if Graham is lucky.*

Otherwise, it's going to be a very long night.

8

DREW

Back at the hotel, Drew jumps out of the shower, towels off, and changes into a summer romper along with the pink flip-flops she grabbed on her way out of Churchill Downs. The cool foam feels heavenly against the soles of her feet. Even her platform sandals were biting into her toes and heels by the end of the day. And now a shower, after a short nap on the bus ride back to the hotel, has revived her.

That doesn't mean she's not still struggling with Nate's bet at the track, though. They're lucky he won. She knows this. But the nagging feeling that her husband is fighting a demon larger than their bills keeps chasing her. His gambling is starting to feel like more of a habit than a hobby. More of an addiction than a fun activity. A little "fix" that his body depends on to keep the adrenaline pumping.

A thousand dollars? It feels like a lot.

She tries to think back to when she first noticed an uptick in her husband's trips to the casino. Was it last month? The month before? But no, it was shortly after her birthday, in the dark, snowy days of February. She remembers because she started binge-watching *House of the Dragon* when Nate rarely seemed to be home. On the weekends, he'd head out with a group of guys, usually to the casino. But these weren't his college buddies, whom Drew knew tangentially and would occasionally bump into around town. No, these pals were a different group entirely, a ragtag bunch he'd apparently met at the casino.

Whenever they came to pick him up, they waited outside the house, the car idling in the driveway. A text would arrive on Nate's phone, alerting him to their presence. As if they, grown men, were afraid to come inside, afraid of meeting his wife and what conclusions she might draw. She imagined big, burly guys sitting in that car who could double as bouncers at the casino, a cigarette tucked behind each ear. The kind of men most women knew to stay clear of, who brought only trouble with them, like missed child-support payments and an occasional roughing up.

Or maybe not. It's possible that they're just a group of geeky salesmen whose egos have been bruised by the bad economy, who need to get out and remind themselves that they can still have fun while winning a buck or two. She hopes that's the case.

Nate doesn't talk about them much. Whenever she asks why he doesn't include Graham in his gambling escapades anymore, Nate shrugs off the question. *Graham wouldn't fit in with these guys. He's too—I don't know—serious.* Drew both understands this and doesn't. She suspects Nate shuns Graham because he doesn't want a babysitter at the casino, reporting back to Leslie or, worse, to Drew. So long as no one can witness his debauchery firsthand, it's impossible for her to gauge how much Nate is really winning . . . or losing. Frankly, she doesn't care to know, would prefer to think of it as Nate's "fun money," much like when she splurges on a new dress, a new pair of shoes.

Which might be why, on a random Thursday night when Nate and Owen were out for a rare boys' night of bowling and pizza, she pulled a bottle of pinot grigio from the cupboard and headed over to Leslie and Graham's. Did she already know that Leslie would be stuck at work? No, that was inconceivable. Drew knocked on their door, in search of company. She can still recall the bright-orange ball of the sun being swallowed by the pink horizon while she stood on the front step, waiting for her friend to answer.

"Drew," Graham said, seeming surprised and maybe a tiny bit flustered when he opened the door. "Leslie's not here; she's working late tonight. And Zach's over at a friend's. I was just reading."

"Oh, I don't want to bother you." A pause, a beat of silence.

"No, no. You're not a bother at all. Do you want to come in? I see you've brought wine. Wine is hardly a bother, is it?"

A hint of playfulness edged his words, and she laughed. "You're right, I guess. Especially when it's the good stuff." And she stepped inside, newly emboldened, following him into the kitchen, where he poured them each a goblet intended for red, not white.

In the living room, he sank into his reading chair, his book tented on the side table. He picked it up, placed a temporary placeholder between the pages, and flipped it shut. She settled herself in the wing chair opposite him, normally Leslie's spot.

"So," he began. "What's new?" He asked it in such a tender, caring way.

Drew had always liked Graham but considered him a bit too stodgy, too professorial to be much fun. But that night she glimpsed in him what Leslie must have seen so many years ago. Concern, empathy, a steadiness that calmed the air around him.

And Drew, without meaning to, said, "Well . . ." And promptly burst into tears.

That was the first time she revealed to anyone that she thought Nate might have a gambling problem (although later, she'd hint at it with Leslie). And Graham nodded his head sympathetically while listening. He didn't so much offer advice as reassure her that everything would be all right. He got up to grab a box of tissues, said Nate was a good man and that he and Leslie were available to help if need be.

But is it a big problem or a little problem? Fifteen thousand dollars is a lot of money. Can she trust Nate to spend his winnings wisely, to fill whatever deep holes might already exist in their finances? Perhaps the cost of this trip alone?

She decides she doesn't want to think about it. Not now. Not on her birthday weekend. Fifteen thousand dollars is a *good* thing, she reminds herself. Leave it to Drew to find the worry in every situation. Instead, while Nate showers, she calls home, eager to hear Owen's small voice on the other end, eager to tell him that she loves him and they'll be home soon.

~

When Nate steps out of the bathroom, the hotel's fluffy white towel circles his waist. Drops of water pool on his shoulders, and muscles that Drew would be hard-pressed to name rope through his bulky arms, across his chest. Even at forty-one, he's still got a football player's physique. A patch of pink sunburn runs along the stretch of his nose.

"Who was that? My parents?"

"Yeah. I wanted to check in on Owen."

"And?"

"And apparently he's doing fine without us."

"I told you so." He jumps onto the bed and wrestles her onto her back before starting to kiss her, his lips tracing the arc of her neck down to the vee of her romper. "Did you tell them about our big winnings?"

"No, I thought I'd leave the honors to you."

"That was thoughtful."

"What," she says, threading her fingers through his hair, "are we going to do with all that money?" His hair has gotten so long that she can tug on it.

"I don't know." He rolls over onto an elbow. "Buy a yacht? Move to Tahiti?"

"How about the French Riviera? I hear it's nice."

"You mean, move there? Or buy it?" he asks.

She giggles. "Can we do that? Buy the entire Riviera? Is it for sale?"

"Sure, why not?" he demands. "We've got $15,000. How much could it cost?"

A laugh travels up her throat. She loves it when he talks like this, as if they'll actually do it. Move to the French Riviera, offer a down payment on the wide expanse of land and the wild blue sea. All theirs to own. Mountains, too.

"I like it," she decides, but his lips have returned to hers, and Drew feels herself sliding down the rabbit hole of desire. When his towel accidently falls from his waist, his gaze skips downward, then back up to her. He grins.

"Oops," he says. "I don't suppose"—he slides the romper down past her shoulders, nuzzling her neck—"you'd be interested in a little playtime before dinner?"

"Oh, honey. You know I would, but Leslie and Graham will be waiting for us."

Nate's lips continue to travel along her body, his day-old beard scratching her shoulders, the inside curves of her elbows, the narrow bands of her wrists. "They can wait another five minutes, can't they?"

Her skin feels electric, as if it could power a small city. "Sure," she mumbles before her romper gets shimmied farther down, their feet entangled at the bottom of the bed.

"You," Nate whispers, "are crazy beautiful." His hands grip hers as they begin to make love, and she tries to recall when they were last this close, so close that she can sense his breath on her skin. But it feels like forever ago. Forever since Nate even glanced her way. When he collapses on top of her, his long, heavy sigh pushes the air out around them, as if to create space for the significance of the moment. "That . . . was amazing. Thank you."

She waits to see what will happen next, but already he's scooting over to the edge of bed. "Give me one minute to hop in the shower and wash off." As if that's what concerns her most right now. A glint of irritation tiptoes across her skin. It's her birthday weekend. Are they really that tight on time? What about her happiness? Especially when it's been weeks? Possibly a month?

She's relieved that Nate wanted to fool around. It means her husband still desires her, even though she's at a place in her life where she's been feeling less than desirable. That's a win.

But why did he thank her, as if it were some kind of exchange? As if she were doing him a favor? Are they that out of practice? She decides not to think about it. *Fifteen thousand dollars.* Drew lets the heft of that number sit on her bare stomach until the shower spigot turns off. She sits up and crawls to her rumpled romper at the bottom of the bed, locates her underwear balled up on the floor. A lot in their lives could change with that number, if it's not already spent.

When Nate steps out of the bathroom for the second time, he's fully dressed. A pair of jeans and a red golf shirt, the shimmer of a gold chain circling his neck. Drew's stomach flips. This is sexy Nate, the one she fell in love with over a decade ago at a random bar in Harvard Square. The guy who asked her if he could buy her a drink, told her she reminded him of Katie Holmes. Drew had been out with her girlfriends that night but was strangely still sober. When Nate asked if she wanted to go someplace else, like his apartment, she said yes willingly—eagerly, even. Within a week, they were a couple.

She remembers the Summer Olympics were being held in London, and they logged a ridiculous number of hours watching the games together over the weekend, ordering Chinese takeout from the Hong Kong, a restaurant down the street from his apartment. The attraction was so intense, so immediate, like nothing she'd experienced with her previous boyfriends. Six months later, Nate proposed on bended knee at a Celtics game, and within a year, they were married.

He grins at her from across the hotel room, his hair still mussed, his eyes edged with that heavy, hungover quality.

"You look like you just had great sex," she says.

He crosses the room and gently, seductively bites her lower lip. "Funny. What gave it away?"

It takes every ounce of willpower in her body, but she pushes him back a step. "Oh, no you don't. We're already late."

Maybe later tonight, she'll get a second chance.

~

In the lobby, Graham and Leslie are already waiting for them. Graham wears a white oxford, sleeves rolled up at the elbow, and jeans. It's a good look on him—that of a hip professor. And were it not for last week's episode, Drew might tell him so. But right now, her mind centers squarely on her husband, the fact that they've reconnected more in the last half hour than they have in the past month.

It's hard not to notice the way Graham looks at her, though, as if he could put his hand right through her, claim her as his own if only she'd let him. Her mind flashes back to that night, over a week ago now, and everything that led up to it.

Drew had begun to look forward to their after-dinner chats on Sunday evenings, once the others had gone up to bed. Graham was always patient, willing to listen. When she talked, he would nod, as if he knew exactly what she meant. Sometimes she kidded that their conversations felt more like therapy sessions than a mutual sharing of stories. And ever so gradually, Drew found herself dropping by the house on the odd weeknight. *We had some leftovers from takeout. I thought you might enjoy this book on the Beat poets. Do you think Zach would want an old Bruins sweatshirt? It doesn't fit Owen anymore.*

Almost without her noticing, the impromptu visits evolved into longer stays. And almost always, he invited her in. Owen, too, who'd run to find Zach. Drew and Graham both shared a love of books. Some of his favorites were her own: *Middlemarch*, *The Great Gatsby*, *David Copperfield*, anything by Virginia Woolf (Drew had minored in literature at Providence). The last time she and Nate spoke about anything other than Owen or work felt like a slipped stitch, a memory impossible to retrieve.

Her talks with Graham lit something in her that Drew hadn't even realized had gone dormant: the realization that there were still more worlds for her to discover, new ideas to explore. If she'd been feeling a tiny bit stuck—turning forty could do that to you—then Graham had stepped in to "unstick" her when she needed it most. It was a gift she'd always be grateful for, this rekindling of, for lack of a better word, her intellectual self. Graham reminded her how to be curious, interested, alive again.

But last Thursday, the air in the room had shifted to something deeper, more tremulous.

He'd baked a chocolate cake in honor of Zach's half birthday (Graham and Leslie were quirky that way—inventing holidays to celebrate). When Drew dropped off a pair of earrings that Leslie had loaned her earlier in the week, Graham invited her in, insisting she try a slice. "Come in, come in. There's plenty left over." On the kitchen island, the cake—shaped like a crescent moon and dripping with chocolate frosting—beckoned. Graham cut a slice for himself and for her, shimmied them onto smaller plates, set out twin forks.

"This looks delicious," she said.

"Try it." He waited for her to take a bite. When she did, she was surprised to discover that inside was a gooey chocolate filling.

"Like a lava cake," she said, groaning at its deliciousness.

He smiled across the counter. "I knew you'd understand. Neither Leslie nor Zach had ever tasted a lava cake before. Can you imagine?"

She shrugged. "A first time for everything, right? Your first step. Your first day of school. Your first lost tooth. Your first . . ." She paused, trying to think.

His head tilted. "Your first kiss."

Drew nodded. "Your first kiss, your first apartment, your first job." She stopped for another bite. Graham circled the kitchen island, dropped down onto the stool next to her with his plate. "This is so good," she said. "I think you've missed your true calling."

"Eating cake?"

She laughed. "Opening a bakery, I mean."

"Ah, you might be right about that." His bright-blue eyes focused on her. "So, next week is the Derby, huh? Excited?"

"Mmm . . . I can't wait. How about you guys?"

Graham grinned. "I'm not sure *excited* is the right word, but yes, I'm looking forward to getting away."

"Oh, I forgot. You're an animal lover," she teased.

He shrugged. "Someone has to be, right?"

"Horses love to run, Graham. That's the whole point. That's what they're born to do."

"If you say so."

She polished off her last bite. "Oh, Graham, please tell me you're not going to rain on my Derby weekend."

A laugh. "Not a chance. It'll be fun to watch all the drunk people walking around in funny hats." A crowd of crumbs sat on the edge of his plate, which he pushed toward her. "Would you like my leftover crumbs?"

She grinned. "Am I that pathetic? Well, I'm not letting your cake go to waste, that's for sure. Crumbs and all." Instead of grabbing her fork, though, he gathered up the crumbs with his fingers.

"Say *ahhh*," he instructed.

Her eyes closed, she let her mouth fall open as he dropped the crumbs in, but somewhere in that simple action, his fingertips grazed her lips—and lingered there, his thumb tracing the bottom edge. Her eyes blinked open; she pulled away.

"What was that?" Her own finger ran across her lips, as if to confirm they were still there.

"You had a few crumbs stuck."

"Was that all it was?"

He paused before answering. "What if it were more?"

"Graham, are you . . . flirting with me?"

His shoulders lifted. "What if I were?"

"I think it would be a very bad idea."

Her heart was careening around in her chest. She liked Graham, enjoyed being in his company, but not that way, did she? They were married! To each other's friends.

Graham had been a catch back in the day; Leslie had told her so. Tall and striking. The lucid blue eyes, the shaggy blond hair, an aspiring professor who could quote Wordsworth on a whim. And Drew could see hints of that person in the man sitting beside her—his carriage, his wit, the mischievous blue eyes. But his hair was starting to thin, a paunch forming around his middle.

Was she attracted to him? Was he attracted to her, or was this all one big misunderstanding? Why didn't she help herself to the damn crumbs!

She pushed his plate away. "Well," she said. "I better get going."

"Drew, I didn't mean anything by it. I was just goofing around."

"Okay, yeah, sure. I know."

"Look at me. Please?"

She turned her head, lifted her eyes.

"I would never be so stupid as to interfere with what you and Nate have, okay?"

She didn't know how to react. Did he mean that were it not for Nate, it could be otherwise? "But you and Leslie are okay, right?" she asked, confused. "Things are good between you two?"

He shrugged. "Depends on the day, I guess. As long as we have Zach around, yes."

"Oh." Occasionally, Leslie would grouse about Graham over a glass of wine, but never in the sense that they were having real problems. Just in the girlfriends-confiding-in-each-other sense. Drew always felt as if *she* were the one in the volatile relationship, whereas Leslie and Graham seemed as steady as the planets in their fixed paths.

Now an entire week has passed, and despite playing it over and over in her head, she still can't determine what exactly transpired that day. She's a smart woman; she knows how to read the signs when someone's interested in her. Has she missed them completely over the last few months with Graham? But it doesn't make any sense. Best friends don't fall in love with best friends' spouses. She's pretty sure there's some sort of rule about it. And yet, she'd felt something in the kitchen that day. A small current of attraction that shot across her chest, gone as quickly as it surfaced.

What if their conversations about art, literature, and music—the very talks that ignited a fresh spark in her—were all foreplay leading up to something else? Is she guilty of flirting with her friend's husband? Of leading him on? Did she befriend him, not because she needed someone to talk to, but because, subconsciously, the thought that Leslie's husband might prefer her over his own glamorous wife would give her a much-needed boost of self-esteem?

If Drew digs really deep, she might admit that layered on top of Graham's ability to calm her frayed nerves is his ineffable power to charm. Intelligence, tenderness, and wit, it turns out, can be as powerful an aphrodisiac as chocolate or oysters.

"We've already called an Uber; should be here any minute," Graham says now. "Even though the restaurant is only a fifteen-minute walk, my lovely wife refuses to do any more physical activity in this heat."

"I'll wilt like a pretty flower if I do," Leslie protests in a Southern drawl. "And my husband refuses to carry me."

Drew laughs, uncertain if they're teasing or accusing each other of being unreasonable. Which is when Graham takes a step away from Leslie, closer to Drew.

"Well, I don't blame either one of you," Drew says amiably. "I don't know if my legs can handle much more walking today."

Then, as if she might prefer to stand alone, Leslie backs away from their group with a few steps. It must look odd to a bystander. *What's going on?* Drew wonders. *Did they have a fight back in the room?*

When Graham moves even closer—so that he's practically standing on Drew's foot—she's grateful when Nate rests a territorial hand on her back.

How does she signal to Graham to cool it? That whatever happened between the two of them last week must stay in last week? Why are he and Leslie acting so strange?

At that moment, their Uber pulls up, and Graham immediately grabs the front seat without a word while the rest of them pile into the back. Nate shoots her a look, then grabs her hand and squeezes it. Drew squeezes back. It's their secret signal. *I love you.* Silly, but it's been their sign for years. She lets her head rest against his shoulder on the ride over, hoping their friends will have shaken off whatever's bothering them by the time they arrive.

The restaurant, like everything else they've seen in Louisville, turns out to be stunning. Its high ceilings and modern, open-concept design create a spacious, airy feel, while the ample bar at the back gleams with row upon row of bottles of locally distilled bourbon. Over the speakers, soft country music plays. Their hostess escorts them to a long table, where Nate pulls out a chair for Drew and Graham does the same for Leslie. Leslie's eyebrows shoot up. "Who knew we married such gentlemen? Or was it something in the juleps?"

"Not sure, but I do know that Nate promised dinner is on him tonight," Drew says.

"Well, I should hope so." Graham drops down in the chair next to him. "I mean, given your good luck at the racetrack today, man, it seems only fair."

And Drew lets go a sigh of relief. It feels as if everyone's back on firm ground again.

A blue ceramic bowl filled with peanuts sits in the middle of the table, and Nate helps himself to a handful. "You'll have better luck tomorrow. Trust me. The Derby is the big one, anyway.'"

"So I hear. Any advice?"

"My money's on Spitting Image, same as a lot of people's," says Nate.

"I was eyeing him," Graham says. "Three to one odds. Not that big of a return, but if he does win like everyone's predicting, that's a pretty good bet if you put down a wad of cash."

"Just not *too* much cash." Drew's eyes dart to Nate.

"Right." He tosses another peanut into his mouth.

Leslie fishes her reading glasses out of her pocketbook and begins to peruse the menu.

"Did you know"—Graham leans in as if he's about to reveal an industry secret—"that every Thoroughbred can be traced back to three stallions on a family tree? It's in the *General Stud Book*, which lists pedigrees dating back to the 1700s in England and Ireland. Almost all of today's Thoroughbreds, including Seabiscuit and Secretariat, can follow their genes back to one of those original three horses."

"That's crazy," says Drew.

"Crazy but true."

"Well, I don't know anything about horse lineages, but I'm ordering the baked mac and cheese with bacon. That, I'm positive about." Leslie drops her menu on the table and removes her glasses. "Carbs are what I'm craving right now after all those cocktails."

Graham forges on as if he hasn't heard her. "I also read that a Derby racehorse can have only eighteen characters in its name, including spaces. And it can't start with a number."

"Well, in that case, when I buy my horse," Leslie says with an eye roll, "I'll be sure to choose a short, nonnumerical name," and the three of them laugh.

Graham, however, stares down at his hands and picks at his cuticles.

After the waitress takes their orders, Drew strives to right the balance of the evening once more. "I'm impressed, Graham," she says brightly. "For a guy who couldn't care less about the racetrack, you're suddenly a font of knowledge about all things horse related."

"Lucky us," Leslie huffs, and Drew exchanges a quick glance with Nate. "Sorry," Leslie apologizes. "That came out sounding meaner than I intended."

"And exactly how *did* you intend it to sound?" Graham asks, as if gearing up for a fight.

"Oh, stop." Leslie waves him off. "Let's not get into it here, shall we?"

"I don't know. I think we're already into it, aren't we? Maybe we should put the question to our friends." Graham turns to Nate, then Drew. "What do you guys think?"

Drew's gaze skips to Leslie, then Nate, and back to Graham. *What's going on?* And then the panicked thought that maybe Graham revealed their little chocolate-cake incident to Leslie flits through Drew's mind.

"Um, I'm not sure," she finally says, her face growing hot. "If you'll excuse me, I need to use the ladies' room." Behind her, Leslie hastily follows.

At the sinks in the bathroom, Drew turns to her friend. "Hey, you. Everything okay?"

Leslie shrugs. "Why?"

"I don't know." She searches for the right words, sudsing her hands beneath the tepid stream of water. "You seemed kind of hostile out there."

"Did I?" Leslie's bright-blue eyes regard her with such intensity that she looks away. "Yeah, I suppose I was. It's just that, well, I haven't wanted to say anything because I didn't want to burden you—"

"Burden me?" Drew yanks a paper towel from the dispenser. "Are you kidding? What's going on?"

"Are you sure? You really want to hear this right now?" Leslie digs around in her pocketbook. Her question stops Drew for a moment. Does she want to hear? What if it's about the chocolate cake? But they might as well clear the air, whatever it is. She nods.

"Okay, honestly? Graham and I haven't been getting along so well."

Drew's stomach plummets to somewhere around her feet. "What do you mean?"

Leslie puckers up in the mirror before running a sheer gloss along her top lip, then the bottom one. "Want some?" she holds out the small tube to Drew.

"No, thanks. I'm good. Keep talking."

"I'm not sure I'm attracted to him anymore—or that he's attracted to me."

"Oh, that's just middle age talking. Marriages go through ups and downs. And of course he's attracted to you! Every man you've ever met is attracted to you, Les."

Her friend smiles at her in the mirror, but her eyes blink back tears. "I don't know. I'm not feeling it anymore. And I think he might be seeing someone behind my back."

"Graham? Oh, honey, no." Drew pulls her into a hug, feeling slightly ill. "Why on earth would you think that?"

"It's just a feeling I get." She pulls away, swiping at her eyes. "He seems so distracted lately. And work has been nuts . . ." Her voice trails off.

Drew does a quick calculation of whether to admit how much she and Graham have been hanging out lately. Will it reassure her friend or only worry Leslie further?

"Hey," she finally says, "I don't think you have anything to worry about. I would notice if Graham were sneaking out of the house—or if another woman were sneaking in. We're only three doors down. Besides, Owen and I have been at your place a lot lately because Nate hasn't been around much either. Work," she explains when Leslie shoots her a funny look.

"Maybe you're right." Her friend hardly sounds convinced, though. "I hope you are." She offers a faint smile. "Maybe I should have an affair. You know, like, to get back at him?"

"Leslie, stop. You're talking crazy."

She shrugs. "Sometimes doing the opposite of what's expected of you is the best revenge."

"But you don't need revenge! Graham's done nothing wrong. Neither have you. C'mon, trust me. Let's go eat our dinner. I'm starving."

Back at the table, Drew slides into her chair and nods at Nate, as if to indicate that all is well again. At least, she hopes all is well *enough* so that the remainder of the evening can unfold smoothly. Because one thing she definitely can't handle this weekend is being the go-between for Leslie and Graham. Her feelings for Graham are complicated enough without her having to choose sides. And she understands that if it comes to that, she'll always pick Leslie first.

DOG AND PONY SHOW

9

GRAHAM AND LESLIE

Graham was an idiot for thinking this trip might fix whatever's broken in his marriage. For every laugh Leslie has given him, there's been a shrouded insult. The little insinuations, the undercurrent of tension that marks each exchange. Not even spending time with their friends, kid-free, has helped to close the gap that's become increasingly apparent. *As deep as a cavern,* he thinks. And then, with grim amusement, *As wide as a horse's ass.*

He will not, however, let it spoil Drew's birthday weekend.

As promised, Nate picks up the dinner bill, although Graham can't help but think that actually *he's* picking up the bill, considering the generous check his wife wrote Nate earlier. They're headed over to Fourth Street Live!, where some fellow Graham has never heard of is playing country music. After draining two generous glasses of chardonnay, Graham has a nice buzz going and has concluded that his wife can do whatever she damn well pleases tonight. He, for one, won't be counting her cocktails.

When they reach their destination (apparently, an acceptably short walk from Third), a giant neon sign advertising Fourth Street Live! greets them. Graham would much prefer to sample brands of whiskey at one of the nearby bars. But then again, no one's asking him.

Like a capable Scout leader, Leslie flashes her phone with their electronic tickets at the gatekeeper, who ushers them through. Inside, a pointed glass canopy stretches above a wide-open street. An assortment of restaurants and bars runs along each side, lending the whole place an aura of a block party on steroids. Near the back, a sea of people wearing cowboy hats already gathers around the stage, awaiting the band's arrival. Somewhere in the midst of the mayhem, Nate manages to procure four beers for their group.

The moment that Jake Owen, barefoot and grinning, walks out onstage, the noise level crescendos. His fans cheer when he calls out, "Good evening, Louisville! So happy to see all your smilin' faces." Without waiting for them to settle, he gives a nod to his bandmates and starts strumming the chords to a song called "Barefoot Blue Jean Night." As if a spell has been cast, the women around Graham immediately begin swaying their hips to the music. When Owen's magnified face flashes up on the wide screen behind him, they scream. He's got that scruffy, enigmatic look of a country music crooner: long hair, chiseled jawline.

Graham tries to get Drew's attention by pointing to his own suede loafers. "Hey!" he shouts. "Does your pal know he forgot his shoes?"

Her arms flutter above her head in rhythm to the music. "What?" she hollers back.

Graham gestures to his feet again. "No shoes!" He points to country music boy on the stage.

"Oh, yeah!" Drew nods. "That's his thing. He likes to go barefoot!"

Graham shoots her two thumbs-up, acknowledging her answer, but it's too loud to carry on a conversation. Meanwhile, his wife's arms now rest across Nate's shoulders, and Nate's right hand moves along with her hips, his left hand gripping his beer. Graham knows it's silly, especially given his own secret crush, but jealousy sneaks up on him nonetheless. He watches Nate's face—mellow, eyes closed, a small smile playing across his lips—and it occurs to Graham that everyone in their group, except for himself, is completely hammered.

Drew shimmies over to him, knocks her hip into his. "C'mon, Graham!" she shouts. "Dance with me!"

He offers a half-hearted attempt, but his body falls out of sync with the beat of the music. His dance partner seems unfazed, though, and wraps her arms around his neck. A shiver of excitement zips up Graham's spine. Isn't this what he's been hoping for the entire weekend? Drew's arms wrapped around him, staring into his eyes? Up close, she seems so small, her five feet three inches to his six feet. He waits for her to maybe mention last Thursday and the cake—*did she feel it, too?*—but she's too drunk for a lucid conversation. And then she's dropping her arms and twirling over to Leslie.

"Dance with me!" she calls out, pulling Leslie off Nate.

Graham watches his wife and his friend's wife twirl under and around each other, holding hands. His eyes should be pinned on Leslie, he knows, but instead they keep catching on Drew. A faint screen of perspiration glimmers on her skin, and her brow knots adorably in concentration while she mouths the lyrics to the song "Homemade."

Lovely, enchanting Drew. The thought pops unbidden into his mind, like one of those balloons floating above a comic-strip character's head. *Drew Starling.* Even her name sounds like something out of a Shakespearean play. He watches the way her raven hair swings over the soft curve of her cheek, then back again, the strobe lights electrifying her. Her face—no, her entire *being*—glows.

If someone were to ask him right now, at this exact moment, Graham would confess that he's smitten. Completely bewitched. By his buddy's wife. By his own wife's close friend. But Leslie and Nate can't know. They must never know. Because it would be the ultimate betrayal to their group.

And Graham wouldn't dare upset that balance. Only if he knew his feelings were reciprocated would it be worth it.

So what the hell is he supposed to do?

~

Jake Owen is as cute and talented in person as he is in his videos. When Leslie's assistant stumbled onto the news that he was playing in Louisville on the Friday night of the Derby, Leslie could hardly believe their luck. That very afternoon, she swooped up the tickets. And even though she wouldn't tag herself as a country music fan, per se, there's something about Jake Owen that makes her want to jump in a pickup truck with a cooler of beers and drive off to a cabin in the mountains. Maybe it's his barefoot persona that implies he's as easygoing as his songs (one is actually called "Let's Go Easy") that turns her to Jell-O, or maybe it's his chiseled jaw and good-boy looks peeking out from beneath the scruff. Whatever it is, he does it for her.

The way Graham used to.

When she first met Graham at the US Open, she'd flirted shamelessly with him. His blond shaggy hair, those brilliant blue eyes. *Robert Redford* was the first thought that popped into her head. He was handsome in an understated, rakish way, or at least that's how he carried himself. Leslie always described meeting Graham as love at first sight. *I just knew,* she'd tell people. And then, when she discovered he was an English professor to boot—well, wedding bells started ringing in her head. He even quoted poetry to her: "She walks in beauty, like the night / Of cloudless climes and starry skies . . ." (Lord Byron). Graham was her Indiana Jones, her Clark Kent—the dazzling professor who also happened to share a passion for adventure. And when Zach came along, it was as if they'd created a mini-Graham, as delicious and sweet as the cracker itself.

But as her marketing career began to take off, Graham's career seemed to simultaneously flag. He went up for tenure, and a jealous colleague blackballed him, more or less forcing him out of a job. After that, her husband taught the odd class at Lesley University, then filled in for a professor on maternity leave at Emerson. But it wasn't until Zach turned five or six that Graham landed his current position as a full-time professor at Quincy College. A step down from his previous position, but the job had its advantages. For one, the campus was only a fifteen-minute drive from their house in Milton. The salary, if not jaw dropping, was at least adequate, and the offer felt like a no-brainer to Graham, who was growing restless with having to switch schools every few years.

Recently, though, her husband's social circle has begun to dwindle as well. He no longer seems interested in going out to fellow professors' lectures or to the symphony in the evenings. He and Nate barely hang out anymore, aside from their shared family dinners. And when Leslie recently planned a fun Saturday for Zach downtown, hopping between the aquarium and the Museum of Science, Graham complained that he had too many papers to grade and couldn't possibly go. As if Leslie weren't busy herself! As if she didn't have a pile of reports in her own briefcase awaiting her review.

When Zach was little, they'd hired a nanny, but whenever the nanny got sick or went on vacation, it was Leslie who picked up the slack. She and Drew would sometimes trade stories late at night, after they'd gotten the kids to bed. They agreed that whoever said that modern child-rearing was evenly split between women and men was full of crap. Leslie had plenty of other girlfriends who could attest to the same.

Even women who were CEOs of their own companies (and their husbands worked at home!) were expected to drop everything when day care or school called. Above Leslie's desk at work hangs a small plaque inscribed with a favorite quote from the late Ruth Bader Ginsburg: "Please alternate calls." It was Ginsburg's response to her son's school when they persisted calling her at work whenever a problem arose. She reminded the school that her son had two parents—and to please alternate calls between his father and herself.

Was it during those early years that a tiny seed of resentment started to take root? That she was arguably working twice as hard as Graham and yet expected to do 80 percent of the work when it came to their child? Graham wasn't the kind of dad who enjoyed tossing around a baseball or shooting hoops in the driveway, and they'd relied largely on Nate, a kind of surrogate dad, for sports. Leslie understood that her husband loved Zach wholly and completely, right down to his perfect, adorable ten-year-old toes, but when it came to the practical stuff, he proved to be utterly useless.

She and Drew have rehashed the same story untold times over glasses of wine, mosquitoes biting at their ankles on sticky summer nights. Leslie, in her own perverse way, never really expected Graham to be that helpful in the child-rearing days, hence the extra boost of a nanny. But once Zach started elementary school, she couldn't justify paying for a nanny, the result being that her workload seems to have quadrupled in recent years.

No one warned her, for instance, that when school finished at 2:20 p.m., you were expected to be there for pickup before shuttling your child around to his various after-school activities. (When Leslie was a kid, she walked home with her friends and fixed herself a peanut butter and jelly sandwich for a snack.) If Leslie were to do school pickup every day, she would need to leave her office by 1:30. In other words, work part-time, which isn't feasible when she's directing an entire team.

"Why don't you hire a babysitter, someone who can take Zach to all his after-school sports if you and Graham aren't available?" Drew sensibly suggested years ago.

Leslie certainly toyed with the idea. "Okay, this is probably going to sound bananas, but if I do that—hire a babysitter—it would suggest that I'm inadequate. That I can't do it all by myself."

"But you can't!" Drew exclaimed. "That's the whole point. It's impossible to handle everything by yourself. There's just too much stuff these days." She started ticking off items on her fingers. "Allergies. Medications. Music lessons. Sports practice. Sports games. The perennial question *What's for dinner?* Laundry. Homework help. Grocery shopping. Changing the sheets. Cleaning the house. Planting the flowers. Not to mention doing anything for yourself."

Leslie started laughing, holding up a hand. "Stop! Please stop. You're stressing me out!"

"But you do understand how crazy it is to assume that you can tackle it all alone?"

"Single moms do it every day," countered Leslie.

"Yeah, but they're probably insane by the time their kids leave the house." Drew traced her finger along a crack in the arm of her Adirondack chair. "Look, whenever I have to work late at school, Owen goes to the after-school program, and I have zero guilt about it. My sister also helps out from time to time, and Nate's parents are great." She paused, thinking. "What about Graham's parents? Did you ever ask if they might pitch in more? They live nearby, right?"

Leslie had shrugged off the same idea when Graham suggested it. "Yeah, maybe." She then admitted, "I think I might have a problem delegating."

"Oh, you think?" Drew laughed. "Hey, what about me? I could take Zach a few days after school. Owen would love it!"

But Leslie drew the line there. She didn't want to intrude on her friend's already chaotic life. It was crossing a line, where Drew would be providing a service for her, and Leslie could imagine things quickly unraveling.

Nevertheless, the conversation stuck in her mind, and she'd resorted to asking Graham's parents to help out occasionally. It made a difference—but not enough. Zach now went to after-school three days a week.

It's not only the childcare stuff that's frustrating, though. The physical attraction between Graham and herself—one that used to be so intense they could barely keep their hands off each other—has taken a deep dive. A dive that she holds Graham largely responsible for. Because her forty-one-year-old husband treats middle age as a foregone conclusion instead of—like most women she knows—a phase in life meant to be skipped over, ignored. This from a man who used to race down the soccer field to score a goal every Saturday afternoon in his men's league.

Leslie finds it especially ironic, considering that she practically kills herself to get to Pilates three times a week, books regular Botox appointments, highlights her hair, and starves herself whenever her skirts start to pinch around her waist. Part of it, she knows, derives from her own vanity. But the other part (okay, maybe the smaller part, but still!) wants to stay in good shape for Graham's sake and for Zach's. She lives in constant fear of being dubbed "the old mommy" at the playground. Meanwhile, Graham proudly crows abouts his expanding stomach, and Leslie watches his once-thick hair receding like a tide pool sweeping out to sea. Where did the hip young teacher she fell in love with go? And who is this apathetic, middle-aged professor with whom she and Zach now share dinners?

It's impossible to pretend that everything is the same, that an attraction still exists. She sees Graham's eyes catch on her when she walks in the door, trying to get a read on her. Senses him wondering if he's misjudging her or maybe projecting his own worries onto her, and she wants to scream, *You're not imagining it, Graham. Something is most definitely wrong!* But how does she do that and still keep Zach's every happiness at the forefront of their tiny family of three?

It's a question she wrestles with daily.

It's all starting to grow old: her husband's lack of enthusiasm for her, for Zach, for their family. His seeming disinterest in the larger world. She twirls to the music, enjoying every minute of freedom in Louisville tonight. It feels good to get away, nice to know that any crises at work will have to wait until Monday. She's about to go back to dancing with Nate when Jake Owen wraps up a song and announces that the band will be taking a short break. When she stops moving, her arms are sheathed in sweat.

"Wow. Amazing," Nate says and flips his hair out of his eyes.

"I think you might have a little country in you after all, honey." Drew twines her fingers through his, sending an unexpected pang of envy through Leslie. It comes so naturally to the two of them, this easy, casual show of affection. Her eyes jump to Graham, wondering if he's noticed it, too. How comfortable and happy their friends seem together and how far apart the two of them are. Whatever tension might have arisen earlier at the racetrack over Nate's bet has dissipated into the Kentucky sky.

"I think I could use some air, maybe even a change of venue?" Leslie suggests. "I mean, I love me some Jake Owen, but I wouldn't mind checking out the PBR bar and that mechanical bull they supposedly have."

"I like your energy," Nate says, nodding approvingly. "I'm game. Graham, how about it, buddy? Wanna take a ride on the ole bull?"

Leslie notices that Drew's body continues to sway, even though the band has ceased playing. Nate doesn't appear to be in much better shape than she is.

"I'm not sure, guys." Graham checks his watch. "It's almost eleven thirty. We've got the Derby tomorrow. Maybe we should think about heading back to the hotel?"

Leslie makes a *pfft* sound. *It's so typical,* she thinks, *Graham trying to ruin everyone's fun.*

Drew pokes out her bottom lip. "C'mon, Graham. Don't you want to have fun? How often do we get to stay out late?"

She's egging him on, but Graham surprises them all by saying, "Oh, fine. But just for a little while. Okay by you, Leslie?"

Leslie, stunned to be asked, says, "Sure. Whatever you guys want to do."

"Yes!" Drew shoots her fist in the air for victory. "I knew you guys would go." She giggles, then hiccups. "Excuuuse me. Now, does anyone remember where exactly this place is?"

Graham's face cracks into a smile before he nods to the building behind her. "I expect you'll discover it's very close."

10

GRAHAM

Apparently, they're not the only concertgoers who've hatched the brilliant idea to head to the bar while Jake Owen and his band sneak a break. The place is spacious enough, but everywhere Graham looks, drunk people congregate like scattered colonies of tipsy penguins.

"What does PBR stand for anyway?" They press through the crowd, trying to make their way to the bar.

"Professhional Bull Riders," replies Nate, his words slurring on the tongue. "Don't you know anything, buddy?" He's kidding, but the comment still stings; Graham is so clearly out of his element here.

Drew nudges him, her elbow sliding past his ribs. "Don't feel bad. I thought it stood for Pabst Blue Ribbon."

"That would actually make more sense, wouldn't it?"

Graham reminds himself that his friends are very, very drunk—to the point where they're not likely to remember much of tonight. He's not quite sure why he agreed to stay out this late, especially when the worst fights tend to start right about now.

"Where's the bull?" Nate shouts. "I'm gonna ride it!"

The upside to Nate's obsession with the mechanical bull is that it might actually distract him from buying another drink, which he most definitely does not need. The guy next to him, dressed in a cowboy hat, jeans, and boots, points to the right and gruffly mutters, "Over there."

"Thank you, appreciate it," Graham says on Nate's behalf and hurriedly steers his friend that way.

"Graham," Nate attempts to whisper, failing miserably, "I might be wrong, but some of the women here, the ones wearing chaps? I think they're only wearing red panties underneath. Check it out. Am I right or am I right?"

Graham gives his friend a gentle shove forward. "Cool it there, cowboy." Of course he couldn't help noticing the "Chaps Girls," as he's already labeled them in his mind. Cowboy boots, black leather chaps, red shorts or undies underneath, and a red bikini top and a cowboy hat. Hard to miss.

"Hey, a fellow can look, can't he?" Nate protests.

Graham tells him to shut up.

"Are you guys really going to ride that thing?" Drew asks no one in particular. "Do you think that's a good idea? I don't know. I don't think it's such a good idea now. How much does it cost? It's probably too expensive, anyway, so you won't ride the horse, right? Or, I mean the bull, or whatever it is." She's talking to herself in a drunken stupor. Leslie tries to shush her, but Drew dissolves into giggles. The sinking feeling that Graham has been left in charge of the children while all the parents go out partying washes over him.

Their group comes to a full stop in front of the mechanical bull. Although, it's not so much a bull as the *shape* of a bull missing its head and legs. There's canvas wrapped around the body that reminds Graham of a pommel horse in men's gymnastics, and a leather saddle with a grip to hold on to. Surrounding the "bull" are thick, cushiony mats, similar to those of a high-jump pit. Graham watches one guy climb up and get tossed after a few seconds before stumbling away.

"Hey, Nate. Buddy, here's a thought," Graham suggests. "How about we leave the bull-riding to the cowboys tonight?"

But his friend shrugs him off, already pawing his way to the front of the line. When he learns it costs nothing, Nate hoots. "You people in Louisville are some of the nicest folks I've ever met. In fact," he says, loudly enough for everyone crowded around to hear, "y'all are so nice, I'd like to buy y'all a drink. Got that?" he shouts, using his best Southern accent. "Next drink is on me!" The announcement is met with a chorus of cheers.

Graham groans.

Drew comes over and tugs on his shirtsleeve. "You're going to do something, right? Nate's in no condition to ride that thing."

Graham is trying to figure out a way to extricate them from the particular hell that Nate, in his boozy moment of charity, has gotten them all into. But Drew's staring at him wide-eyed, panicked. He can't let her down, not in this moment.

"Nate!" Graham cries out in a last-ditch effort. "I thought you wanted me to ride first." Heads turn, and he can feel all the eyes in the joint sizing him up. There are a few chuckles, grins, and nudges in the crowd. "I know, I know. I may not look like a cowboy, but I used to ride horses when I was younger," he lies as he makes his way toward the front.

"You're right." Nate steps aside, slapping Graham on the shoulder. "I'll be a gentleman and let you go first."

A distinct feeling of dread gathers in Graham as he kicks off his shoes (only socks are allowed). Scenes from the stoning in Shirley Jackson's short story "The Lottery" flash through his mind as he trudges over to the bull, his feet sinking into the mat's divots. It takes a few tries before he manages to swing himself up into the saddle. His eyes search the crowd, eager for reassurance, and land on Drew and Leslie, both of their faces twisted in worry. Nate, meanwhile, shoots Graham a confident thumbs-up.

"Where am I supposed to hold on, again?" he asks.

The crowd yells and gestures. "Right there! The grip in front of you, dumbass," someone shouts.

He stuffs his socked feet into the stirrups and grabs the leather grip with both hands, having regrettably passed the point of no return.

"One hand, one hand," people clamor, reminding him of bull-riding etiquette. He releases his left hand and throws his arm out in the air, that is, until the mechanics kick in and the bull starts to spin and buck. *What happened to giving the signal?* He manages to hold on, his body bucking for maybe ten seconds, before his right arm wrenches, launching him through the air and into the pen's padded wall with a distinct thud.

"Ooof," someone says. "Man, that must have hurt."

Graham remains immobile for a moment, eyes closed, silently taking inventory of all his limbs. Nothing feels broken—a good sign.

"Oh my gosh, is he okay?" Drew's voice cuts through the fog, and he gives himself a moment before slowly pushing up into a sitting position. He waits to see if he's about to vomit, but the feeling passes. His new fans cheer, and on his hands and knees, Graham begins to crawl across the mats. Cowboy Bouncer Man helps him to his feet.

"Graham, are you all right?" Drew grabs his left arm and ropes it around her shoulder. "Here, let me help you."

"I'm fine. Nothing to worry about." If fear flooded his veins earlier, embarrassment thrums through them now. As well as humility. Also, a sharp pain cuts into his right side. She guides him over to a chair.

"Well, that was a *spectacular* idea," Leslie snips, her arms crossed.

"What would you rather I have done, honey?" Graham feels his frustration mounting. "Nate was about to get on that bull, and we all know that *really* would have been a bad idea. Consider me the sacrificial lamb."

"More like the sacrificial dodo bird."

"Leslie!" Drew exclaims. "I really appreciate what Graham did. He probably saved Nate from breaking his back or worse." Nate, meanwhile, remains oblivious to the entire conversation because he's befriended another cowboy.

"Are you okay, buddy?" One of the bouncers, his arms the size of tree trunks, approaches with a glass of water.

"I'm fine. Just a little flesh wound," he jokes, gratefully accepting the water. "Never watched Monty Python, I take it?" The bouncer stares back at him blankly. Graham sighs.

"Thanks for the water. Sorry for the trouble." He's unsure why he's apologizing but understands that their group should probably beat a hasty retreat. At least before anyone starts cashing in on Nate's offer to buy a round of drinks.

To his left, he overhears Drew asking Leslie, "Are you sure we shouldn't take him to the emergency room? Just to get him checked out?"

"He's fine. Graham's had much worse than this. Rember that time when he got conked in the head with a baseball at Zach's championship game? It's his pride more than anything else that's been wounded."

Graham frowns. Does his wife think that his collision with the wall has left him deaf? Hard of hearing? He wouldn't have climbed up on that bull if Nate hadn't won fifteen grand today. And Nate wouldn't have won, he's quite certain, if she hadn't lent him ten grand in the first place! That Drew seems more concerned than his own wife about his well-being feels oddly backward, and wrong.

Can he do nothing right in Leslie's eyes? It's beginning to feel that way.

As he sits in the uncomfortable wooden chair, waiting for a new wave of nausea to pass, it occurs to him that, in fact, it has felt this way for quite some time. The complaints are endless: He doesn't spend enough time with Zach. Why can't he help with the grocery shopping? If he wants to take a family trip this summer, he'll have to plan it. Why does he insist on never pushing in his chair?

Leslie's promotion (over a year ago) apparently makes it impossible for her to accomplish any of the tasks she once willingly tackled with gusto at home. Graham needs to pick up the slack, she tells him. Yet no matter what he does—cooking dinner, baking a cake for Zach's half birthday, taking her BMW to the car wash on Saturdays, mowing the lawn—it never seems to be enough. Begging the question: Was Graham *ever* enough for her?

The thought that the answer might be no pains him. That all his insecurities about this dynamic, gorgeous woman falling in love with him—seemingly too good to be true—were based on very real instincts after all. He even confessed his secret fear to her on their honeymoon in Nantucket, their bodies stretched out on a blanket at Surfside Beach. *What if you wake up one day and decide you don't love me anymore? What if you decide you want someone else in your life?*

She quickly shut him down. *Stop it! We're on our honeymoon. Of course I'll always love you. We took a vow, remember?*

Oh, how he remembers. But now he wonders if his worries had been prescient.

Graham suddenly, desperately needs to get out of the bar.

"Whoa there, buddy." The friendly bouncer grabs him by the shoulder when he attempts to stand. "Let us help you, okay?"

"I think we might need an Uber," Graham urges.

"I'm on it." *Ah. Sweet, beautiful Drew.*

"I'd like to go back to the hotel, please."

"You've got it." Drew's voice drips with concern while his wife stands by mute, frowning.

"Coming through," the bouncer yells. "Make way!"

"You feeling okay, buddy?" Nate asks, propping up his other side. "You're doing great."

Graham thinks he might ask the same of Nate, but he's too tired to care. Too tired to look out for anyone else tonight. Except for maybe Drew.

When they reach the front door, a blast of stale air hits them from the street party, but it's preferable to inside. They find their way to a picnic table, and Graham mentions that his head is starting to feel marginally better.

"I still think it's a good idea for you to lie down at the hotel. Don't you, Leslie?" Drew asks.

But Leslie appears to have checked out of the drama entirely. "Sure," she says. "Whatever. I kind of want to hang out longer, though. Nate, what about you? Want to listen to a little more Jake Owen with me?"

Drew, whose hand rests on Graham's shoulder, presses hard, as if willing him not to speak. Not only does his wife refuse to show him any sympathy, but she also plans to keep partying as if nothing has happened? As if Graham didn't try to avert disaster for their friend by putting himself in harm's way? Why did she let him go ahead in the first place?

He hates to consider the answer, so wants to believe that she didn't stop him because riding a mechanical bull didn't strike her as imminently dangerous. The alternative—that she didn't care—is too discouraging to contemplate.

Graham watches while Nate eyes Drew, seeking her permission to stay out later. "Go ahead," Drew says finally, sounding much more sober than she did half an hour ago. "Don't let us get in the way of your fun. I've got Graham covered." Her phone pings. "In fact, our Uber just arrived. We'll see you guys back at the hotel."

"Um, do you want some help out to the car with him?" Nate asks.

"No, thanks. Graham and I've got this. Don't we, Graham?"

And all Graham can think is, *Bless your heart, sweet Drew.* "Yes, I think so. You two have fun." He refrains from saying the rest: *You two deserve each other! Don't spend the whole fifteen grand tonight! You've still got the Derby tomorrow.*

When he and Drew step out onto the sidewalk, the air has cooled, the night sky turned an inky black. They're quiet while they walk to the car, a small green Honda Civic, waiting at the curb. But Graham can't stop thinking about what Drew said . . . and whether she's as upset with Nate as he is with Leslie.

They climb into the car silently, and Graham, heavy with his own thoughts, leans his head against Drew's shoulder, where she lets it remain for the entire ride to the hotel.

11

LESLIE

"And then there were two," Nate says.

Leslie swings an arm around his shoulders. "Just like old times."

"You know Graham will be fine, right?"

"Of course," she says.

"Can I buy you a beer?"

She narrows her eyes. "You know that you can always buy me a beer."

"It's good to see some things never change." He grins and heads off in search of drinks.

Leslie watches Jake Owen and his band reappear onstage, tuning up their instruments before the next set. The crowd has thinned a bit from earlier, but it makes for a much more comfortable space. They can dance without banging into other people's elbows and knees. She wishes she'd thought to bring her cowboy hat to Louisville, but she'd been so focused on her Derby hats that she completely forgot.

Now she tries to determine where, exactly, tonight took an unpleasant turn. Back in the room, when Graham more or less accused her of being a drunk? Of being loose with their finances? Or was it at dinner, when she jumped on him for his annoying Derby trivia? At the concert or the bar? Everyone seemed to be having fun dancing together. Drew danced with Graham, and Leslie with Nate, and then she and Drew had twirled together. Admittedly, Leslie's buzz added to the warm feeling, but now she wonders if her dancing with Nate perturbed Graham further. It's possible that Graham, not nearly as drunk as the rest of them, was less than charmed to see her hanging on her old college pal.

Leslie knows her husband harbors a jealous streak. But whatever happened between Nate and her back in college is ancient history, and Graham knows this. In fact, the first time he asked, she told him the truth. That Graham had homed in on it so quickly—the easy relationship that she and Nate shared—surprised her. It was the first time he'd met Nate, at a bar in Brookline with a bunch of Leslie's friends, and Graham detected a vibe right away. When they got home later that evening, he was distant, not his usual self.

"What's wrong?" she asked.

"What's the story between you and Nate? Old boyfriend?"

"No, nothing like that," Leslie quickly assured him. "We never dated. We're just good friends."

Graham, cupping a fresh tumbler of whiskey in his hand, waited patiently.

"But . . . ?" he asked. "Why do I feel like there's a 'but' coming?"

They were seated across from each other on their old blue corduroy couch, living in a high-rise apartment in Brookline. From their living room window, they could make out the lights of the Back Bay, the Prudential Tower looming in the distance. Leslie was working as a marketing associate at a financial firm downtown at the time, and Graham had begun teaching at Northeastern. Their salad days.

Leslie shrugged. "Do you want the whole truth, half-the-truth, or a lie?" she asked playfully. The phrase had become a running joke between them whenever they were discussing a potentially fraught topic. A way to ease into the ugly.

"I think I'll pick the whole truth for this one."

His voice was so stern, so serious! It was the first time it struck her that an indiscretion from her past might impede her future with the man she now loved. She knew to choose her words carefully.

"It's not really a 'but,'" she explained, then shrugged again, trying to downplay the story while struggling to come up with the right word. "It's more like an asterisk, you know, a footnote to the main text? You can read it if you'd like a slightly fuller picture, but it's not necessary."

"I guess I'll take my chances."

And so she launched into it, describing how she and Nate met during freshman year. He was on campus in August for football training; she was working dorm crew, cleaning the rooms and bathrooms for all the students who'd be returning to campus in a couple of weeks. Nate was a football star from Newton; she was a scholarship kid from Dorchester. During that first week, Leslie and some of her girlfriends wandered over to an off-campus party, in search of something to do. The party, at a derelict house in Davis Square, was filled with athletic types, all in town for preseason practices. Soccer players, golf, football. Leslie and her friends stood out like the nerdy, dorm-crew kids that they were. They were about to leave when Nate approached her with an extra beer in hand and perhaps the world's worst pickup line: "I didn't know that smart girls could be gorgeous, too."

"How do you know I'm smart?" she asked.

He grinned. "You're confident. I like that. Most girls would say they weren't pretty."

She flipped her long, blond hair over a shoulder. "You still haven't answered my question."

"You're at this party, aren't you?"

"For the moment." Her friends, behind her, snickered.

"Well, only Tufts students were invited, so I'm assuming you go to Tufts. And therefore, you're smart."

"I will be at Tufts once school starts."

An eyebrow shot upward. "So you're a freshman, then, like me."

"A freshman, but definitely not like you."

He tilted his head, confused, as if trying to determine if she was pushing him away already. Trying to play it cool in front of her friends? The truth was, she was terrified. She didn't know what to do. She wasn't accustomed to cute college guys flirting with her, and without question, Nate was cute, and tall. Thick, curly dark hair; soulful brown eyes. Her heart thumped so loud she was sure he could hear it above the music.

"Tell me more." A small smile danced at the edges of his mouth.

"I will if you invite me out for coffee," she said boldly, as if already trying to set the parameters on their relationship. He needed to know that she wasn't one of "those girls." The easy ones. If he wanted her to be his girlfriend, he'd have to work much harder.

His eyes skipped over to her friends, then back to her, as if trying to ascertain if she were kidding, trying to make him appear foolish in front of her buddies. But then he shrugged as if he didn't care one way or the other.

"All right." He cleared his throat. "Will you go out for coffee with me, cute girl without a name?"

"Leslie." She held out her hand. "My name is Leslie. And yes, I'd love to get a coffee with you, tomorrow."

He awkwardly handed her the other beer to free up a hand, then shook hers. "Hi, Leslie. I'm Nate. Glad to meet you. Coffee tomorrow, then. Could you maybe write your number on my hand?"

She pulled a Bic pen from her purse, inking it on his palm. He double-checked, as if he didn't trust her, thought she might have scribbled gibberish there instead, and grinned when he saw an actual number.

"Great. I'll call you tomorrow. We can figure out a place and time."

And Leslie and her friends had marched out of that party as if they'd found precisely what they were looking for. Afterward, her friends teased her. *You were so bold! I loved it! Where do you get the confidence?* Her place in the social hierarchy was established early on. Leslie Bowler was no one to mess with.

But then Nate's high school girlfriend, Stephanie (whom he'd neglected to mention at that first coffee date), showed up on campus the following week. Also a freshman, also from Newton, also very pretty. Leslie was heartbroken for an afternoon and angry for a week.

"So, you *were* boyfriend and girlfriend," Graham interrupted.

Leslie shook her head. "No, that's not right. The next time I saw him he was walking across campus holding Stephanie's hand. Later in the year, we became friendly, but we didn't cross a line until junior year."

"Uh-oh." Graham's face had looked so dejected. "I hate line-crossing," he offered, decidedly without humor.

She sighed and took a breath before launching into the part of the story she knew would upset him. "So, junior year, we'd both broken up with the people we were dating, and there was this party, like a costume party. It wasn't Halloween, though; it was for something else . . . I can't remember. Anyway, I dressed up with my friends, and we were all flappers."

"Flappers?"

"Yeah, the girls who wore short dresses and stockings and fancy hats during Prohibition?"

"Yeah, I know."

"And Nate and his buddies dressed up as gangsters. It was funny, almost like we'd come up with our costume ideas together. Gangsters and flappers. They went together. So we all proceeded to drink too much and go out dancing. Nate and I kind of hooked up that night. It wasn't anything major, it was just that night . . . and then, um, one other time senior year. But trust me when I tell you they were drunken hookups. We both should have known better."

"Did you sleep together?" And there it was: the question that could derail all her plans to marry this man. But that was crazy, she reasoned. Graham had girlfriends in college. Leslie didn't expect him to be a virgin. Why would he expect it of her?

"Yeah, we slept together. It was college," she emphasized, as if that explained it away. "It meant nothing."

"Except it happened twice. Are you sure you're not still in love with this guy? I mean, you say you're just friends, but what if you really still love him?"

"First of all," she replied slowly, "I was never *in love* with Nate. Maybe I love him like a brother because he was always helping me out, like paying off part of my tuition when I was about to get kicked out of school. But we were never *in love*."

"Sounds to me like he might be in love with you."

"You're joking, right? You know that he's with Drew. And she's perfect for him. Drew's like a Girl Scout cookie—sweet and wholesome, a Thin Mint. She spends her days working with kids who have developmental needs. She's the all-American girl. She's exactly what Nate wants in a partner."

"Huh."

And that had been the end of the conversation. Afterward, they made love as if it were their first time.

But now Leslie wonders whether those questions from more than a decade ago resurfaced for Graham tonight while he watched her dancing with Nate. Is that why he was acting so ridiculous over the mechanical bull? Was he really trying to protect Nate or show off for her? A pang of regret stirs inside her as she hopes it wasn't the latter.

"Here you go, my lady." In a weird flashback, Nate hands her a beer. It takes her a second to remember where she is—at the concert.

"I was just thinking about that time when you came on to me, freshman year. Do you remember? You brought me a beer at that lame party." She sips.

"How could I forget? You were the prettiest girl I'd ever seen."

"Yeah, right. Although you neglected to mention that you already had a girlfriend."

He lifts a finger. "Those two things, I'll point out, are not mutually exclusively."

Leslie rolls her eyes. She's heard this excuse before, Nate's theory that you can still think someone is empirically beautiful without wanting to date them.

"It's like admiring an incredible painting," he says drunkenly now. "It doesn't mean I want to go out with it."

"Right." The band is playing, but they're not as loud as their first set. She and Nate can actually carry on a conversation in the corner where they're standing.

"Guess Drew and Graham are kind of pissed at us, huh?"

She turns her head. "Yeah, I was getting that feeling, too. What's going on?"

Nate shrugs. "I was hoping you could tell me."

"Not a clue, unless she found out about the money I lent you. Graham did."

"Oh, shit. He did? What did he say?"

"Well, he wasn't thrilled, especially that I didn't tell him. He noticed the money missing in our checking account."

"He's not going to tell Drew, is he?"

"Why would he? I asked him not to."

"Man, he must think I'm the biggest loser. Not being able to handle my own debts."

Leslie studies him for a moment. "No one thinks you're a loser, Nate. You brought your wife to the Kentucky Derby for her birthday. That's pretty awesome. Besides, we're all friends here. But I will say that the sooner you pay me back, the better you'll feel."

"Why? Are you going to break my thumbs if I don't?"

She laughs. "Let's just say, I hope I don't have to. Remember: I know you won fifteen grand today."

"True." His gaze drifts to somewhere above her shoulder. "Hey, don't look now." His voice drops. "But some guy is walking over to us, and I don't think it's to say hi to me."

Curious, Leslie spins around. When her eyes land on the young man, she contemplates hiding behind Nate, maybe diving under the stage, but it's too late.

"Hey, Leslie. I thought that was you. Is this your husband?" Jackson turns to shake hands with Nate, whose eyes crinkle in mild amusement. Leslie groans internally. *What must Nate be thinking?*

"Um, nope. I'm just an old friend. Nate. Nice to meet you."

"Nice to meet you." A mixture of relief and happiness falls over Jackson's face before he addresses her. "I was watching you across the dance floor. Funny how we keep running into each other, huh?"

"Yeah." Leslie hopes for a small miracle, that somehow the street beneath her might open up and swallow her whole, make her disappear. "That's one word for it," she says now. Then she flashes her best flight attendant smile and finishes the introductions. "Nate, meet Jackson. He's from Louisville and a lawyer."

12

DREW AND LESLIE

The hotel manager at the front desk hands Drew an ice pack, a gauze bandage, a bottle of Extra Strength Tylenol, and two bottled waters. *What doesn't this hotel have?* she wonders.

"C'mon. This way, mister." She steers Graham toward the elevator after thanking the manager for the supplies. "Let's get you into bed."

Graham's earlier bravado, claiming he felt fine, has begun to crumble. It's obvious that he's in pain and that his right side, in particular, got pretty banged up. Anytime she inadvertently brushes up against it, he winces. He'll likely have a sizable bruise on his rib cage tomorrow morning. As in, sirloin-steak size.

"You know, it's nice to see there are a few chivalrous men left in the world." She pushes the button for the ninth floor and waits for the doors to close.

"I don't know how *chivalrous* I am. *Stupid* is more like it."

"Oh, I don't think so. Not at all. What you did back at the bar, climbing on that ridiculous mechanical bull—that took courage." She laughs at the memory. "You up there, your arm whipping around, your torso flying in the air . . . You were something else."

"Ugh. I can only imagine. Thank goodness no one was filming me."

"Oh, I think there might have been a few. Not me!" she hurries to add. "But I wouldn't be surprised if you went viral on TikTok by tomorrow afternoon."

Graham leans against the elevator wall and groans. "Please, no." When the floor pings and the doors slide open, she waits for him to shuffle out into the hallway. He's moving even more slowly than back at the bar.

"Here we are." Graham swipes his room key through the slot, then turns to her. "I hate to ask, but would you mind coming in for a minute? Just to help me get set up?"

Drew stops, holding the door open for him. "Um, sure. I guess so." And even though there are a million reasons not to, it's as if someone gives her a solid shove from behind. She's gotten him this far; how can she abandon him now? What if he needs help getting into bed?

Inside, he grabs his pajamas from the bureau and heads for the bathroom. "I'll just be a minute."

"Take your time."

She notes that, like herself, Graham unpacks his clothes and folds them neatly in the hotel dresser, as if he's still at home (Nate generally leaves everything crammed in his suitcase and pulls out items as needed). She moves about the room, placing the water bottles on the bedside table and shaking out two Tylenol for herself, then two more for Graham. She turns down the bedsheets, fluffs the pillows. The ice pack is one of those self-activating ones that Zach's coaches bring to every soccer game, and she bends it in half until it cracks, starts to grow cold against her hand. On the side of the bed, she sits down to wait.

It turns out that Leslie and Graham's room is more or less identical to theirs, except laid out in the reverse pattern. The bathroom and coat closet have swapped sides, and the wallpaper is gold instead of burgundy. Paintings of horses dot the walls. There's the sound of the toilet flushing, the water running in the sink. A wave of exhaustion rolls over her. It's difficult to believe all that's happened in the last twenty-four hours. And they haven't even been to the Derby yet.

When the bathroom door opens, Graham offers a weak smile. He's wearing blue-and-white-striped pajamas, a line of white buttons marching down the front of his shirt.

"Well, this wasn't quite the way I had envisioned tonight," he jokes.

"No," she says, standing up so that he can crawl into bed. "I don't imagine so." She hands him the Tylenol and the water and watches him swallow. When he lies back against the pillows, he attempts to hold the ice pack to his ribs.

"I think that's what the bandage is for," she explains. "To help you keep it in place while you sleep."

"Ah, right." Sitting up elicits a wince, and he works to wrap the bandage around himself, unsuccessfully.

"Here, let me try." Sitting down beside him, she takes the bandage and directs him to lift his arms—"Ow!" he cries—and then gingerly winds it around until the ice pack is firmly in place.

"There." She tucks in the ends. "That ought to hold it for tonight. Is it too tight?"

"No, it's perfect. You're a natural Florence Nightingale." Their faces haven't been in such close proximity since last week in Graham's kitchen, and without thinking, Drew leans toward him. His hands lift to cup her face . . . and then, ever so gently, he begins to kiss her.

A minute later, she pulls away. "I'm sorry. I don't know what I'm doing. I think maybe I'm still a little drunk."

"No, don't apologize. I'm the one who kissed you first."

She can feel herself bending, yielding. "I think it takes two." She leans back in, her lips pressing against his, a hint of whiskey on his breath. A rush of heat travels along her body, goose bumps up and down her arms. His lips are tentative, questioning, and then, suddenly, hungry.

When he moans, she stops. "Oh no! I'm hurting you."

His eyes study hers. "Not at all. Quite the opposite, in fact."

An electric moment passes between them, that interstice of time where the future could unfold along two very different paths. Graham is extremely handsome; Drew can admit this in her addled state. She's always thought of him as older and wiser than the rest of their group, but the fact is, he's only a year older than she is.

"You're beautiful, did you know that?" He pulls her hair behind an ear, studies her face. Then softly, "Are you sure you want to do this? Not that I'm trying to stop you," he adds quickly.

When he says it, though, it's as if a switch flips in her brain. The truth of what they're doing here—the wrongness of it. The urge to keep kissing him, to run her hands across his chest. Her friend's husband! She's sober enough to know that the sense of abandon empowering her right now comes from a long day of drinking. And if Graham—the very person who instigated all this with the simple brush of his thumb across her lips a week ago—is questioning it, then it must be a very bad idea, indeed.

Awkwardly, she leaps up from the bed, smooths her dress. "You're right. This is a terrible idea."

He falls back against the pillows, his eyes heavy with sleep and perhaps . . . regret? "Okay, but I hope—"

"Get some rest, Graham." She cuts him off and retrieves her purse from the bedside table before shutting off the light and seeing herself out. Leaning against the door in the hallway, she can feel her body trembling. *What was I thinking?* And then her next thought: *What am I going to do?*

Down the hall, the elevator dings, and a woman in a bright-pink dress emerges, heading toward a room a few doors away. She looks vaguely familiar, but Drew can't place her. Before she does anything else she might regret, Drew pilots herself to her own room for some much-needed sleep.

~

"Well, that was fun to see you in action again. I'd forgotten," Nate says after Leslie has paid their Uber driver.

"What are you talking about?" She grabs his arm to help him up the steps to the hotel lobby, but it's a wobbly affair. She's had a few too many cocktails herself.

"That kid, Jackson. Clearly, he had the hots for you. The way he kept looking at you, offering to buy you another drink."

"Um, he was about half my age."

"Doesn't matter. Must feel good to have a twentysomething lawyer coming on to you."

"Please. I'm not a cougar. Not to mention, I'm married."

"Yeah, I know. I'm just giving you a hard time. How did you meet him again?"

She shrugs. "In the pretzel line." When Nate grins, she adds, "It was a long line."

"That's how all the great love stories begin," he teases. "In the pretzel line at the Kentucky Derby."

"Stop it. You're not funny."

"Then when you blew him off at the end, told him we had to get back to the hotel to check on our spouses." Nate claps his hands together, laughing. "I thought he was going to fall over. His face dropped like ten feet, poor guy. Think he was pretty disappointed you weren't going home with him."

The elevator finally arrives, and Leslie scoots him inside. Thankfully, no other guests are around to eavesdrop on their conversation. "Not sure what planet you're living on, but nothing was ever going to happen. He saw my wedding ring."

"Oh, right. The old flash-your-wedding-ring trick."

"Speaking of which, where is yours?" Earlier at the racetrack today, she'd noticed it was missing—a pale band of flesh where Nate's wedding band usually was—but hadn't wanted to ask about it in front of Drew.

"Home. Didn't want to risk losing it here; I have to get it refitted. Guess I've lost some weight. It keeps sliding off."

She narrows her eyes. "Are you sure that's all it is?"

"What do you mean?"

"I mean, you didn't hawk it for gambling money, did you?"

He rakes his fingers through his thick hair, leaving a tuft sticking up in the back. "Jeez, Les, give me some credit, would you? I'm not that stupid."

"Good."

"And don't worry. I already told Drew that I left it at home so she wouldn't freak out."

There's a pause before either of them talks again.

Then Leslie dives in. "Do you remember what I told you on your wedding day?"

Nate holds up a finger. "I believe you said"—he clears his throat—"'Drew is the best thing that has ever happened to you. Don't screw it up.'"

"That's right. And do you know what I'm going to remind you of tonight?"

"Drew's the best thing that's ever happened to me?" His words are fuzzed with alcohol.

"Yup. And guess what? I think maybe you're screwing it all up, Nate. Your marriage. You've gotta stop with this gambling stuff."

"But we're at the Kentucky Derby! For her birthday. That's gotta count for something."

"Sure. You know what I mean, though. Going out every weekend with the guys, leaving her home alone with Owen. Not being straight with her about how much trouble you've gotten into financially. I don't even know the extent of it, Nate, and I'm scared for you. *Can* you stop it? Or do you need, like, professional help?"

His eyes roll drunkenly in his head. "I'm not some kind of basket case who needs professional help."

"I wouldn't be so sure. Gambling has a way of becoming an addiction. Remember what you told me about your dad? Didn't he have a problem with the slots? It's like smoking or alcohol. A brain thing, not a willpower thing. If you need help, I'm here to drive you to sessions, do whatever you need. Just tell me. We'll make it happen."

He shakes his head. They've made it back to his room. "Leslie, Leslie, Leslie. You've always been like my little sis, looking out for me. Everything's under control, though. You're gonna get your money back, don't worry. And soon."

"That's not what I'm talking about, Nate." She pauses, striving to underscore the gravity of her words. "You've gotta rein in this gambling stuff; otherwise, I'm going to make sure you get help."

When he tries to salute her, his hand misses his brow completely. "Okay, Captain. I'll get right on that."

"Good." She waits till he's safely inside before she leaves.

~

When she lets herself into her own room, Graham's snores travel over from the bed. He keeps forgetting to pack his nasal strips, the only things that help him sleep peacefully. Her hands feel their way along the wall to the bathroom light switch. When it flicks on, Graham doesn't stir. He's out cold, thankfully not in enough pain to prohibit sleep. She washes her face, brushes her teeth.

"Hey," she says softly when she climbs into bed. He shifts position, tries rolling onto his right side, then rolls the other way, asleep through it all. She jiggles his good shoulder. "You feeling okay?" Her question is answered by a snore, and she flops back on her pillow.

It was unfair, she thinks, *to judge him so harshly back at the bar.* Graham was simply trying to spare Nate humiliation and injury, and as a result, he'd taken one for the team.

A hero, Drew said. But Leslie, his own wife, called him a dodo bird. Honestly, how cruel could she be? She searches inside herself for a glimmer of affection left for this man to whom she's been married a dozen years. In her heart, she understands that Graham is a good person, better than most. Loving and kind and generous. And smart. He can hold a fascinating conversation with almost anyone.

And yet. Somehow, it never seems like enough.

Is it because she expects too much? Unreasonably so? That's what Graham would say, she knows. Because he *has* said it. *Maybe,* she thinks, *if I cut back on my work hours, show him some longed-for affection, we might find our way back to each other. It's possible.*

But what is it that she wants, exactly? Sometimes she feels like that teenager back in her poster-lined bedroom in Dorchester, dreaming about how her life would unfold. She had big plans! Mostly, to become a famous ballerina. She would imagine the places she'd travel once she'd been accepted into Boston Ballet: New York, Vienna, Paris. Her teachers said that she'd been gifted the body of a ballerina, coupled with the requisite grace. Unfortunately, while teenager Leslie may have possessed such traits, older Leslie was less driven. She grew tired of the hours-long practices, the bruised toes, the constant reminder to relax her shoulders and pull up through her core. She quit it all, redirected her focus on getting into college, moving to New York, building a life that included a husband and a family.

But as she's come into middle age, she understands that it's not enough. There needs to be something for her, too. A sense that her mind, her hands, her heart are being used not only to care for the people she loves most but also to create something of her own. To be more than a wife or a mother. One day, she will try to explain this to Zach—this feeling of being at odds with herself, the restlessness, this constant longing for more—so that her decision will make sense. She'll tell him how hard she loved him and his dad, but that sometimes a crossroads presents itself in life.

That sometimes you have to choose.

13

GRAHAM

The next morning, Graham asks her if he was dreaming. He'd been playing it over and over in his head, and when Drew texted him back, agreeing to meet him downstairs for breakfast, his heart leapfrogged. *Drew Starling kissed him last night.* Why on earth did he ask her if she was really sure? What possessed him to say such a thing? He should have kissed her, made love to her, folded her in his arms and held her for as long she'd let him. If he could go back in time, he would shake himself back to his senses.

Because not only did his secret crush help him into bed last night but she also *kissed him* of her own volition. Her lovely face next to his, the softness—and the boldness!—of her lips. He recalls thinking, *So this is how she kisses Nate.* An odd thought, perhaps, but that's what swam through his mind. That Nate, the lucky bastard, probably got kisses like this every night.

It must have been a combination of the booze and Tylenol, the awkwardness of having an ice pack tied to his ribs. He couldn't exactly be at his best, given the circumstances. Maybe she'd give him another chance? They still have the entire day ahead of them. And even though his right side remains tender to the touch, only the slightest hint of a bruise is evident. He'd been expecting (maybe hoping for?)

a dark-purple smudge imprinted on his rib cage, evidence of a grave injury. Yet apparently, the memory itself is graver than the actual event.

Now Drew sits across the table from him and averts her eyes, perhaps considering how best to answer his question about last night. Eventually, her gaze returns.

"No, certainly not a dream," she confirms. "But it would make things easier if it had been."

His body sags at her response. He can't tell if it's disappointment or regret or anger that edges her voice. Whatever it is, it doesn't sound promising. Doesn't sound as if she, like him, has been floating on the idea that they might pick up where they left off last night.

"Hey," he says quietly, thinking perhaps she's embarrassed. "You know I would have gladly kept going if you'd wanted to. I think you're sensational in every way."

A distinct blush flames across her cheeks. "It seems so strange to hear you talk that way. To me, at least."

"Why?"

"Because you're married to one of my best friends!"

"True." He sighs, debating how much to reveal. Surely Leslie has confided in her about their problems. "Although, Leslie and I have been having our own issues lately."

Drew nods as if she's familiar with the idea. "That doesn't make what we did right, though."

"But we hardly did anything!" he exclaims. Her eyes dart anxiously around the room. Both Leslie and Nate are still asleep upstairs, and nobody else at breakfast seems to be paying them any mind. "Sorry." He lowers his voice. "But it's true. It was only a kiss. Two kisses at the most."

She shakes her head. "We both had a lot to drink. I think maybe we got a little carried away."

Graham grunts. "If that's your definition of getting carried away, I'd hate to see what your idea of taking it slow is."

This prompts a laugh, and Graham is grateful for anything to cut the tension. "I guess I've been thinking about that day in your kitchen," she admits. She lifts her fingers to her lips, brushing them as Graham did that day. "What if we'd kept going? After you wiped the crumbs from my lips."

"If I had kissed you, you mean?"

She nods, bites her lip.

"Believe me, I've thought about it, too. And I would have if you hadn't pulled away. I assumed you were mortified. That I'd ruined everything."

"You surprised me, that's for sure." She cuts into her french toast. "But then, for some strange reason, I kept thinking about it. What if we'd acted on it? I guess last night was about that—the wondering. The *what if?*"

"And?"

A faint smile crosses her face. "It was nice. I liked it." She bows her head. "Does that make me a terrible person?"

Oh, how he wishes he could hold her and reassure her that she's the furthest thing from a terrible person! "I don't think so. If it does, then I'm terrible, too."

"What are we going to tell Leslie and Nate?"

Graham frowns. "What do you mean?"

"Well, we have to tell them, don't we? I was thinking we admit what happened. I was helping with your bandage, and we were both pretty drunk, and one thing led to another, and it was only a quick kiss, that it didn't mean anything."

"Huh." He takes a bite of his scrambled eggs while internally screaming, *Hell, no! Telling them would be the worst thing we could do!* And then, *It didn't mean anything to you?*

"If we're honest about it, they can't really be angry with us, can they?"

"Well," he says, "that part, I'm not so sure about. My wife knows how to hold a grudge."

Drew leans in, lowers her voice. "It's not like we slept together or anything."

"Right." He stretches his arms out in front of him, cracks his knuckles.

"Eww. You should really stop that."

"Sorry, bad habit. Leslie's always on me to stop, too. I do it when I'm thinking."

She waits, her big, beautiful brown eyes staring back at him as if he might provide a better, more plausible explanation for last night's events. "I guess I was thinking," he begins, "that maybe we don't need to mention it? That it could be our little secret. Kind of like their little secret from college, you know? Tit for tat."

Across the table, she clears her throat. "I'm sorry. What?"

"I mean, admittedly, theirs happened a long time ago."

She sets down her fork, leans back in her seat. "Seriously, what are you talking about, Graham? You're scaring me."

"Oh, um," he says slowly, buying time. "Nate never told you?"

"Told me what?" Her expression dims.

"About Leslie and him?"

She pauses. "All I know is that they've been friends since college. He said they never dated. *Leslie* said they never dated."

Graham nods. "Right, I think that's true." If he knows what's good for him, he should stop right now, push back from the table, and leave immediately. But how can he lie to her? After all she did to help him last night?

"What else, Graham? What aren't you telling me?"

An image of himself in a canoe, feverishly trying to paddle backward, surfaces in his mind.

"Shit." He throws his napkin down on the table. "This is *not* how I imagined our brunch going."

"I think," she says, eyeing him cryptically, "that you have a very big imagination."

Graham leans back in his chair and considers what his takeaway from *that* comment is supposed to be. That there's been no spark between them at all? That she hasn't enjoyed their late-evening chats the way he has? That he's imagined it all? Well, if she wants transparency, if she wants truth, he's more than happy to provide it.

"A few other things may have happened," he adds.

"Such as?"

"It's not worth getting into, really; it was back in college. You should ask Nate."

"What are you saying? They *slept* together?"

He shrugs. "I guess they fooled around a couple of times. Just like we all did back then. We were kids. Stupid."

"So, Nate and Leslie had sex?" Her voice sounds small.

"I'm sorry. I shouldn't have said anything. I assumed you knew."

She tilts her head back. "Um, nope. Never came up, funny enough."

"I'm sorry."

"If you'll excuse me," she says, pushing up suddenly from her chair. "I need to go talk to my husband."

"Drew—"

But she's already flung her napkin onto the table. He watches her strut out of the dining room and wonders what sweet hell he's launched their group into now.

~

She flings open the curtains, sunlight flooding the room. Nate, still in bed, curls up in the fetal position. "What the . . . ?"

"Time to wake up," Drew says much too loudly.

"Ouch. My head. Do you mind?" He yanks the covers over his eyes. "That sun is excruciating."

"Do I *mind*?" she says. "It's funny you should ask that question."

She drops down heavily beside him on the bed. "Because I just had a very interesting conversation with Graham."

"How's he feeling? Is his side okay?"

"Oh, he's fine. A little sore, but nothing major." She continues, "Anyway, we got to chatting about last night."

"I know, I'm sorry. I'm an idiot. I shouldn't have let him climb up on that bull. It was bound to be a disaster. I'll make it up to him today."

"That's not what I'm talking about." If she weren't so angry, it would almost be comical that they're having this discussion while Nate's head is hiding beneath the covers.

"Oh."

"So last night," she continues, "I was helping with his bandage and getting him into bed and, well, one thing led to another, and we kind of kissed." She pauses. "But it didn't mean anything."

This makes Nate bolt upright, ripping the covers off his head. "I'm sorry. Did you say that you and Graham *kissed*? As in, each other?"

She nods. "Yeah, I thought you should hear it from me first."

He rubs his eyes as if he might still be asleep. "But why?"

"Why?" Drew shrugs. "I don't know *why*, exactly, but you and Leslie stayed behind at the bar last night instead of helping me take care of him. Maybe I felt a little sorry for him. Maybe I was pissed. Maybe it was my way of thanking him for taking the fall for you."

This explanation comes out so easily that it grabs her by surprise. Graham's truth-telling has ignited a fire in her.

"What the hell, Drew? That's messed up."

She tilts her head. "I don't know. Not as messed up as you telling me that you and Leslie never hooked up in college, that you were like *brother and sister*."

She waits for his reaction, curious to see whether he'll deny it or confirm it. "When, in fact, it was a lie," she tacks on.

"Who told you that?"

"Hmm, I don't know. A little fairy? Graham did!"

"Okaaay." Nate scoots over toward the bedpost, farther away from her. "I'm not saying it didn't happen, just that I didn't lie to you intentionally about it."

This will be interesting, she thinks. "So you're admitting that you guys *did* sleep together but that you *unintentionally* forgot to tell me about it? How does that work, Nate?"

"Honey, please, settle down. You're out of control."

"Ha!" She leaps off the bed. "*I'm* out of control? I love that, how you spin things so that it's me who sounds crazy."

"Not crazy. Just calm down a little, would you?"

"Honestly, Nate, sometimes it's so exhausting being married to you. What else aren't you telling me? Have there been other women? While we've been *married*? And what's going on with all your gambling lately? Should I be worried?"

"Okay, can I *please* take a shower, and then we can discuss this over some coffee? Of course there haven't been any other women, but my head is frickin' jackhammering right now."

She leans back, arms folded, considering. "That might give you more time to think of a cunning excuse." She hesitates. "I suppose I'll allow it, but only because I have to get ready for the Derby. The buses are leaving in half an hour. You'd better hustle if you plan on going."

"I'm going, I'm going," he repeats as he swings his legs out of bed. "Jesus, this is already turning out to be *a day*."

Indignant, Drew ignores his comment and marches directly to the closet, where her kelly-green gown and fabulous hat await. While she dresses, she resolves that today, against all odds, will be a *good* day. She'll make certain of it.

Because, as a close friend once told her, doing the opposite of what's expected of you is often the best revenge.

HATS OFF TO YOU

14

NATE AND DREW

Nate understands he's in deep, deep trouble, that his buddy Graham has opened a Pandora's box, and now, on Drew's birthday weekend, he'll be forced to explain why he never told her about his history with Leslie. He struggles into his khakis, then a white shirt and a red jacket the color of a McIntosh apple. Normally, he'd ask Drew to help him with his tie, but he doesn't dare this morning. She's in the bathroom putting on her makeup—and giving him the silent treatment.

He knots the navy tie with red roses scattered across it, trying to gauge if there's time to grab coffee and a doughnut before hopping on the bus. Coffee, he decides, is a necessity if he has any intention of surviving today. And he'd better let Leslie know that their little secret is out. Although sending her a text doesn't feel right. No, he should tell her in person. Try to track her down before Drew does.

And then he'll throttle Graham.

He grabs his hat. "I'm heading downstairs to see if I can get breakfast. I'll meet you at the bus?"

"Sure. Whatever." Drew doesn't bother glancing away from the mirror when he pokes his head in the bathroom.

"Wow, you look amazing."

"Thanks." Still no eye contact.

"Okay, then. I guess I'll see you down there."

"I guess so," she says tartly.

Then, stupidly, because he can't help himself, he says, "You really kissed Graham?"

Her eyes shoot daggers at him in the mirror. (It was better when she refused to look his way.) He holds up his hands. "Okay, okay, I'm going."

Nate takes a packed elevator down to the lobby. Everyone chats animatedly, dressed in their Derby finery. Someone's wearing a heavy floral perfume that makes him hold his breath till the doors open on the lobby, where a preparty appears to be in full swing. A swarm of guests hovers around the bar and buffet table. Nate sets off in search of caffeine.

He's pouring cream into his cup when there's a tap on his shoulder. *Graham.*

His first instinct is to throw a punch. But then he takes a long, hard look at his friend. "Jeez, you look like hell."

"Thanks to you." Graham stares back at him through bloodshot eyes.

"Yeah, I'd say I'm sorry about last night," Nate begins, "but it sounds like you're the one who owes me an apology."

"That's what I was coming to tell you. Drew and I were talking at breakfast this morning, and somehow I let it slip that you and Leslie hooked up in college."

Nate debates playing dumb, asking Graham what the hell he's talking about. String him along, prolong his agony.

"I'm really sorry, man," Graham says. "I thought she knew."

"Yeah, well, she didn't." Nate sips his lukewarm coffee, reminds himself he's only drinking it for the caffeine. "In fact, I'm kind of surprised that *you* knew. I guess Leslie told you, huh?"

"Of course she told me. Years ago. I asked her if you two ever had a thing, and she said you'd had a couple of one-night rendezvous."

Nate groans. "How terrific that you two have such an open relationship."

Graham, ignoring the sarcasm, says, "I'm curious. Why didn't you ever mention it to Drew? After all this time?"

Nate shrugs. "Seemed best not to dredge up old news. Plus, she's always had a thing about Leslie and me. Like maybe she's jealous of our friendship. I didn't want to add fuel to the fire."

Graham nods, but Nate can tell he doesn't really get it, that he probably assumes Nate has been dishonest with Drew throughout their entire marriage.

Across the room, Leslie watches them from her table. "I should probably warn your wife."

"Oh, I already told her," Graham confirms. "That Drew might be, you know, a little upset with her today."

"Perfect."

Graham stands there, unmoving, blocking his way.

"Was there anything else that you wanted to tell me?" Nate snaps.

It's slight, but there's a definite flicker that passes across Graham's face. *He's probably wondering if he should own up to kissing my wife,* Nate thinks. *Probably trying to decide if Drew already told me.*

"How about I make it easy for you, so long as we're being truthful and all?" Nate suggests. "Like, did you want to mention that you made out with my wife last night?"

Graham's face blanches as he holds up his hands in surrender. "Buddy, it's not how it sounds."

"Yeah? Explain it to me, then." Drew's own words from this morning echo in his head.

Graham leads him over to a corner of the bar. "Look, we were drunk. She was helping me get into bed with my beat-up ribs, and one thing led to another. It was just a kiss. Nothing like what you and Leslie had."

"Oh, right. So that makes it better? Because Leslie and I weren't married when we fooled around. I don't know. Given the two scenarios, yours actually seems a little worse to me."

At that very moment, Leslie comes over to join them. "Good morning."

"Hey," Nate says. She's wearing a black dress stitched with a field of red roses and a hat dripping with faux roses.

"So I hear the cat's out of the bag?"

"Yeah, thanks to your husband."

"Graham didn't know, Nate. I mean, he didn't know that Drew didn't know."

"Yeah, and now she thinks I've been keeping all these secrets from her."

Neither of them says a word.

"What?"

Leslie shrugs. "Maybe it's time we stop hiding things from each other."

"Hey, *you* didn't tell Drew, either, so let's not paint this as if I'm the only bad guy here."

"I didn't tell her, Nate, because you specifically asked me not to, and I respected your request. *For years*, I might add."

Graham interrupts. "If I can ask, what's the big deal? You guys hooked up in college a couple of times. So what?"

"Because we denied it when she asked us if anything ever happened between the two of us," Leslie says softly. "It's a betrayal of trust."

~

The milliner Louise Green once said that "wearing a hat is like having a baby or a puppy: everyone stops to coo and talk about it." And this is precisely how Drew feels about her hat today. It's a showpiece, a showstopper. And while not a designer hat, per se, it *is* a cheap knockoff of a Vivien Sheriff. Browsing at home one night, she found it online and knew instantly that it was meant to be hers. A train of orchids, dyed the cheerful color of a green apple, twist around the wide white brim, and emerald-green peacock feathers sprout from the back. It's a hat masquerading as art, and Drew adores it.

Around this hat, her entire Derby outfit has been assembled—the kelly-green dress, the handbag, the delicate green earrings shaped like horseshoes. The only thing missing is a pair of chunky apple-green heels to match (she'd no idea of the importance of stylish footwear at the Derby, or she would have splurged). Instead, she's wearing her platform sandals again. But the hat! The hat will distract from the shoes.

As she swings through the hotel doors and heads to the line for the bus, she can feel the admiring glances being tossed her way. One woman stops her to say, "I *love* your hat. And your dress. That color! My goodness, you remind me of a young Jackie O."

Drew couldn't be more pleased. She'd been striving for a similar sense of style and elegance to that of the former First Lady, whom she sometimes gets compared to, mostly because of her hairstyle—a modern take on Jackie's bob.

As she walks, a line from a Lilian Jackson Braun character pops into her head: "I myself have twelve hats, and each one represents a different personality. Why just be yourself?" And Drew thinks, *Why, indeed? When there are so many other options. Why be myself when I can be the woman in the green orchid hat today?*

She will be elegant and poised, a true Southern lady. She will not linger on her husband's past transgressions, just as Jackie rose above her husband's infidelities, his half-truths. She will not obsess over a drunken kiss last night that will likely become meaningless in the larger scheme of her life. Beneath this hat, she will be become someone else entirely. Not a tired, slightly hungover forty-year-old mom who works with school children in Boston. Not a woman who has looked the other way for an impossibly long time.

Pinched waist, full skirt buoyed by layers of tulle, a boatneck, and cap sleeves. Even Drew will admit that, if anything, her dress errs on the side of being *too* fancy, especially now that she understands the

Kentucky heat means business. *But it's part of the costume,* she thinks. *My disguise.*

As she approaches the line for the bus, she spies Nate, Graham, and Leslie hovering off to one side. They're all staring at her. It crosses her mind that she could ignore them, go straight to the line. But then, what fun would spending the day by herself at the Derby be? No, she'll take the high road, the path of grace and elegance.

"Hi, everyone," she says from beneath her very large hat.

"Drew, you look incredible. That hat is to die for," Leslie comments.

"Thanks," she says coolly. She wonders whether Leslie knows that she knows about her and Nate's little secret. Did the guys warn her? Surprisingly, Drew doesn't feel the least bit guilty about her kiss with Graham last night. More like embarrassed that they'd both been so careless, so thoughtless.

Still, out of the entire crew standing before her, Graham's face is the only one she can stomach seeing this morning. "Hi, Graham."

"Drew." He tips his hat. "You're a vision."

"Thank you." She refuses to acknowledge her husband. "Should we get in line?" The heat, already pressing on her skin, leaves behind tiny thumbprints of perspiration.

"Sure, good idea," everyone hurries to say, as if they're afraid she might bite.

When they climb onto the bus, Drew immediately drops into an empty seat near the front. The rest of her group stops in surprise, then continues to the back once they realize she has no intention of sitting with any of them. Not a one. At the very least, she'll give herself the duration of the bus ride to corral her anger, salve her hurt feelings. They should be grateful that she chose to sit alone; it's her small gift to them.

She places her hat on her lap and turns to the woman beside her. "Hello, I'm Drew," she says, offering her hand. "Nice to meet you. Whereabouts are you from?"

DERBY DAYS

15

LESLIE AND NATE

If Churchill Downs was crowded yesterday, people flood every possible corridor today. Oaks Day was clearly the dress rehearsal for the Derby. It takes twice as long to reach the entrance gates, and the outfits on display are doubly bold, three times as wild. Except now the color palette extends beyond pinks and purples to bright reds and oranges, fluorescent yellows and rich greens. There are homemade hats fashioned from cardboard, tin, colorful socks. One woman walks with a field of faux butterflies fluttering above her head. Another man's hat is made from cigars, and Leslie wonders if he'll pass security, because, *Dude, isn't that a fire hazard?*

In truth, though, she understands that she's looking for someone, *anyone*, to distract her. To get her mind off the fact that her friend is barely speaking to her. Looking back, Leslie knows it was wrong to hide her dalliances with Nate, but he asked her not to mention them. And what did it matter to Leslie one way or the other when she first met Drew? Leslie's allegiances were to Nate. As her friendship with Drew evolved over the years, though, she should have guessed it would come up eventually. How she regrets not telling her!

Nate walks alongside Drew, probably trying to reassure her that it all meant nothing. But after a few minutes, he drops back and shoots Leslie a pleading, desperate look.

She scoots up next to Drew. "Hey, can I talk to you for a sec?" she asks.

"Not really interested right now." Drew keeps walking.

Okaaay. She and Nate exchange glances. *Uh-oh. This feels bad.*

But the whole thing has been blown out of proportion! Leslie needs to make Drew understand this. She and Nate figured out a long time ago that they worked better together as friends than boyfriend and girlfriend. The two times they fooled around, it had felt almost incestuous. Of course, now she can see everything through Drew's eyes: the deception, the lying, the sense of betrayal that they never told her. That they've shared this one secret for all these years.

Their group passes through security before being handed new wristbands at the escalators. As they ride up, Leslie notices that today's wristbands are forest green. Yesterday's were orange.

"Hey, honey," Nate calls out. "Our wristbands match your dress."

Drew holds out her arm to inspect it. "Close, but they're not apple green." As if to say, *Nice try*.

"But they *are* the color of money," Graham points out. "Very symbolic, wouldn't you say? The rich get richer, and their money gets greener. Or something like that."

"Would you stop with your symbolism," Leslie pleads. "No one cares about that stuff except your students."

"And probably not even his students," Nate jokes, although it feels a little mean.

"Hey, guys, hold up a minute." They all stop in a semicircle near the escalator while Graham's gaze follows an older couple, also wearing green wristbands, who continue to the escalator leading up to the next floor. Graham strolls over to chat with the guard and returns a minute later with a mischievous smile.

"So, guess what? Green wristbands mean Millionaires Row."

"What? No way." Nate shakes his head. "They're very strict around here."

"But how is that even possible?" Leslie demands. "Did they give us the wrong color by mistake?"

"Apparently so." Graham smiles like the crook he's quickly becoming. "Well, are you all going to stand there, or are you joining me?"

"Are you kidding?" Drew steps forward. "I'm so coming with you."

"I'm not missing out on Millionaires Row," says Leslie, grateful for the distraction. Maybe this will be just the thing to cut the tension in their group.

"But what if we get caught?"

"Seriously, Nate?" demands Drew, incredulous. "You, of all people?"

"C'mon, Nate," Leslie coaxes, amazed that he might actually pass up the opportunity to sneak back into his wife's good graces. "What could be more fun than crashing Millionaires Row?"

"Okay," he says. "But trust me, it's not gonna work."

When they reach the guard, however, he whisks them through to the escalator without so much as a glance at their wrists.

"Huh, look at that," Drew quips. "Guess you were wrong about something, Nate. What a surprise."

And for the remainder of the ride, no one else dares to utter a word.

~

"Well, well, well." Graham clicks his tongue. "Guess we've been promoted from the Lexus Club to the Aston Martin League."

Leslie would laugh if it all weren't so preposterous. Upstairs, Millionaires Row consists of a formal sit-down dining area flecked with white-clothed tables and a buffet stretching the entire length of the room. In the corner sits a well-appointed bar. Wide-screen TVs, broadcasting the races live, line the walls. No sticky floors here. It's all very civilized, *très* chic.

Then she sees him. "Uh-oh."

"Uh-oh?" Graham frowns.

Leslie nods to a man dressed in a black coat and tie, who appears to be signing in guests, placing checkmarks next to their names on a list. "Looks like we might need more than a wristband to get in."

"Oh, please." Graham trills his lips. "What's a little list? Follow me." He parades past the podium while waving at the maître d' as if their party already awaits them. Then he aims straight for the buffet table and grabs two plates, passing one first to Drew, then Leslie.

"You're good," Drew says, clearly impressed. "Do you break into parties often?"

"The trick is to be discreet." Graham snatches plates for himself and Nate.

If they were enjoying the chicken fingers and fruit kabobs yesterday, it was only because they'd no idea what they were missing. Leslie marvels over the decadence on display. Artfully arranged shrimp that hang like commas around the edge of an enormous glass bowl. Fresh fruit and crudités. Scones bursting with blackberries, the official fruit of Kentucky. Finger sandwiches and pasta salads. Chicken parm and fettucine alfredo. A carving station with roast beef and ham.

They load up their plates and flock around the dessert table, heavy on the blackberry pie and bourbon balls. Graham coaches them not to appear "so obvious" while they scour the room for a place to sit. But when Drew asks, *Where's the silverware?* Leslie suddenly realizes that they've grossly miscalculated. Rather than being placed at the buffet, the napkins and silverware already sit on the tables. *Next to name cards.*

"Oh, that's rich," Nate says. "You can get your food but not your silverware unless you have a name card."

"Let them eat cake with their fingers?" Leslie jokes, referencing Marie Antoinette's famous quote. She shrugs. "I'm not above eating with my fingers."

"Nonsense," hisses Graham. "This is where we pretend that we're the Thortonbachers from Beacon Hill in Boston."

"The who?" Drew asks, her brow knitted in confusion.

Graham sighs, as if disappointed by her lack of imagination. "The Thortonbachers. If anyone asks, just go with it." He strides over to a table with two empty chairs while the rest of them observe.

"I'm afraid," says a blue-haired woman seated at the table, the light winking off her bejeweled hand, "that those seats are already taken."

"Oh, my mistake." Graham's voice booms with faux sincerity. "I forgot we all have name cards. Silly me. I'll have to check what table I'm at. Sorry to bother you." And he sets off, as if to confirm with the maître d', before making a beeline to the drinks table.

"Oh my gosh," says Leslie. "I can't watch. He's going to get us all kicked out."

To the contrary, though, Graham begins chatting with the fellow ahead of him in line as if he were here yesterday.

Leslie ducks her head. "What are we supposed to do without silverware?" She can feel the burning stares of those who do belong here. Two women travel down the buffet line while discussing the designers for their dresses, one in Versace, the other in Vera Wang. When they reach the dessert table, they glance in Leslie's direction and—is she imagining it?—crinkle their noses!

"Hey, no one knows we snuck in. Just act like everyone else," whispers Drew once the women are out of earshot. And Leslie, both surprised and grateful that Drew appears to be speaking to her again, nods. When Graham finally returns to their corner, he's holding a gin and tonic in one hand and a half-eaten plate of food in the other. A fork rests on the edge of his plate.

"Hey, where'd you pilfer a fork?" Leslie exclaims.

"From one of the tables." Graham shrugs. "It looked clean enough."

"Eww. That's disgusting." Leslie sets her own plate down on a butler's tray. "I feel so out of place. I'm going to the ladies' room, and then I'm getting out of here. I liked our seats better yesterday."

"So soon?" Graham raises a questioning eyebrow, clearly enjoying the chance to rub elbows with the ridiculously rich and potentially famous. "But we haven't even seen a celebrity yet."

"You know what?" Leslie says. "I'm okay with that."

"Oh, come on, please stay," Drew pleads. "Just a little longer? You owe me that much, don't you think?" Her words are suddenly ablaze with innuendo, and Leslie sucks in her breath, waits for her friend to berate her here in Millionaires Row. *How could you?* Drew will ask. *How could you keep a secret from me for almost eleven years?*

And Leslie will have no answer. Except to say, *I don't know, and I'm so sorry. Please forgive me?*

She just wishes she could predict what Drew's response will be.

～

Nate is trying to figure out how to make it up to his wife. He will buy her a hundred roses and have them delivered to their room. He'll find her a lucky horseshoe necklace inlaid with diamonds. He'll get their flights changed tomorrow so that she can spend an entire day relaxing at the spa.

"So I was considering not talking to you at all today," Drew says, turning to him at last. "Because I'm mad at you. You know that, right? Like *really* mad."

"Yeah, I was getting that feeling." Nate sips his 7UP. No booze for him this afternoon. "Honey, I'm so—"

"I can't believe you lied when I asked if you and Leslie ever had a relationship."

"But we didn't! That's why this is all so bizarre."

She lifts a finger to his lips, shakes her head. "Don't try to explain it, okay? Not now. It'll only make me angrier. I want to enjoy today. I've pretty much been waiting my whole life to come to the Kentucky Derby. And now that I'm here, I plan to enjoy it." She pauses. "Besides, it's my birthday present."

At the mention of her birthday, Nate internally cringes. He can't believe how screwed up everything has gotten. But he's not a complete fool; he knows when to shut up.

"Okay, sure. I can do that. Does that mean you're talking to me again, though?"

She gives him the smallest of smiles, that crazy dimple winking at him. "If you're on your best behavior, sure."

Relief pools in him. Maybe the few cocktails she's had have helped pave the way to this momentary reprieve. Suddenly, laying into her about kissing Graham last night strikes him as petty and insignificant. Besides, as far as Nate is concerned, the fault all lies with Graham on that one. A buddy doesn't mess with another buddy's wife. It's part of the code.

Whatever it takes to get back into Drew's good graces, he'll do. He's about to suggest that they head out to the terrace when everyone's cell phone starts buzzing simultaneously. It feels weirdly apocalyptic, as if someone just shouted, *Fire!* in a movie theater.

Nate grabs his cell and begins reading the news alert.

"Spitting Image scratched! A bruised knee!" A man wearing star-shaped glasses calls out, prompting a wave of exclamations and curses around the room. Many of the millionaires (and Nate's pretty sure there are a few billionaires here, too) have probably already placed hefty bets on Spitting Image. That was going to be Nate's pick, too. The odds for Spitting Image (3–1) were about as sure as you could get in horse racing.

At least, that's what Phil told him.

But now what's he supposed to do?

Nate feels a little bad for the horse's owner and the trainer, whoever they might be. Having your horse scratch on race day must be one of the toughest experiences for a team. To invest so much time and money, only to discover that it's all been in vain, really stinks. Yet with such high stakes at the Derby this year (given the number of casualties a couple of years ago), Nate understands that officials are more likely to pull any horse who could risk further injury. Maybe Spitting Image will be healthy enough to race in time for the Preakness and the Belmont. Better to rest him today than push him too far for later.

Nate gets it. No one wants to see a horse with a broken leg get carted off the track in an ambulance only to be euthanized later. He also understands that a bruised leg bone can be particularly dangerous for an animal who stands on four legs most of the day, even while sleeping. And if the bone breaks, the odds of it healing properly can be slim. For one, the bones in a horse's leg are relatively thin compared with the thousand-plus pounds they support, so even a cast won't necessarily keep it straight enough to heal. And try telling a Thoroughbred to stop using his injured leg when it's in a cast! Add to that the high risk of infection when you've got a horse trucking around in the dirt and mud, and oftentimes the most merciful act is putting the animal down.

It's a shame, but it's also always a risk.

And now, thinks Nate, *hugely inconvenient.* He was so confident that Spitting Image would deliver a huge win that he's refrained from placing any other bets today. His phone buzzes—Phil. "Hey, sorry, honey, but I've got to take this," he tells Drew. "I'll be right back."

She rolls her eyes as if to say, *Of course you do.*

In the foyer, he searches for a sliver of privacy, but other guests appear to have the same idea. Everyone's scrambling for a new horse.

"Phil," he says, holding a finger to his other ear. "What the heck are we supposed to do now?"

"Just sent you a text. Check your messages."

"Hold on a sec."

Nate's blood starts pumping a little faster when he reads it:

Horse Cents to win.

Horse Cents and Best Neighbor for an exacta box.

So maybe there's still hope after all. He's debating whether to place his bet now or hold off a bit longer when he spots Phil walking around the corner. They both start to laugh and switch off their phones.

"Fancy, fancy. I didn't know you were up in Millionaires Row, too."

"I'm not," Nate corrects. "They gave us green wristbands by mistake today. Thought we'd take advantage of it while we could."

"Good for you. And don't worry—I won't tell."

"So listen. Got your text. Horse Cents? Are you sure? Why not Big Dipper? Last time I looked, Big Dipper had 4–1 odds, Horse Cents 5–1."

"Because everyone else is going to start betting on Big Dipper." Phil's voice drops an octave. "And there've been murmurings that Big Dipper has been off his game in morning training runs. He's hardly a sure thing." Phil pauses. "Horse Cents, on the other hand, has been clocking consistently good times all week in practice. Short of a complete upset, he'll almost certainly be today's Derby winner."

Nate nods. Those are the words he needs to hear. *Almost certainly a winner.* "Okay, I like it. You may have just saved me from a panic attack—or a heart attack," he jokes. "Thanks."

"No problem. Hey, good luck today."

"Yeah, same to you." Nate heads back into the dining area to find Drew. *Maybe,* he thinks, *if I win really big today, Drew will forgive me.* It's as if a light bulb goes off in his head: *Yes, that's the way to make this all go away.* If he plays it smart and brings in even more money than he did yesterday, Drew will have to overlook his tiny white lie, won't she? She'll see how it pales in comparison with everything else about this weekend. A tiny lie about something that happened more than twenty years ago? *C'mon,* he thinks. *Let's not overplay it.*

When he sees her waving across the room, her silver bracelets jangling on her wrist, he begins to stride in her direction, certain he's figured out a plan for how to win her back. A plan that will ensure her birthday weekend turns right side up once again.

16

DREW

"Uh-oh. Look out," Drew mutters under her breath when Leslie rejoins her with fresh cocktails. Even though she hasn't forgiven her friend, Drew has consumed enough alcohol to table their discussion (or argument) until later, maybe even until they're back home in Boston. Earlier, when she more or less guilted Leslie into staying in Millionaires Row because neither she nor Graham was ready to leave, it felt as if an entire conversation passed between them. As soon as the words, *You owe me that much, don't you think?* were spoken, Drew watched the color drain from Leslie's face. And Drew thought to herself, *Aha! We understand each other, then. Enough said for now.*

"Three o'clock. To your right," Drew directs.

"Yoo-hoo!" Trixie Fairfax, waving her hand, is headed their way in a royal-blue gown and a fabulous blue hat, feathers spilling out the side.

Leslie groans.

"I *thought* that was you!" Trixie exclaims, rushing over to embrace Leslie, their hats colliding. A wave of floral perfume, like gardenias, wafts through the air. "Don't you look darling in your magnolia dress! Is it a Versace?"

Leslie musters a smile. "Thank you. So do you. Not Versace," she notes, without offering an alternative, but Trixie doesn't seem to notice. "And you." She turns to Drew. "My goodness, dear. Green is your color!"

"Thank you."

"I'm so happy to see you, ladies. What have you done with your handsome husbands?"

"Graham and Nate are helping themselves to more food."

"Excellent." Although, it's unclear what exactly is *excellent* about it. Maybe because Trixie assumes that means they'll be hanging out in Millionaires Row indefinitely? She hasn't questioned how their crew got up here in the first place, which is a relief. "We missed you guys on the bus this morning. Benton decided he wanted to splurge on a limo for the big day." She winks at them, as if to say, *Can you believe my crazy husband?* Drew eyes the drink in Trixie's hand—by the looks of it, her third or fourth of the day. "So, tell me. Are you two having the *best* time?"

Drew wonders if the woman always speaks in superlatives or if it's the Lilies talking. "We are," Drew coos in response, channeling her best Southern charm. "How could we not? It's everything we imagined the Derby would be—and more." Even to Drew, her own voice rings false. "What about you and Benton? Having fun?"

Trixie waves a drunken hand in the air. "Oh, you know Benton. He likes to have his own fun. He's off smoking cigars with some of the fellows right now. Don't ask me who they are." A rush of something like sympathy washes over Drew for the briefest of moments. Loquacious and affable Trixie has no other friends up here in Millionaires Row? "Plus"—she leans in—"between us girls, he's kind of grumpy since his horse just scratched."

"Oh. Yeah. I think a lot of people are feeling that way," offers Drew.

"It wasn't just the horse he was betting on. It's *his* horse."

Uncertain glances pass between Drew and Leslie. "His horse?" Leslie asks for clarification. "As in, you guys *own* Spitting Image?"

Trixie nods, her hat bobbing up and down. "Yep. Don't tell anyone here, though. Benton doesn't want them beating him up, in case they're angry. He and maybe twenty other guys went in on the horse together a couple of years ago. I think they all own an equal share, whatever that means."

"I'm pretty sure it means that they pooled their money together to buy the horse as an investment," says Drew.

"That sounds right. Anyway, I always tease Benton about it. 'Which part did you get, honey?' I'll ask. 'The leg or the ass?'" Trixie snort-laughs as if it's the funniest thing she's heard all day. "Anyhow, have you ladies had any big wins so far? We're doing lousy. Throwing money away left and right."

"Mmm . . . not so much," Drew answers quickly for them both. For whatever reason, mentioning Nate's winnings to Trixie feels wrong. Is it because she doesn't want to brag, or is she still too angry to feel happy for him?

"But we're having fun," adds Leslie.

"Ain't that the truth?" Trixie says, before exclaiming, "Oooh!" when Benton sneaks up from behind and gives her a friendly slap on the derriere.

"Why, hello there, ladies. Good to see you again. You both look beautiful. It's Leslie, right?"

Leslie answers in the affirmative, then says, "And this is Drew. I think you met her on the bus yesterday?"

"Oh, right, yes, Drew. How're you doing, honey?" Benton, who reeks of cigar smoke, twirls the ice in his cocktail nonchalantly. He's wearing a cream suit, red roses twining down the lapels, and a cream fedora with a red rose tucked into the hatband. Drew can tell by the way he won't meet her eyes that he doesn't remember her at all. Considering his horse scratched, though, he appears to be in good spirits. Maybe Trixie got it wrong? Maybe he doesn't actually own Spitting Image?

Trixie lays a hand on his arm. "Poor Benton's been scouring the charts for a winner today, but we haven't had much luck—have we, honey? If only Spitting Image hadn't up and hurt his knee on us."

She makes a pouty face as if it's personal, as if the horse intended to disappoint them all along.

"The day's still young, honey," he says, patting her bottom again.

"Oh, stop it!" Trixie slaps his hand away. "Honestly, you'd think my husband was sixteen, not sixty-six."

"Well, it was really nice seeing you both," Drew says quickly, eager to be rid of them. "We're headed out to the terrace to watch the races."

"Have fun, ladies!" she calls after them.

Drew drags Leslie by the hand. "Oh my. I hope Trixie finds her way home tonight."

"No kidding."

The terrace for Millionaires Row turns out to be practically sitting on the finish line. Around them, a mix of young folks (new money) and octogenarians (old money) converses. Drew questions if they're all somehow related or if the younger crowd, mostly in their twenties and thirties, is independently wealthy. It's hard to imagine having that kind of money, especially at such a young age. It seems that she and Nate are always struggling, trying to save, only to have another emergency deplete their funds all over again.

Leslie turns to her, rests a hand on her arm. "Listen, I know you're really angry at me right now," she says. By now, they're both a few cocktails deep into the day. "But I want you to know how sorry I am. I should have told you about Nate and me in college."

Drew narrows her eyes, says nothing.

"We were never boyfriend and girlfriend. That part was always true."

Drew waits for her friend to continue, won't give her the satisfaction of making her confession easier. *If you want to apologize right now,* she thinks, *then have at it.*

"But we did fool around. Only twice! But still. We were both trashed. Once junior year and once senior year. It was stupid. It should have never happened in the first place."

"Okay," Drew says slowly. "But you know that's not the part that really upsets me, right?"

Leslie bites her bottom lip and nods. "Yeah."

"Both you and Nate lied to me when I specifically asked if you'd ever been together. I don't understand why you'd do that." The hurt in her voice slips through.

"Listen," says Leslie. "When Nate asked me to keep it a secret, I'd only just met you. He was afraid it would put you off. And then when things started to get serious between you two, he was worried that if you found out, you'd break up with him."

"But that's crazy! Maybe I would have been a little freaked out, but I wouldn't have broken up with him. Besides, it was college."

"Right, but he was so worried about screwing things up with you. I could tell that he was totally in love."

When she hears those words, Drew feels herself softening a little. "You could?"

"Absolutely. He used to drone on about how cute your kids would be, and I'd tell him to shut up, that he was pathetic." She laughs now. "Not very nice of me, I guess, but honestly, it was annoying."

Drew laughs despite herself. "That's funny to hear."

"Anyway, I wanted you to know that I'm so, so sorry. I never meant to hurt you. Especially on your birthday weekend."

"I know," Drew says quietly.

"And I'm pretty sure that Nate wanted to keep it a secret because he thought he was protecting you. As nuts as it sounds."

"Maybe." Although Drew's not completely convinced of this.

"Factor in Nate's bad instincts with those of my husband, who, for reasons still unclear to me, set off a marital bomb this morning . . ."

"I think we were both a little discombobulated," Drew says. "I mean, after our kiss last night."

Leslie's eyes grow wide, and a strange feeling sweeps over Drew. The sensation that maybe she's gotten the better of her friend without meaning to. That maybe Graham hasn't told her yet about last night.

"I'm sorry, but what are you talking about?" Leslie asks.

Which is when their husbands materialize by their sides, fresh drinks in hand. "Are you ladies ready to head back to our fancy-adjacent seats?" inquires Graham. "Not much longer till the Run for the Roses."

"Perfect timing." Drew, feeling lighter already, gladly accepts her new cocktail. "Let's get out of here. I've had enough of the rich and famous for one day."

"Leslie?" Graham asks.

"Yeah, I'm coming." But she spins back to Drew. "This?" she whispers, pointing between the two of them. "To be continued."

And Drew nods her pretty hat agreeably.

17

GRAHAM AND LESLIE

Whatever Leslie and Drew discussed in Millionaires Row, it seems to have worked its magic on Drew. Graham even pulled a smile from her when they were walking back to their seats. He longs to tell her how he can't stop thinking about their kiss. How he regrets that their conversation at breakfast swerved so quickly to the topic of Nate and Leslie. How he wishes he could go back in time and rewind it! Explore whether there might be real feelings there, grounded in authenticity and not just alcohol. Graham already knows how he feels about Drew. But what about her? Now that her lips have touched his, it's as if he's sipped the whiskey and craves the bottle.

And even though Graham's already declared himself not a betting man, it seems as if the odds might have shifted in his favor when it comes to Drew. *Is it possible,* he wonders, *that I intentionally let it slip that Leslie and Nate had a tryst in college? So that Drew could see her husband for the man that he is?* But that's nuts. Graham counts Nate as one of his closest friends. No way would he try to sabotage his marriage on purpose. And he wasn't even aware that Drew didn't know!

With his program, he fans the humid air across his face while he and Nate wait on their wives, who've ostensibly gone off in search of sustenance. Their fancy-adjacent seats in the sun are not nearly as cool (or as comfortable) as those up in Millionaires Row, and Graham shifts awkwardly in his chair, crossing one leg over the other, then recrossing the other way. The question of how—and whether—to revisit the subject of his own mess up this morning (and last night!) runs through his mind. Nate has barely said a word all afternoon, and Graham gets the distinct feeling that his friend is simply waiting for the right moment to turn and sock him in the mouth.

"Why so antsy today, Graham? Nervous about your bet?" Nate doesn't even bother to glance up from the article he's reading in the program. Something about the history of jockeys who've raced at Churchill Downs.

"Ha! Yeah, that's probably it." He waits to see if Nate will offer anything more, but his reply is met with silence. Which isn't surprising, really, given that it's pretty much the way things have always gone between them: Nate's the alpha male in their motley gang of two. If he prefers not to rehash recent history, then that's how they'll play it. Besides, Graham's not in any rush to justify his actions of the last twenty-four hours.

He opens his own program and pretends to study the odds for the Derby, only a short time away. Big Dipper's odds still beat those of Horse Cents. "Hey, are you sure we shouldn't be putting our money on Big Dipper?"

Nate pulls his gaze away from the program and stares out at the track. "Not according to my source. Phil predicted which horse was going to win yesterday, and that was based on terrible odds. I've gotta believe Phil knows what's going to happen in today's race, too."

"True. Good point. All right, then," Graham says, taking out his phone. "A hundred bucks on Horse Cents, it is." It's stupid, he knows, but maybe taking Nate's advice will help to ease the friction between the two of them.

He puts his phone away and glances around. "I wonder where our seatmates from yesterday disappeared to?"

Nate shrugs. "Maybe they snuck up to Millionaires Row by themselves."

Just then, Leslie and Drew return with pretzels in hand, and Graham hops back a row so he can sit beside Leslie, and Drew next to Nate. But he doesn't miss Drew's quick glance as she passes him to her seat. *Are you thinking what I'm thinking?* Graham is dying to ask. *That maybe we can grab a cocktail tonight, just the two of us?* There's still so much they need to discuss.

And while he sits beside Leslie, who quietly munches on her pretzel and reviews the odds for today's big race, he can't help but ponder what lies ahead for their marriage. Their Derby getaway hasn't exactly brought them closer, but it hasn't torn them asunder either. Not for the first time, with the sun glancing off her hat, Graham is struck by how classically beautiful his wife is, this woman he has slept beside for more than a dozen years. But do they have anything left in common? Does she even *like* him anymore?

When he tries to imagine whom his spirit most aligns with, it's Drew, not Leslie. He and Drew both enjoy a good bottle of cabernet, a little Beethoven playing in the background, relaxing without a lot of fuss. They share a sweet tooth and a passion for books. (Leslie always complains that she doesn't have time to read.) But Drew will sometimes stop by the house to drop off a title that she thinks he'll enjoy. Joyce Maynard's *How the Light Gets In.* Katherine Heiny's latest collection of short stories. James McBride's *The Heaven and Earth Grocery Store.* And then later, they'll discuss it over a glass of wine, their own private book club. A sense of serenity infuses their togetherness, no one making demands of the other. Nothing expected.

"Have you made your final pick?" Leslie asks.

Her question, so on point, jolts Graham out of his reverie, and he stumbles to answer. Is she asking him if he's made his final pick between Drew and herself? As if Drew were a choice! As if he's at liberty to decide.

"Are you okay?" Her brow knits. "You just turned instantly pale. Here, have some water. It's hot out."

He sips and struggles to regain his composure. "Thanks. Um, I placed a bet on Horse Cents a few minutes ago. How about you?"

"I'm thinking either Good Enough or Second Chances." She flips her hair over her shoulder. "I like the sentiment behind both those names." For an instant, he considers the possibility that his wife is sending him a veiled message. Perhaps she's made her peace with their slowly disintegrating marriage. Perhaps she's decided he's good enough. That she'll give their relationship another chance.

"Makes sense." He refrains from pointing out that the odds for Good Enough are a ghastly 30–1. But Second Chances, with 11–1 odds, could prove a worthy competitor. To Graham's way of thinking, it's anyone's guess which horse will thunder across the finish line first today. Ever since the news broke that Spitting Image scratched, the odds have been shuffling and reshuffling, as if they themselves can't decide.

It's funny, but before this weekend, Graham always considered betting on horses akin to reading tea leaves. The past two days, though, have given him a new appreciation for the statistical analysis involved in handicapping. Calculating the number of prior wins, a horse's average speed across a number of races, and the untold other variables turns out to be a bit of a science. For a literature professor who tends to view the world in terms of nuance, quantifying things has always made Graham slightly nervous.

But what if he's missing something? What if the rest of the world could be similarly understood, through quantification rather than qualification?

And if so, would it be useful?

For instance, if he were betting on whether he and Leslie would go the distance, their marriage surviving all the way to Zach's high school graduation, he might give it 8–1 odds. Not crazy good, but not crazy awful either. If he had to wager on whether he'll retire before age sixty-five, he'd give it 3–1 odds, as in excellent. And if he had to guess if his crush on Drew is reciprocated, he'd wager maybe 6–1.

But the odds were forever shifting, weren't they? Right up until the horses made their way to the starting gates. And therein lay the rub. Because the odds couldn't always accommodate the shifts quickly enough. Nor did they necessarily dictate success. Drew might have feelings for him, but then what? Where did they go from there? There were too many nuances in life, too many variables for any particular scenario to boil it down to one absolute, guaranteed outcome.

It occurs to him suddenly that maybe he hasn't been giving Leslie a fair chance. If she's annoyed at him, it's quite possible that Graham is *being* annoying. If she's uninterested in him, maybe it's because he's allowed himself to become a slightly overweight, unfulfilled community college professor who'd prefer to sit at home rather than venture out to an art museum or a concert. If she rolls her eyes when he launches into a discussion about a book he read and why she should read it, perhaps he *does* sound a tad condescending. It never occurred to him that he might be the problem, the one who's closed off and missing all the signals, not his wife.

He reaches over to squeeze her hand. "What is it?" she asks, surprised.

"Oh, nothing. Just saying hi."

~

So that's it, Leslie thinks. *He's not going to tell me.*

Tell her that when he and Drew got back to the hotel last night, Drew played nurse, tucked him in, and the two of them kissed.

It feels strange, sitting next to her husband, pretending she doesn't have a clue. Especially given all that's already transpired today. And that

Graham, the newly self-appointed Solicitor of Truth in their group, appears to have skipped right over himself.

Over the last hour, Drew has divulged to Leslie every detail about their unchaperoned time back at the hotel last night—not that there was much to tell. Perhaps Drew offered it as an olive branch, or maybe it was her way of sticking it to Leslie. A way of saying that while Drew's husband may have slept with Leslie back in college, Leslie's husband wanted Drew *last night*. Over the last few months, Drew has mentioned having a case of the "middle-age blues," and Leslie understands probably better than her friend can imagine.

Oddly enough, though, upon hearing Drew's retelling of "the kiss," Leslie's reaction had been one of inaction. She knew they'd been spending a fair amount of time together over the last few months, that Graham enjoyed Drew's company. But did Leslie suspect actual physical contact? No, not really. Nate was such a catch, and Leslie couldn't fathom Drew being attracted to her husband in that way. Nate and Graham were so different!

But maybe what surprised her most was not that it had happened, but the feeling of indifference that settled over her as Drew spoke. Leslie didn't feel angry, or jealous, or any of the other emotions she might have expected. When Drew told her the details, she nodded her head and said, "Don't worry about it. Stuff happens."

And Drew, her close friend of over a decade, stared back at her with those huge brown eyes. "You're not mad? I don't understand."

Leslie downplayed the whole event. "It was just a kiss, right? You guys were drunk. What's the big deal?" Maybe she was playing it too cool, hoping Drew would follow her lead when it came to Leslie and Nate's history, but she didn't think so. Drew didn't need more guilt piled on her. "Seriously, don't sweat it. It only seems fair, given that I never told you about Nate and me. Tit for tat."

"That's funny. That's exactly what Graham said. 'Tit for tat.'"

Leslie raised an eyebrow. "Is that right?" So maybe, she conceded, it was her own husband who'd been out for revenge.

She studies him now, sitting next to her in his Derby finery, and asks herself whether she even knows this man anymore.

"What?" he asks, but she shakes her head.

"Nothing. Just thinking about my bet." She pulls out her cell and logs it: fifty bucks on Good Enough. Because Second Chances suddenly sounds like a loser to her.

18

NATE

Nate excuses himself under the pretense of going to fetch a cool drink. For all his hair-of-the dog-that-bit-you bravado earlier today, he found he couldn't stomach a single mint julep. He's been sucking down sodas exclusively. The real reason for his sneaking out, however, is that he's yet to post his bets. In less than an hour, the uniformed men and women of the US Navy will stride onto the field with the garland of roses meant for today's winner. The national anthem will be sung, followed by the walkover, the Call to the Post, and finally, the starting bell. He needs to get his bet in before the window closes.

And he wants to place it alone, away from curious, prying eyes. One person's, in particular.

In the back of his head, Drew's voice begs him not to go crazy, reminds him that even after taxes, fifteen grand is *a lot* of money. She's unaware, however, that this trip, her birthday present, has yet to be paid off, all on a credit card that's accumulating interest. That he still owes Leslie, and then there's the matter of paying off his other credit card, as well as his buddies who spotted him a few grand last weekend at the roulette table. As far as he knows, Drew's only aware of the few thousand due on the kitchen renovation—peanuts compared with the rest.

The thing is, as much money as fifteen grand *sounds* like, it's only a fraction of what he needs. To make all their debts disappear, it'll take a truly big number. Like fifty grand. And so he's been debating whether to heed Drew's cautious—and probably wise—advice to bet $5,000 at the most on Horse Cents. It would leave him with $10,000, which he could at least use to pay down his credit cards or pay Leslie back.

But what if he trusts Phil's instincts and bets the whole farm, which, assuming Horse Cents wins, would bring in *$75,000*? Nate understands anything can happen, and that 5–1 odds aren't by any means a sure thing. But Phil's been texting him all afternoon, urging him to leap, saying Horse Cents looks very promising.

It's tempting. And Phil was right on the money yesterday. But if Nate loses, Drew will never forgive him for betting all his winnings. She'll accuse him of being shortsighted, possibly call him out for having a gambling problem, which even Nate himself is beginning to suspect. It's just that every time he's gotten into a hole like this, he's managed to climb his way out. Usually at the casino, but cards are similar enough to horse racing. A bet is a bet.

Does he dare risk losing it all?

Some freak accident could occur. Horse Cents could collide with another horse, break a leg. Not likely, but possible. On the other hand, Nate didn't have $15,000 last week, so what's the big deal if he loses? It's more or less play money. *Play money that could reap significant, life-changing benefits.* It would take so much pressure off, and man, lately he's been feeling it. Seventy-five thousand dollars. Wrapping his head around that large of a number takes some work. But if Horse Cents wins, Nate could finally take a deep breath, maybe spend more time with Drew and Owen, help out around the house. That would make her happy.

He calls up the app on his phone, logs on, and selects his race and horse to win. Now it's just a matter of deciding how much and how many bets to place. Phil recommended an exacta box—a wager on two horses to place first and second in any order—but Nate's not feeling it today. It seems like a tremendous risk, praying for *two* horses to perform the way you want in the Derby.

Better, he decides, to place his bet on a single winner. He considers $1,000, but that feels paltry. Five thousand? That means his return would be $25,000, plus the $10,000 that he'd hold back. Thirty-five thousand sounds pretty nice. That could work. If he boosts that number to $10,000, though, it'll earn him $50,000. That's a boatload of cash, plus the extra $5,000 he'd have from yesterday's winnings. That might just do the trick, give him a clean slate to start over debt-free.

He decides that's what he'll do: place $10,000 that he never had in the first place on Horse Cents for the win. He starts to type in the figure when the announcer comes on to say that Shania Twain will soon be taking the stage for the national anthem. Nate's thumb hovers above the "Post" button. Fifty-five thousand or seventy-five thousand? Which one sounds better?

Well, dang it, he thinks. *Seventy-five, obviously.* He digs deep, tries to feel the race in his gut. Phil sounded pretty confident about Horse Cents. To bring home $75,000 would clear out all his debts and then some. They could even take a real vacation over the holidays, the whole family. Drew keeps talking about wanting to see Hawaii someday. It would make his little white lie disappear.

To hell with it, he decides. He deselects $10,000, scrolls down to $15,000, and hits "Post" before he can change his mind. As soon as he does, his stomach churns. A tough decision, but one that had to be made for his family. It's what they need to break free of their current situation. Drew will thank him later. At least, that's what he tells himself when he steps up to order four Cokes with a side of fries at the kiosk. It's all about doing what's right for his family.

FEELING YOUR OATS

19

DREW

Drew has been texting back and forth with Owen, who wants her to put five dollars down on a horse called Runs the Gamut. He tells her that he likes the way the horse looks, and he'll pay her back when she gets home. She laughs when she reads it. Her son's bets seem about as well thought out as her own. But she's happy to hear from him, glad to know that he's watching the Derby on TV with his grandparents and that they've fashioned their own hats from construction paper.

It's also nice to be reminded of what counts most. She's been so consumed with the drama of this weekend: Nate and Leslie's secret; her kiss with Graham; the fact that Graham didn't tell Leslie, so Drew told her. She practically needs a scorecard to remember who's being truthful with whom!

She appreciated Leslie's leveling with her, apologizing and explaining why she never told. How she'd promised Nate and thought it was his responsibility to convey the truth to Drew, not hers. And for that honesty, Drew repaid Leslie with her own, detailing the events of last night with Graham. But after the initial surprise, Leslie hardly seemed bothered by Drew's confession.

It was as if she already knew—or perhaps didn't care?

Drew's head spins from all the emotions in play this weekend. And now she's especially anxious for Nate to get back from his soda run, because 1) she's dying of thirst, and her body is severely dehydrated from last night's antics; 2) because the entire spectacle of the Derby is about to begin and she doesn't want him to miss it; and 3) as much as she loves her husband, she doesn't completely trust him to bet a safe amount. As if he's read her mind, Nate materializes beside their seats holding a gray cardboard box, four sodas and a side of fries stuffed into the slots. As he starts to pass them out, he apologizes to Betsy and Della, who only recently arrived, for not having anything for them.

"We're all set, but thank you, honey," Della says, holding up an enormous Styrofoam cup. Mother and daughter joined them about ten minutes ago, explaining that they kept mostly to the tents and air-conditioned rooms today. Yesterday's heat, understandably, drained them. Betsy is wearing a red sundress, a straw hat with a red ribbon circling it, and white cowboy boots. Della, on the other hand, appears to have abandoned her fashion sense today and is dressed in a short-sleeved blouse and black polyester pants. But her hat—an explosion of red roses and feathers—is outstanding.

"Are those cardinal feathers?" Drew asks, leaning in closer.

Della laughs. "Oh, dear, I wish I could tell you, but the truth is, I have no idea. A nice young man downstairs noticed that I didn't have a hat for today, so he took this one right off the table and handed it to me. Told me it was mine to keep."

Betsy cries, "Can you believe it? My mother is wearing a centerpiece for a hat!"

"It suits you," Graham says good-naturedly. "Truly."

Nate holds up his phone and insists that they capture "the centerpiece hat" for posterity before he cajoles a guy in the adjacent box to take a photo of all six of them.

"You better get ready to plug your ears," Della warns. "Because Betsy and I will be doing some serious hollering today. Runs the Gamut is supposed to race like the wind. That's who our money's on."

They flutter their white tickets in the air, a first-rate advertisement for why everyone should bring their mother to the Kentucky Derby at least once.

"That's the horse our son wants," Drew shares. "I just placed a bet for him."

"Well, we've been hearing positive things about him all day," Betsy says. "Less so about Spitting Image, though."

"Is that right?" Graham asks.

"People are talking. Saying it wasn't a bum knee at all that kept him out of the race." Now she's got Nate's interest.

"What was it, then?"

"What you might expect. Drugs." Her delivery is very matter-of-fact. "I don't remember the name, but it's supposed to help protect the horse's lungs."

"I'll bet it's Lasix," Graham supplies. "It used to be legal. It only recently got banned on race day."

"I'll be damned." Nate shakes his head. "Phil didn't mention anything about it."

"Well, it's not official yet. Just rumors, so who knows."

"Okay, hush now," Della says. "The uniformed men and women are walking the rose garland out."

Drew can hardly believe that the Run for the Roses is less than an hour away. They watch the dignified procession onto the field, the officers in their pressed whites carrying the long, narrow glass case that holds the garland. There's applause, and then it's time for the national anthem, Shania Twain jumping up onstage and dazzling the entire audience with her voice, transcendent and brazen at once. When she hits the high note on "free," the audience goes bananas.

Drew, meanwhile, struggles not to think about the fact that Graham is sitting directly behind her. That if he wanted to, he could easily reach out and tap her on the shoulder. That he could bend forward as if to ask her a question, but instead might whisper that he can't stop thinking about her. She knows it's silly, but despite her downplaying the whole episode as a drunken nonevent to Leslie and Nate (and herself), the spark she felt last night when they kissed still lingers.

As if for reassurance that he's still there, she keeps turning her head, trying to glimpse him out of the corner of her eye. Does last night keep replaying through his head? Did it mean anything? She attempts to eavesdrop on his conversation with Leslie, but there's not much to hear. If Drew were sitting next to Graham, they'd be having so much fun. Instead, she's trapped beside Nate, who's nervously jouncing his leg.

If only she could channel some of Graham's calm! Maybe she could scoot her chair back a row, blaming it on the woman's hat that's partially blocking her view? But when she glances across their box, there's definitely only room for two folding chairs across. No, the only option would be for her to swap seats with Leslie, or Nate with Graham. And how on earth can she suggest *that* without causing a scene?

She sighs, resigns herself to her seat being where it is, and busies herself with people-watching. Eventually, the announcer directs everyone's attention to the edge of the track, where the horses and their owners are beginning to gather for the esteemed walkover to the paddock.

Drew's skin prickles, a fresh rush of adrenaline shooting through her veins. "So, are you going to tell me how much you bet?"

"For me to know and you to find out," Nate offers cagily. She rolls her eyes, gives up. She refuses to worry about it.

As the horses begin to step onto the track, the stadium hums with electricity. The animals' sheer physicality is striking, their enormous bodies rippling with muscle. If the fillies in the Oaks impressed yesterday, they seem like mere amateurs now, compared with the regal line of Thoroughbreds parading down below. These horses walk with a distinct swagger, as if they know they're the real deal. A certain gravitas further infuses the event, as if everyone understands that up for grabs are the bragging rights of a lifetime. Not to mention an enormous pot of gold (some $5 million in the winner's purse alone).

That fifty thousand more fans than yesterday pack the stands also means the arena practically vibrates from the energy and noise. Drew spots her horse, Good Enough, as soon as he enters the track. He's a beautiful bay with white stockings around his ankles. "That's my horse," she proudly tells Nate. Maybe not quite as fierce-looking as Horse Cents, but to Drew's untrained eye, powerful and focused.

"Nice," Nate comments without even looking.

She won't let it bother her, though. He's nervous, which is natural. Her husband knows what he's doing, and even if he doesn't, this guy Phil seems to. Odd, she thinks, how she's counting on a man she's never met to give her husband solid advice. For all she knows, he's a fortune teller, a medium, a charlatan.

Breathe.

"Oh, there he is!" Betsy cries when Runs the Gamut starts down the track. Whatever their horse might lack in size, he more than compensates for in good looks. A gorgeous gray with a mottled white coat, he's apparently as fast as quicksilver. A certain bravado marks his walk, as if he knows he's the best-looking horse out there. Since this morning, his odds have climbed substantially. Betsy and Della wave their hats in the air and cheer like they're high school girls at a state championship football game.

Soon enough, the famous command from the paddock, "Riders up!" goes out, and the jockeys climb onto their respective horses. When the bugle sounds for the Call to the Post, Drew's stomach twists into knots. This is it. They're about to witness what's famously known as "The fastest two minutes in sports. The best two minutes in sports. The Run for the Roses."

The day she has dreamed about ever since she was a little girl watching in her family's living room. Incredibly, the Kentucky Derby, finally within her grasp.

One hundred and fifty thousand spectators sing or hum along to "My Old Kentucky Home" while the university band plays. Drew understands the controversy swirling around this tradition because of the song's references to the Old South, but no one in the stands today can deny the deep sense of nostalgia that sweeps over the arena. Men and women alike clasp their hats to their chests, out of respect for those who are about to race—and those who've come before.

Down at the far end of the track, the racehorses have begun to emerge from the tunnel, the jockeys mounted and dressed in their sharp-looking silks. Some don multiple pairs of goggles strapped to their helmets, in case their lenses get fogged or muddied during the race. But that shouldn't be a problem today. There's been no rain, and the track appears to be dry and in good condition for racing.

Drew watches as Good Enough gets led over to his gate. The horse goes in willingly, smoothly. Horse Cents, on the other hand, swings his head from side to side, taking a moment to settle before finally entering Gate 12. Ordinarily, twenty horses run in the Derby, but today there are only eighteen. When she asks Nate about this, he explains that Blazing Sun pulled out at the last minute, though no one knows why.

Her hand reaches for Nate's; the waiting is intense. As the final horse gets shoehorned in, Nate squeezes her hand hard enough that her fingers pinch. And then, almost as soon as the last horse is secured, the buzzer rings and the gates swing open. Drew's heart might as well be down on the track with the horses.

The call goes out. "And they're off!"

It looks like a fair start, and by the end of the first length, it's Horse Cents, Runs the Gamut, and a horse named Sheer Luck in the lead. Good Enough moves into tenth place, then ninth, but still lags several lengths behind the top horses. Betsy and Della start screaming when Runs the Gamut moves up to command the lead after the first turn, Horse Cents nipping at his heels. After those two follows a cluster of Thoroughbreds jockeying for position, among them Good Enough. From up in the stands, it appears as if all the horses might be racing on top of one another down the backstretch. The crowd screams and hollers, cheering on their favorites.

Going into the turn, five or six horses vie for first position, including Horse Cents. One of the horses suddenly bears toward the inside rail, and Drew holds her breath, thinking a horse—or a jockey—is about to go down. But thankfully, it's a false alarm. Horse Cents and Sheer Luck pull ahead of the pack. Runs the Gamut has fallen back to third. Incredibly, Good Enough continues to advance, pulling up alongside Steady Does It, who's in fourth.

"Come on!" Drew screams.

"Let's go, Good Enough!"

Nate, meanwhile, bellows so loudly that Drew has to cover her ears. "You've got this, Horse Cents. Kick it!"

Starting down the homestretch, Good Enough passes Steady Does It and then Runs the Gamut. Drew grabs ahold of Nate. If Good Enough wins, she'll get three thousand dollars!

"Run!" Leslie cries. "Run!"

With less than a hundred meters to go, the jockeys are laying on their whips, urging the horses to give them every last ounce of speed and muscle left in their already depleted bodies. Drew watches them on the Big Board, their heads straining, their manes flying, their entire bodies leaning in. Horse Cents, Sheer Luck, Good Enough.

Good Enough, in third, fights to get ahead. Watching him race is inspiring and exhilarating and heartbreaking all at once, and suddenly, inexplicably, tears prick at Drew's eyes. The emotion of it all is overwhelming. These gorgeous creatures are being pushed to their absolute limit, and yet still, she hopes her horse wins. It's an odd battle of wills inside her, this both wanting them to stop but also to push harder, run faster, give it their all.

And as they speed across the finish line, Drew realizes that's exactly how she feels about this entire weekend. Overwhelmed, conflicted, uneasy, adrenaline fueled. She wants all the secrets to stop. At the same time, she wants to win.

Determining what that means, exactly—the winning part—remains to be seen.

TROJAN HORSE

20

Nate and Leslie

Nate's screaming his vocal cords raw. "Run! Damn it, run!"

He tries to will Horse Cents to the finish line, as if he might drag him by an invisible rope. Horse Cents has *got* to get there first, but Sheer Luck's making him work for it, up to the brutal end, as is Good Enough in third. "C'mon," he says through gritted teeth. "C'mon."

In the last few lengths, he watches as Horse Cents pulls ahead by an inch, only to have Sheer Luck draw up even again. Nate's hands are clenched into fists, his entire body taut as a stretched rubber band. The odd sensation that he's watching the race in slow motion falls over him.

"Come. On." And then, as if by some miracle, Sheer Luck starts to fade. Only a few inches initially, but that distance grows to half a length, which then extends to a full length. Good Enough falls back, too. It's all the impetus Horse Cents needs, as if he's been waiting for everyone else to step aside. As if he won't brook having another Thoroughbred in the finish line photo, a photo that'll be plastered across the front page of every major newspaper in the country tomorrow. Churchill Downs has given his horse the perfect stage on which to shine.

Nate and one hundred and fifty thousand other fans scream and holler when Horse Cents crosses the finish line a full length ahead. *First place.* And Nate, stunned into silence for a moment, starts whooping.

"He did it! We won! We won! Horse Cents for the win!" He leaps up, throws his hat in the air, and pulls Drew into a hug. She's crying, probably because she's elated that he hasn't bankrupted them. She still has no idea that they've gone from being broke to practically loaded in two minutes. *The best two minutes in sports, for sure,* Nate thinks.

"Horse Cents! Horse Cents!" chants the crowd. Nate high-fives Graham, whose money was also on Horse Cents.

"You did it, honey," Drew says softly. "You beat my horse." As if that's all that matters.

Nate grins. "I can't believe it. Wow," he says. "Wow, wow, wow." He keeps repeating it like a scratched record.

Suddenly, everything that seemed so important—so upsetting only hours ago—fades away. What does it matter that Drew shared a drunken kiss with Graham? What does it matter that he kept a small secret from her? Once she learns exactly how much they've won, all will be forgiven. She'll understand how much he has always loved her—only her—and she'll learn to trust him again. Yeah, he may take huge risks on occasion, but look where it's gotten them! All those hours at the casino have been leading up to this one shining moment; he's sure of it. The moment when he won $75,000 at the Kentucky Derby.

He grabs Drew and kisses her, long and hard.

"And Good Enough came in third," he cries.

"I know!" She laughs, swiping at her tears. "It's crazy."

"Did you bet on him to win or to place?"

"Just to win, but I don't care. You won!"

Nate's fingertips start to tingle. "Man, I've gotta sit down for a minute."

"Good idea." She drops into the chair next to him.

Behind them, Graham is shouting, "Five hundred bucks! I won five hundred bucks!" Leslie starts laughing, tells him to calm down.

"Wanna know how much we won?" Nate asks Drew.

"I don't know, do I?"

"Seventy-five." The words hang in the air between them. "Thousand."

Drew smirks. "You did not. You're fooling with me. Tell me, really."

He shakes his head. "Not fooling."

Her eyes widen. "What?"

"Seventy-five thousand dollars, babe. You and me."

She mouths their son's code for amazement. *OMG.*

"Buddy, how much?" Graham demands after he's come down from his own winner's high.

Nate hesitates, glances at Drew, who nods. "Seventy-five."

"Get out. No way. You made seventy-five hundred?"

Nate grins sheepishly, shakes his head. "Thousand. Seventy-five thousand."

"Holy crap," Graham says and collapses in his seat. "You bet the whole fifteen?"

"Yup. And I'm glad I did. Pretty unreal, huh?"

He can almost envision the stress of the past several months taking leave of his body. A dark-gray funnel cloud being sucked up into the sky. *We're going to be okay,* he thinks.

But then a collective gasp ripples through the stadium, and Nate's eyes cut to Drew. "What? What is it?"

"Um, I'm not sure, actually."

He turns to check the Big Board, where a single, incriminating word flashes:

INQUIRY

And Nate's entire world starts spinning.

~

"Nate, honey, are you okay? You seem kind of . . . I don't know, pale."

They're all staring at him. He can see their lips moving, but whatever they're saying doesn't make sense. A low humming starts in his ears, right before a sudden wooziness descends. Graham reaches out for him, and Nate hears him say, "Whoa there, buddy. Let's get you lying down," right before everything goes dark.

Nate doesn't feel his body drop from the folding chair onto the cement (later, they'll tell him that he was out only for a minute), but when he comes to, three sets of worried eyes hover above him. Someone official looking crouches next to him.

"Hey, buddy," he says. "Welcome back. How're you doing? Feeling okay?" There's some talk of getting a medic and moving Nate to a space inside—somewhere cooler—but Nate, his lips dry and cracked, tries to protest. He doesn't want to go anyplace; the world is slowly beginning to shift back into focus. If they move him, he's pretty sure he'll be hit by a wicked case of vertigo.

"Water," he manages to say.

The man, with a stocky build and a thin white wire trailing from his ear, asks Nate if he knows where he is while Graham holds a water bottle to his lips. The water dribbles down Nate's neck and into his shirt when he sips. For a minute, he's back at the PBR bar, thinks maybe he's fallen off the bull. There's an official patch of some kind on the guy's shirt. His eyes dart around until they find Drew. When he lifts his hand, she grabs it.

"You're going to be okay," she says. "You fainted. We're going to rest here for a few minutes until you feel like getting up, all right?"

He half nods, but Nate knows the officer asked him something important and he can't remember what. Someone places a cool paper towel across his head. There seems to be a discussion about whether he's suffering from heatstroke or if he's had too much to drink.

"No, I don't think he's had anything to drink today," Drew says matter-of-factly. "We kind of overdid it yesterday."

There's more mumbling, then Drew's voice again. "I think it might be shock, actually."

He tries to shake his head, but it won't move. "It's okay," Drew says, coming up behind him, cradling his head and gently massaging the back of his neck. "You can lie here as long as you need to." Everything goes dark again. When he opens his eyes, Graham is standing in front of him, acting like a human shield against the sun's glare. A current of air rides over his face, and he spies the younger woman from their box waving her program, sending a tepid breeze his way.

"You gave us all a good scare," she says in a thick Midwestern accent.

He should thank her, but a wave of exhaustion envelops him. A small crowd has gathered, and someone says that she's a doctor. Nate feels the press of cool, firm fingers against his wrist, checking his pulse. Then she shines a pen flashlight in each eye. "I don't think he's concussed." Around him, there's a low hum of conversation.

Nate's desperately trying to remember what happened before he fainted, but it's all a blur. Someone says, "I really think we should get him inside." And the next thing he knows, he's being propped up on either shoulder and carted away from their section. A frosty blast of air-conditioning hits him, and a voice says, "In here. You can move him in here. There's a couch where he can lie down."

And the last thing Nate remembers is the sensation of cool leather against the backs of his forearms and neck, his shoes being removed, and the soft brush of a thin blanket being thrown over him.

~

Blood, broken bones—even scrapes, for that matter—have never sat well with Leslie. Whenever Zach would come home from the playground with a bloodied lip or a gouge in his knee, she'd point him to his dad. If Graham weren't home, off he'd go to Nate and Drew's. There were always boxes of Band-Aids and Bactine falling out of Drew's medicine cabinet when you opened it.

And Nate, who grew up with three brothers, would examine the injury and invariably act as if it were no big deal. *Looks like you might need a couple of stiches, bud,* he once told Zach as if he were merely suggesting that her son finish his vegetables. (Zach had been goofing around with a Swiss Army knife and sliced his pinkie finger wide open.)

Nate drove them to the emergency room and held Leslie's hand while she held Zach's (she doesn't remember where Graham was at the time; probably off teaching class). Later, Leslie joked that she could walk over with her femur bone sticking out of her right leg, and Nate would think nothing of it. *Oh,* he might say. *Let's just pop that back in for you, and then we'll get you stitched up at the ER.*

So when Nate slides off his folding chair and hits the ground with a thud, Leslie's first thought is that he's dead. A heart attack like her dad, at the age of forty-seven. She screams. Drew and Graham, however, are visions of calm under duress. Drew immediately drops down next to Nate and scoots the chairs back so he can lie flat. Graham hands her his jacket, and she rolls it up like a burrito before sliding it under Nate's feet. "There's a pulse," she says as others start to crowd around their box, asking if they can help, if they should dial 911.

"I think he's okay," Drew offers a bit shakily. "I think he fainted. Maybe it's the heat."

Then the Derby attendant is at his side, radioing for help. Nate's eyes flutter open, then close again. *He's not dead* shoots through Leslie's brain, as if she needed a direct signal from him that he was okay. He mumbles something, and Graham gives him a sip of water. A local doctor in the stands offers to help and checks his pulse, then his eyes. Listens to his breathing. *I think we should try to get him inside, someplace cooler,* she says. Multiple people assist, clearing the way, while the Derby attendant, a big guy, ropes his arm around Nate and practically carries him single-handedly upstairs and inside.

Leslie follows behind Graham, who follows behind Drew. She thinks she might be in shock. Once he's settled on a couch inside someone's office, they chat with the volunteer doctor just beyond the door.

"He should be all right," she says. "My guess is that it's the effects of the heat, or maybe a combination of heat and stress. People get dehydrated here without realizing how quickly it can happen. Alcohol doesn't help."

"Do you think we should take him to the hospital?" asks Drew.

"He might need an IV if he's severely dehydrated, although I don't know how much luck you'll have getting an ambulance. Do you have your own car?"

"No, we're with one of the Derby tour groups," Graham says.

"Let me see if I can help. I have a few connections to local drivers for instances like this." She walks away to make a call.

Leslie struggles to find her voice. "Um, Drew? What do you want to do? Would you prefer not to move him?"

"No, I think we should get him checked out."

"Okay," Graham says. "Then that's what we'll do."

Leslie nods. Her role here is to be supportive, helpful in any way she can, so long as it doesn't involve blood or broken bones.

When the doctor returns, it's to let them know that an Uber will be waiting for them out front in ten minutes. Their driver has already been instructed to take them directly to Norton Hospital.

"Alrighty," announces Graham. "Let's see if we can wake our patient and get him downstairs."

Given the circumstances, it's probably inappropriate to ask, but Leslie really wants to know. "Wait, what happened with the inquiry? Any word yet?"

Drew and Graham exchange glances. Are they worried? Offended by her question? Leslie can't read their expressions.

"Not yet," Graham finally says. "I'm sure we'll hear soon enough." No one needs to mention how significantly the decision, whatever it might be, could impact their lives—for better or for worse. *Maybe it's just as well,* Leslie thinks and goes to help with Nate.

21

DREW

Drew focuses on remaining calm for her husband's sake, a man who's currently hooked up to so many wires and IVs that it's difficult to believe he's perfectly healthy, as the doctor who checked him out assured them. She's sitting beside Nate in Louisville's Norton Hospital, where she, Leslie, and Graham brought him to the emergency room. Just to be safe. All his tests, aside from an elevated blood pressure reading and low electrolytes, have come back normal.

The doctor ascribed the fainting to a combination of factors, including dehydration, low electrolytes, and stress. *I think you had a little panic attack,* he explained, his tone upbeat and chipper. *It happens. It's the Kentucky Derby. People get excited. I wouldn't worry. Throw in the heat and dehydration on top of that, and you put yourself in the eye of a perfect storm.* A couple of Ativan later, Nate was sleeping soundly.

But despite her calm demeanor, internally Drew feels herself growing more and more agitated. If Nate were truly in the midst of a health crisis, she'd be worried, of course. Sympathetic, even. She's having difficulty, though, overcoming the conclusion that her husband bears the responsibility for his current situation, lying here in a johnny underneath the harsh, fluorescent lights of a hospital. Thousands of miles away from home.

You have deep wells of patience, people have told her, and Drew prides herself on this fact. She works with children who demand no less of her, but those children have special needs. Her patience for adults who put themselves in harm's way, on the other hand, knows its limits. Particularly when they've made the same mistake once before! Nate knew perfectly well her thoughts about betting $1,000 on the Oaks race. How foolish—and how lucky—he was! But instead of counting his blessings, namely $15,000, he went and blew it all on the Derby.

Drew has been silently coaching herself not to throw a tantrum here in the hospital ever since Graham gave her the devastating results of the inquiry: one of the jockeys called foul on Horse Cents for interference, cutting off another horse. After about forty-five minutes of deliberation, the stewards of the Derby agreed. Horse Cents was demoted, stripped of his first-place ribbon. Which means that she and Nate have been stripped of seventy-five grand.

How will she tell Nate when he comes to? When he fainted, he'd no idea what the outcome of the inquiry would be. What will he do when he learns that Horse Cents is out and that he's lost it all?

How could he be so stupid? Drew thinks. Even if he'd had the good sense to wager only $5,000—still a ridiculous amount, to her mind—they'd have come out ahead. There'd still be $10,000 left over from yesterday's winnings, plenty to pay off whatever bills might have piled up.

While Nate slept, her fingers flew over her phone, researching the history of other contested races. It turns out that only three other times in Derby history was a first-place winner stripped of his title. Once in 1968, once in 2019, and again in 2021. Back in 1968, the winner, Dancer's Image, failed the postrace drug test and was disqualified. The race in 2019 was eerily similar to today's. A jockey called foul against the winning horse, Maximum Security, claiming he impeded his horse's path during the race. After a review, the stewards agreed and disqualified Maximum Security, moving Country House (65–1 odds) up to first place (apparently, there'd been quite the brouhaha around the upset).

And then in 2021, Medina Spirit placed first only to be stripped of his title after failing the postrace drug test.

So, out of 151 Derbies, Horse Cents is the fourth winner to be stripped of his title. What are the odds of that? Something like a 2 percent chance?

The entire time Graham was delivering the news to her at the hospital, Drew's emotions ping-ponged between panic, anger, and disbelief. If you'd asked her last week how she spent her weekend at the Kentucky Derby, the answer, *At the hospital, after my husband lost fifteen grand,* would have never occurred to her. Nor would she have thought, *Funny, I spent some of it in my good friend's hotel room while kissing her husband.*

She sat in the sterile hallway beside Graham and Leslie while the doctors continued to check on Nate. Graham's lips moved while he spoke, but all Drew could think was, *You'd never do such a stupid thing, Graham. You bet a reasonable hundred dollars! What is wrong with my husband? What was he thinking?*

Now she wonders if Nate actually believed he'd be lucky enough to win two days in a row, then realizes what a ridiculous question that is. *Of course he believed it!* That's how addicted gamblers think. She's read enough to understand a bit about the psychology behind the so-called sport. Addicted gamblers convince themselves that they'll win everything back with the next bet. *Just one more time,* goes the reasoning. Until they're broke, or utterly bankrupt.

But Nate is a dad! Betting that much money was irresponsible. It's the first time that a tiny alarm goes off in her head that her husband may need professional help. That he can't break this habit, this cycle—whatever it is—without outside assistance. And Drew can't do it alone. It will take someone experienced, someone wise to the denials and subterfuge that accompany addiction. Because that's what she imagines lies ahead for them. Drew will become a babysitter of sorts for her husband, checking his pockets for poker chips, locking in his schedule, their bank account. Telling those guys idling in her driveway on the weekends to get lost.

Nate's imaginary defense rings in her ears. *But if we won—which we thought we did for a brief, exhilarating moment—we wouldn't be having this conversation. How can you say I'm addicted when I only bet on the weekends for a little fun? We're at the Kentucky Derby, for Pete's sake. You're expected to place big bets! Do you think every wife here is having the same conversation with her husband because he took a chance on Horse Cents? Who, I might add, won the race but lost on a technicality.*

Even as she argues on his behalf in her head, she grows more irritated.

But Horse Cents didn't win. That's the point, Nate. That's the rub. You might even say he stole the race from the other horses as soon as he cut them off. He's a cheater. That's nothing to crow about.

Maybe not, but I still think it proves my instincts were right.

Your instincts? she imagines herself saying. *Don't you mean Phil's?*

And that's when it occurs to her. Where is this mysterious Phil? Has he gone into hiding, escaped to the Caymans, knowing that his advice has cost his clients and friends probably millions of dollars? She'd like to get a piece of him, tell him her thoughts.

The blame, however, still circles back to her husband. Nate is the one who made the call on how much to bet. That burden falls squarely on his shoulders.

Graham sticks his head back into the room. "Hey, did you hear the other news?"

"No. What?" Honestly, Drew doesn't know how much more she can take.

"Sheer Luck turns out not to be so lucky." His eyebrows waggle on his forehead. "The stewards ruled that he was involved in the skirmish on the track, too, so he moves to the back of the pack."

"That's unbelievable."

"Agreed, but you know what it means, don't you?"

Drew can't imagine how Sheer Luck's being at fault would have any bearing on Horse Cents' fate. *Unless.* "Horse Cents has been cleared of any wrongdoing?" she asks, hopeful.

His shoulders droop. "No, I wish. But your horse, Good Enough, moves up from third to first place in a spectacular stroke of luck."

"Woo-hoo." Muted enthusiasm is all she can muster at the moment. "After all the bad news we've had today, I suppose it's nice to hear."

"You bet a substantial amount, right?"

She shakes her head, then half smiles. "A hundred bucks. I'm much more conservative than my husband, I'm afraid."

Graham nods, as if he understands her particular heartbreak. "Still, with 30–1 odds, that means you made $3,000. Not bad!"

That he's working so hard to buoy her spirits is sweet. Drew appreciates it, but somehow, after all the ups and downs—from wining $15,000 to winning $75,000 to plummeting back down to zero—that number sounds pitifully small. "Nice," she says, and when he doesn't move to leave: "Thanks."

"Anything I can get you? Twinkies, CHEETOS, Starburst? The vending machine down the hall is loaded with stuff that will send your cholesterol soaring."

That gets her to laugh. "No, thanks. I'm all set for now."

"Okay, well, I left Leslie down in the waiting room. Our plan is to head back to the hotel, if that's okay with you."

"Oh, right, of course. Sorry, I should have told you guys earlier you didn't need to stay. Thanks for your help."

He gestures to Nate. "Any word on when they're going to spring the patient?"

"Not yet." Her phone says it's 8:30 p.m. "I'm hoping he'll be out in a couple of hours, but they may keep him overnight. I'm waiting for the doctor to come back and reevaluate in a bit."

Graham's hand clutches the doorframe, as if he's afraid of both intruding and leaving her. "All right. Well, you know where to find me if you need anything at all. Leslie, too." He pauses. "At least it looks like he's sleeping peacefully now."

"Yeah."

"Hey, Drew?"

Her gaze flickers from Nate back to Graham. "Yeah?"

"Don't be too hard on him, huh? He was only trying to do the right thing."

She snorts. "I suppose that's one way of looking at it."

He starts to say something else but then stops, as if thinking better of it. "I'll leave you be. Try to get some sleep tonight."

"Uh-huh." Her voice reflects the weariness she feels. Gone is the flirtation, the stolen looks, the rush of seeing Graham. Her bank of emotional energy has flatlined. There's a dusting of white powder—maybe from a doughnut?—on his chin, and rather than be overwhelmed by the urge to go over and brush it off seductively, Drew feels slightly repelled. Under the fluorescent lights, Graham looks like the tired, overworked professor that he is. Why she found him so attractive—why she kissed him—suddenly makes no sense to her. She has the strange sensation that she's been stuck in a dream all weekend.

When he ducks out, she's left alone with her husband.

Her eyes trace the curve of Nate's face, his strong jaw and dimpled chin. She reaches out to take his hand, but he doesn't stir. Yes, she's still angry about what he's done, but beneath her indignation lies something bigger, heavier, stronger—her unwavering love for this man.

The memory of the sharp pain cutting across her chest when Nate collapsed, then fell from his chair at the track resurfaces. Because there was a terrible, horrifying moment when she thought maybe she'd lost him. That her husband's heart—so robust, so full of love—had given up and quit. The man with whom she has shared everything that has ever mattered in her life—their son, their home, her happiness—for a brief moment, seemingly gone.

HORSING AROUND

22

GRAHAM AND LESLIE

When they get back to the hotel, Graham tosses his jacket on the floor and throws himself on the bed. "Well, that didn't go quite according to plan." He loosens his tie. Leslie stands at the full-length mirror, unpinning her hat before sliding out of her dress and pulling on sweatpants and a Red Sox T-shirt.

"Oh, yeah? Was there a plan? Because if there was, I was unaware."

He watches her brush out her hair in long, even strokes. Two days under the Kentucky sun have given her skin a healthy glow.

"Well, no written plan. I mean, according to Nate's grand plan. You know, as in, win seventy-five grand, celebrate, and life goes back to being fabulous when you get home."

"Mm-hmm. Well," she finally says, "at least he's going to be all right."

"Yes, that's a relief." Graham crosses his arms behind his head, waiting to see if his wife will begin the conversation he's been expecting to have all weekend . . . or if it will be up to him.

"I wonder if Drew's told him yet." She pulls her hair up into a ponytail. "About Horse Cents being disqualified, I mean."

"Don't know the answer to that one, but I doubt it. When I said goodbye, he was sleeping." Graham moves his neck around, stretching it in one direction, then the other. "But maybe he doesn't even recall winning? In that case, it will be like losing found money. No big deal."

Leslie's eyebrows, delicate and precise, arch on her forehead. "Fifteen thousand dollars lost?" She flops down onto the bed next to him and stares up at the ceiling. "I'm pretty sure he's going to feel awful about it."

"You're probably right."

"Maybe we could give him the fifteen hundred I won on Good Enough. Oh, and Drew won three grand."

"So what are we up to now? Forty-five hundred?"

"Yup."

"It might take the sting out a little."

She rolls over onto her elbow, facing him. "Do you think he has a serious problem? With gambling, I mean?"

Graham sighs. "Not sure. I'm no doctor."

"But betting all that money when he already knew ten grand was spoken for, as in, he has to pay me back? It just felt a little, I don't know—desperate. I'm worried that it's much worse than we think."

"Why?"

"Drew mentioned a few times that Nate's come home from the casinos with empty pockets—after having left with envelopes stuffed full of cash. I don't think she has any idea how much money is involved, though."

"No," Graham agrees.

"Will you talk to him? I tried the other night, but I'm pretty sure he was too drunk to remember anything I said."

There's a pause, until he asks, "Do you think I should? It's not really our business."

"But they're our friends. Drew might appreciate it."

And Graham thinks, *Ha!* "I'm not sure about that. I don't think she's very happy with me lately."

Leslie sits up. "Why wouldn't she be happy with you?"

He shrugs, feeling as if the tables have suddenly been flipped. "I don't know. There's been a lot going on lately. Maybe she thinks I let Nate down by not keeping an eye on him."

"Huh. That's funny, because I'm pretty sure it was *me* who asked you to keep an eye on him."

Graham's skin starts to turn warm. He has the sense that he's lost his page in the book he was reading. *What are they talking about, exactly?*

Leslie rolls her eyes. "I was hoping you'd tell me first."

"Tell you what?"

"Seriously? Come on, Graham."

He's about to tell her everything . . . but then stops. He can't bring himself to say it aloud, to admit to his wife that he's secretly fallen for Drew. That just last night, his lips were pressed against hers. That he thinks—hopes—she might have feelings for him, too.

"You and Drew made out last night. She told me. After you got back to our room and she helped you into bed. She said you guys kissed."

Graham's stomach drops. Not thinking, he immediately says, "Well, we were drunk." As if to imply, *What did you expect? Of course we kissed! Alcohol does that to a person. To two people.* He hates himself for not being honest.

"Yeah, I get that," Leslie replies almost thoughtfully. "I also get that maybe you were trying to even the scales. As in, since Nate and I hooked up in college, why shouldn't you and Drew hook up now?"

"That's twisted thinking, and just wrong." Although when she says it, a tiny explosion goes off in his head as if she's just struck a nerve.

"Whatever the motivation, it happened, right? You're not denying that part of it."

"No, I told you we were drunk. And it only involved kissing."

This prompts her to throw her head back and laugh.

"What's so funny?"

"Oh, Graham," she says, as if she might be talking to a child. "It's the way you said it, all serious." She mimics his deep voice, making him cringe. "'It only involved kissing.'" She laughs again. "Sounds pretty passionate."

A dart of anger shoots through him. How dare she make fun of his feelings for Drew. Spending time with Drew these past few months has made him feel more alive than he has in years! When she's in his presence, she's fully present. Graham can't recall the last time he could say the same about Leslie. "It actually was," he admits now.

"Huh. That's not what Drew said. She said it was a mistake. 'Disappointing' was the word I believe she used."

Graham's heart rips in half as if his wife is holding it up before him, tearing at both ends. He's been beaten, fooled. Drew and Leslie's friendship is such that she's admitted not only to the kiss but also to its insignificance. Graham was a dalliance, a drunken fling, just as she described it to Leslie. Whatever soulful connection he's been imagining between the two of them never existed. At least not for Drew. *Could it be true?*

"What's wrong, Graham? Cat got your tongue?"

He sits up, swings his legs over the edge of the bed. "You know, sometimes you can be really cruel."

"*I'm* cruel? Because you fooled around with my friend, with Nate's *wife*?"

Graham's mind flashes back to all the times that he and Drew have been together. He'd felt something, and he was certain that Drew had felt it, too. What about last week? The cake crumbs? When her eyes opened wide with surprise as he ran his thumb along her bottom lip. How badly he'd wanted to kiss her! The hooded glances they'd been giving each other throughout the weekend. And none of it had meant anything to her? It's impossible to believe. He should talk to Drew. Maybe she lied to Leslie to protect him.

"I'm sorry," Leslie offers, pulling her knees to her chest. "Maybe that was a little mean. I just don't want you getting your hopes up. Because Drew and Nate, they're the real deal, you know? Despite all the gambling stuff, Nate's crazy about her. And she loves him. They've got to work through their money issues, but Drew will never leave him. You know that, right?" Her voice is softer now, gentler.

He recalls trying to comfort Drew at the hospital when they first arrived, but when he'd gone to put an arm around her, she pulled away. *Stop,* she said. *My husband is in the* hospital, *Graham.* As if he were dense, as if he couldn't fathom what she was going through. Now he tries to replay their interactions through a stranger's eyes. Has Graham been acting like a schoolboy with a crush all this time? Has he merely been a convenient distraction for Drew while Nate's been off gambling? Someone to give her fortysomething ego a shot of confidence?

"What I know," he says in response to Leslie's question, "is that I could use a drink." He pushes himself up off the bed. "I'm headed down to the bar. I'll see you later."

"Okay," she says. "But, later? Can we talk?"

A maniacal, crazy laugh escapes from his throat. "Talk? About what? Haven't we covered it all?" But he shakes his head. "Never mind. I don't want to know right now."

~

Later, much later, there's a knock at the door. The sky has grown dark beyond the window. Leslie startles awake and dresses hurriedly. When she goes to answer it, Drew stands outside in the hallway.

"Hi, there." Her friend appears completely exhausted. "I just wanted to let you know that we're back from the hospital—Nate, too—and well, I wanted to thank you for all your help this afternoon."

"Of course. Do want to come in for a minute?" When Drew hesitates, she adds, "Graham's not here."

"No. Thanks. It's late. Like midnight, I think. I should go shower, and Nate might need me." She's still wearing her kelly-green dress, and the likeness to Jackie Kennedy is so stunning that the image of Jackie, in her pink Chanel suit, oddly leaps to Leslie's mind.

"Right, of course. Is there anything I can do?"

Slowly, Drew shakes her head. "No. You guys have done so much already."

Leslie steps halfway into the corridor and wraps her arms around her friend. "Oh, Drew," she says. "I'm so sorry today turned out to be crummy." She squeezes her tightly. "It's going to be okay. Whatever's going on, we'll figure it out."

"I don't know what to do." Drew pulls away. "I think it's pretty evident that my husband has a gambling problem, right?"

Leslie shrugs. "It's not really my place to say."

"No, I'm *asking* you, as my friend." Drew's voice quivers. "Do you think Nate has a gambling problem?"

Having this conversation in the corridor of the Brown Hotel is less than ideal. "Are you sure you don't want to come in for a few minutes?"

Drew appears to reconsider this before declining once again. "No, I'd better get back."

"All right. We can talk later."

"Yes, please. Later."

Leslie watches her friend pad down the hall in her bare feet, the straps of her platform sandals draped over two fingers, before letting herself back into her own room. She worries that perhaps she's just made a grave error, that she should have been more forthcoming with Drew if she really wants to help Nate.

HORSE OF A DIFFERENT COLOR

23

GRAHAM

Downstairs in the bar, Graham orders himself a Hot Brown and a whiskey, neat. For not the first time this weekend, he regrets having played the fool. To think that in the past forty-eight hours, he's nearly killed himself on a mechanical bull, kissed his buddy's wife, gotten terrifically drunk, lost more than five hundred bucks (counting the small races), and received a dressing-down from his wife strikes him as, well, both unlikely and incredibly disappointing. For all his intentions of going to the Derby to have some fun, the weekend has come up frustratingly short.

Turns out that the crowd at the bar is fairly scarce at midnight. A man and woman, probably in their mid-sixties, sit at one end of the counter and talk in hushed voices. There are a couple of loudmouths scattered about, either boasting about their winnings at the track or bemoaning money lost. Three seats down, an attractive woman with long, dark hair plays on her phone while drinking what appears to be a gin and tonic, a slice of lime wedged on the side. Oddly enough, Graham's not even vaguely interested. His conversation with Leslie has sapped every flirtatious fiber out of him. He can't understand how he got everything so wrong, how he could have misread his interactions with Drew so completely.

Was it simply wishful thinking?

The bartender sets his Hot Brown before him, refreshes his whiskey, and sends Graham's mind racing back to breakfast in this very room yesterday, before they all set off for the Oaks. *Was it only yesterday?* he thinks. Drew looked exquisite in her pink sundress and enormous pink hat, so much so that Graham had hardly noticed his own wife. But everyone was always noticing Leslie, which somehow made it less important that *he* noticed her. Maybe that was pure nonsense, just a way of letting himself off the hook, but after twelve years of marriage, what more was there to say?

The shine has worn off; even Graham can see that plainly now. All the hope he felt on the bus ride to Churchill Downs that first morning, thinking perhaps all they needed was a change of venue? That their marriage could be rekindled over a long weekend? It's gone, as surely as Nate's winnings. That optimistic feeling was a quirk, a blip on the radar, not the blinking light they'd needed to lead them to a better place, a happier destination.

Graham doesn't want to give up on his marriage, certainly not on Zach. They've created a family that, from the outside looking in, is enviable. Beautiful house, glamorous wife, precocious child, professorial husband, a solid network of friends. And he likes to think he hasn't taken any of it for granted, that they've worked hard to build this world for themselves—he and Leslie both. Even Zach.

But behind the shimmer, behind the facade, lurks an unhappiness that he can no longer ignore. Perhaps that's why he gravitated toward Drew in the first place. She'd been struggling with her own demons, confiding to him that she felt as if her "best days" were slipping through her fingers. Soon enough, Owen would be in college, her body would get creaky, and Nate would lose interest in her. Graham laughed at her oddball summary, told her she was being ridiculous, but in a strange way, he thought he understood. Her life as she knew it was losing its shine, its gloss; Graham felt the same way about his marriage—and pretty much everything else.

But when Drew came along, some of that sparkle had started to return. A reason to get up in the mornings. A reason to crawl into bed, if only to dream and wake up again.

Considered in this light, his relationship with Drew doesn't feel quite as pathetic as the one Leslie painted back in the room. Because maybe he and Drew weren't meant to be lovers so much as they were meant to help each other through a difficult time. A time when they were both casting about for answers, for a deeper understanding of what their futures might hold.

Graham decides he'll permit himself to draw some small comfort from their conversations over the past few months. That it wasn't only his secret crush that drove them, but a shared need for companionship, for someone to talk to. That they've both come away with more than when they began. An intimacy that perhaps he mistook for a physical attraction, but an intimacy nonetheless. He doubts that there will be any more late-night talks, suspects that the family dinners between the two houses will come to an abrupt halt. But he's grateful for these past few months. Grateful for Drew.

His thoughts get interrupted when the woman a few seats down scoots over. "Drowning your sorrows in bourbon?" she asks. "Mine are drowning in gin."

Graham looks up from his drink and sees now that her eyes are a striking green, all the bolder against her tanned skin and dark hair. *Arresting* is the word that leaps to mind.

"Something like that." He chuckles. "How's it going?" he asks. "The drowning-your-sorrows bit?"

"Not so great. Ever since Horse Cents got disqualified today. I lost a ton of money. Me and a bunch of my friends."

He clicks his tongue. "Sorry to hear that. I bet on Horse Cents, too. Only a hundred bucks. My friend lost considerably more, though."

She raises her glass. "Welcome to the losers club."

Graham clinks it. "Not the best club to be a member of, I suppose, but at least there's good company in it."

She smiles and extends a hand. "I'm Philomena, by the way. Phil for short."

"No kidding?" he says, unable to hide his surprise. "Well, hello, Philomena. Would you believe I've actually heard a lot about you?"

24

NATE AND DREW

When Nate wakes the next morning, his head feels as if it might explode, his body as if it weighs three hundred pounds. He swims up from his dreams and catches himself. He's not at home. Thick, heavy drapes shield the windows, and it hits him that he and Drew are at the Brown Hotel, here for the Kentucky Derby. And then, *Oof!* It all comes flooding back: the feeling of euphoria when Horse Cents crossed the finish line, the cheering and screaming, the delight in Drew's eyes. And then the word INQUIRY flashing on the screen. He'd fainted before the final results were displayed, but Drew broke the news to him before they left the hospital. Fifteen thousand dollars wasted, no winnings to speak of, aside from Drew's bet on Good Enough, who clinched first place after both Horse Cents and Sheer Luck were disqualified.

Talk about a spiraling fall from grace.

To say that Nate is disappointed in himself would be an understatement. Even he finds it difficult to believe that he screwed things up so royally. All he had to do was bet a modest amount, and he could've walked away with five or ten grand, despite a Derby loss. Why did he have to get greedy? What was *wrong* with him?

It's not until he slowly pushes himself up in bed that he realizes Drew's not lying next to him.

"Good morning." He startles before realizing she's sitting in the lounge chair across the room. In the dark.

"Hey, babe." His throat feels dry and scratchy. "Good morning to you." Her knees are pulled up to her chest, her hands cupping what looks like a mug of coffee.

"How are you feeling?" Her voice is level, matter-of-fact. Nate can't get a read on whether she's tired or mad. There are so many possibilities, given the events of the past twenty-four—make that forty-eight—hours. The fact that she didn't strangle him in his sleep, though, is probably a good sign.

"Um, okay, I guess? Still a little groggy. Not sure what the doc gave me, but I haven't slept that well in months."

"Yeah, same here. I asked him for an Ativan, too."

"Good idea." He glances around the room. "You don't want to open the curtains, let some light in?"

"I was thinking of you, trying to be considerate while you slept." But now she gets up, sets her mug on the desk, and yanks the cord that sends the curtains flying back. "Although, I'm not really sure why."

"Why what?"

"Why I'd want to be considerate, given your behavior yesterday—and actually, the day before that, too." She drops back into the chair.

"Babe, I'm really sorry. Look, I didn't—"

But she holds up her hand, signaling for him to stop. "You know what's funny? Here I thought all I wanted from you was an apology. But now that doesn't seem like nearly enough. You've been so cagey with me all weekend. First, you don't tell me how much you're betting on Glory Days, but fortunately that turned out to your advantage. Fifteen thousand dollars! I was so excited for you, so happy for us. But then you stayed out with Leslie instead of helping me get Graham home, who more or less sacrificed the health of his own body for yours."

Nate flinches at the mention of Graham. *She's right,* he thinks. *I'm such a crappy friend.*

"Honey, we've already been over that night. I apologized. I was an idiot and super drunk. I shouldn't have let Graham climb up on that bull in the first place. And you're right, I definitely should have come home with you and Graham."

"Correct." She nods, but if there's such a thing as a sarcastic nod, his wife has mastered it. She pauses, sipping her coffee, leaving Nate to worry where this conversation is headed. "And then, of course, there was the stunning revelation—thanks to *Graham*, I might add—that you and Leslie actually did hook up during college."

"Babe, you're freaking me out a little. Maybe we should get some breakfast and we can talk then?"

"You owe me *at least* this, Nate. You can lie there for a few more minutes and hear me out."

"Okay, yeah. Sure, sorry. Go ahead."

"And then, how should I put it? When it comes to Derby time, you decide not to bet a thousand or even five thousand or perhaps ten thousand. Because, you know, a bet of ten grand would have left you five grand from the Oaks, and why would you do that?" She guffaws at her own rhetorical question. "Why on earth, when you have a family to support, and you've already been fortunate enough to win at the track once, would you risk everything? That's the question I keep asking myself: Why would my husband behave so irresponsibly? Especially when he knew that his wife was worried about his losing it all?"

"Drew, I can explain . . ."

"Can you?" Her voice climbs an octave. "Because I'd really like to know what your explanation is. I've been sitting here in the dark for the last few hours, wondering what it could be. So please, enlighten me. I'll stop talking."

Nate sighs. "Look. I screwed up. I'm sorry. This was supposed to be a special weekend for you—for us. And I blew it. But, babe, if we *had* won—and we were so close; Horse Cents crossed the finish line first!—just think of how excited you would have been. Can you imagine bringing home seventy-five grand? We'd be singing a very different tune right now."

"Huh." She tilts her head and squints at him. "You really believe that, don't you? Because right now, I'm pretty sure the song that's playing in my head is 'You'd Better Think Twice.'"

"I hear you. It's a valid point. But think of it this way: all the winnings we lost? That was found money; we never really had it. And then you went and won three grand with Good Enough, so in fact, we're technically up a little bit. That's not so bad, is it?"

Drew has yet to tell him that her bet on Good Enough, the little white piece of paper, has disappeared. While Nate slept this morning, she tore the room apart looking for it. Nothing.

"And here's the thing *I* want to tell you," she continues. "I'm pretty sure you've got yourself a gambling problem. Like an addiction. And I think you should see someone about it. Figure it out. Because I'm starting to think I have no idea how bad things might be. You keep track of all our big expenses in your account. I couldn't tell you how much you have in checking. Is there any money left at all?"

"Listen, money is definitely tight right now, but I didn't want to burden you. I keep thinking I can dig us out of this hole—Horse Cents was going to be our ticket out—and then it just keeps getting worse." He runs his fingers through his hair. "Do you really want to hear what we owe?"

It's a moment that hangs in the balance. *Does she?* It doesn't matter whether she wants to or not. She must know. Because someone has to get them out of this mess, and it's certainly not going to be her husband.

~

Drew braces herself as Nate begins to share the lengthy, ugly list of bills past due, starting with the few thousand dollars left on the kitchen renovation; to his gambling debts (around six grand, he estimates); to their credit cards, which have maxed out at ten grand each. It's enough to make her want to run down the hall screaming. How could he do this to them? Why didn't he tell her that their finances—and his gambling—were spiraling out of control? They're lucky that the bank hasn't foreclosed on their house.

She grabs the complimentary hotel notepad and pen and starts writing it all down. As the column of numbers grows before her eyes, so does her frustration with herself. Why didn't she ask Nate about all of this sooner? When he'd head out to the casinos with his buddies on a Saturday night, long white envelopes stuffed with cash, only to return home with empty pockets, she didn't question it. She figured if an occasional night at the casino brought him happiness, so be it.

She knew friends whose husbands golfed all weekend, spent their fun money on expensive clubs and trips to the world's finest courses. Gambling wasn't so different, was it? As long as Nate wasn't being overly reckless with their money, it seemed harmless enough.

Now she regrets failing to define *overly reckless*.

"There's something else I need to tell you," he says softly.

Drew's still trying to wrap her head around the fact that both their credit cards are apparently maxed out at ten grand. The only credit card she uses is her debit card, which deducts all charges directly from her account. She quickly adds up the list so far—$29,000. Almost $30,000!

"Uh-oh," she says. "You're not going to tell me that you have another child with a different woman and you need to pay child-support payments, too, are you?"

Despite the pressure in the room, Nate laughs. Honestly, at this point, Drew considers anything to be possible. She can't believe she's been sleeping beside this man for years and had absolutely no idea of the trouble he was spinning for them. "No," he says. "I think you're safe on that account, at least."

"Thank goodness."

"But, um, I kind of asked a friend for a loan to help me out."

"This is in addition to the twenty-nine thousand we already owe?"

He nods. "Unfortunately, yes."

"And how much was the loan for?"

"Ten grand."

She falls back in her chair. "Jesus, Nate! What the hell? How could you get us into so much debt and never say anything to me?"

He shakes his head. "I wasn't thinking clearly. I had some other gambling bets that needed to be paid off quickly."

"Ten thousand dollars' worth?" The question sounds absurd to her own ears.

"Not all of it. I used some of the loan to pay our mortgage, too. I couldn't let that slip."

And this is the moment when she shrinks so far down in her chair that she might as well disappear. "You mean to tell me that we don't have enough money to pay the mortgage?" she asks in a small voice. "But I checked. There's five thousand in savings."

Nate nods. "That's our money. For emergencies only. I won't touch it."

Drew scoots back up and levels her gaze at him. "I want you to know that should we need money for our mortgage in the future, you should *always* feel free to pull it from our savings account. It constitutes an emergency."

"Duly noted."

"And who's this friend? Do I know him?"

Nate laughs. "You do, but trust me when I tell you that you don't want to know who it is."

She's uncertain what to make of this comment. Who could possibly be lending her husband money that would upset Drew more than she already is? Tony Soprano?

"It's Leslie," he says softly, without any prompting. "I asked Leslie for ten grand, and she gave it to me. With the stipulation that I pay it back by the end of the year. Interest-free."

Drew bites her lower lip, nods her head. "Figures. More secrets, huh?" The fact that they haven't really dealt with the other "secret" yet—that he and Leslie lied to her about hooking up in college—still gnaws at her. And yet, somehow, its import, held up against these latest financial revelations, pales in comparison. What was once the elephant in the room has shrunk to more of a groundhog, maybe a mole.

"Babe, I'm sorry. I didn't know what else to do. Leslie was my only out. I made her promise not to tell you."

"Of course you did."

At that moment, her cell dings, and she laughs, can hardly believe it. "It's a text. From Leslie."

Drew reads aloud: Missed you guys at breakfast this morning. Do you want to meet for a quick bite before we head to the airport? I've arranged for an Uber to pick us up at 1:30. That should give us plenty of time for our 4:30 flight. Hope Nate's feeling better today. xo

Drew laughs. "Perfect timing."

"What time is it now?" asks Nate.

"Twelve forty-five."

"Oh, man. I still have to shower. Can we pass on lunch with them? I mean, I'd love to eat something, but I was thinking maybe room service?"

Drew gasps.

"Or not. I can always grab a bag of chips from the vending machine."

"I love how you're considering room service when you basically told me minutes ago that we're in debt up to our ears, like forty thousand dollars in debt." She's added Leslie's loan of ten grand to the roughly thirty thousand already calculated.

He shrugs. "And you think a twenty-dollar room service charge is going to change all that?"

She jumps up from her chair. "Help me out. What's not computing for you, Nate?" she shouts. "We have no money!" She paces the room, back and forth. "This is how you got us into trouble in the first place. Thinking that none of it mattered. That you could just charge expenses left and right and deal with it later. That's how people end up in *jail*."

Drew has a few thousand dollars in her checking account, but not nearly enough to set them free. On the other hand, they've blown through so much money this weekend already, would room service be so terrible? She's craving a Hot Brown right about now.

"I'm sorry," he says for the millionth time. "But some of that debt—some of that includes the expense of this weekend. The Derby's not cheap, you know."

She can't believe he's dragging her birthday present into this. "And if you'd told me about all our debt, I would have told you we shouldn't have come."

"Babe, don't say that. If you could have seen the look on your face when you opened the envelope with the tickets inside? It was worth every penny."

There's a part of her that softens. "Honey, I love that you do nice things for me, for our entire family. But obviously, we're in trouble here."

"I know." His head hangs, as if he's let the entire world down.

"But we can fix this. I know we can. We'll meet with a financial adviser as soon as we get home. They'll tell us what to do. And we'll get you some help. For gambling."

"Okay?" he says it like a question. In that moment, he seems so young, so vulnerable, as if someone has stolen all the quarters from his piggy bank. That he's not fighting back even a little bit tells her how bad things really are.

"I'm heading down to the lobby," she announces suddenly. "My bag's already packed. It's by the door, along with my hat box and dresses. Bring everything down when you're ready to go to the airport, okay?"

"Okay." Then he calls out, "Hey, Drew?"

Her hand rests on the door handle. "Yeah?"

"You know I love you, right?"

She pauses. "Yeah, and I love you. That's why this sucks so much."

When she leaves, the door slams closed behind her, providing a sharp jolt. Maybe it's the big exclamation point she's needed. That *Nate* needs. Maybe it will finally drive home her point to a man who doesn't want to listen.

THE HOMESTRETCH

25

GRAHAM

It's their last hurrah, lunch at the downstairs Bar & Grille. Both he and Leslie have ordered Hot Browns and mint juleps to bring things full circle. Although, truth be told, it doesn't really feel like a full-circle moment without Drew and Nate.

Graham's hands are resting on the table at nine and three o'clock. *Time's a-wasting,* he thinks. He and Leslie have left it until the final hours of their trip to discuss their situation, but maybe it's for the best. Now they'll only have to endure the plane ride home together as opposed to the entire long weekend.

"So," he asks, "should we talk about *us* now?"

Leslie meets his gaze, her bright-blue eyes blinking back at him. "Sure . . . Do you want to go first?"

Graham understands that this will be a defining moment when, as an older man, he'll reflect back on the totality of his life. Whether or not he says the right thing, whether he's sufficiently diplomatic, will matter years from now.

He clears his throat. "Okay, sure, why not? I think it's fair to say that we've grown apart."

Leslie's eyes drop to her plate. "Yes."

"And I don't know about you, but going into this weekend, I was hoping that might change. That we might find our way back to each other, remember what made us so great as a couple."

She nods but doesn't say anything.

"And, well, I think it's pretty clear that nothing's changed—not really."

She shakes her head, and to Graham's surprise, swipes at her eyes.

"Tell me if I'm wrong," he continues more gently. "*Please* tell me if I'm wrong in thinking that you don't have feelings for me anymore."

Her lips are pulled into a tight line. "Of course I still have feelings for you." She offers a half-hearted laugh. "Not always the best feelings, but feelings. I still love you, Graham." She shrugs. "I don't think that will ever change. You're Zach's dad."

Hearing those words is difficult, and he forces himself to look away for a moment while composing himself. "Good to know. For the record, me too."

"But I agree," she continues. "We haven't been close in a while. I've been thinking about it a lot lately, and I can't really put my finger on any one thing that started it."

"Me either."

"I feel like work has been so crazy, and then there's Zach to consider . . ." Her voice trails off, and Graham can feel himself starting to fold in two. *Here we go,* he thinks. *The words I never hoped to hear.*

She takes a deep breath. "I was going to wait until we got home, but since we're talking about it now . . . I should probably just say it." She hesitates, looks him in the eye. "I think I want a separation. I think we should try living apart for a while."

He nods, sucks in his lips. "I know."

"You do?" Her eyes widen. "Did Drew tell you?"

"No. Um, I wasn't aware that Drew knew before I did."

"She didn't! She doesn't. I mean, I didn't tell her directly. Only that we were having some issues."

"I see. Funny. Why is it that everyone in our group has been struggling with something, but no one has been talking with the very people who are most affected by it? It's all a bit ironic, don't you think?"

She shrugs. "I suppose so." The air crackles between them. "Anyway, I was postponing a separation because I was worried about how it would affect Zach."

"Right." Graham heartily agrees with this point.

"But then I realized," she says thoughtfully, "that we're not doing Zach any favors by tiptoeing around him all the time."

"Probably not." Graham refrains from pointing out that maybe if she actually came home at a reasonable hour and acknowledged him in the evenings, they might feel like more of a family.

"Anyway, Zach is ten now," she says. "And kids are so resilient. I think he'll be fine if we work out an arrangement that's amenable to him—and to us. As long as we keep everything civil, you know?"

"Civil, right." He nods. "Don't you sound like a lawyer?" A sense of doom, that his wife has gotten much further ahead in contemplating next steps than he has, sweeps over him.

"I haven't talked to a lawyer yet, if that's what you're suggesting. I'd like to see how things go with the separation first. See how Zach handles it all."

"That's smart." It feels as if someone else is talking for him, as if he's handed the reins over to another rider entirely. "Who knows?" Graham can't resist a joke. "Maybe we'll discover we can't live without each other."

It gets a smile. "Maybe," she says. "I've always loved your sense of humor."

When he can think of nothing else to say, he checks his watch. "Well, look at that. Uber's coming at one thirty, right? That's in ten minutes. We'd better get the check." He signals to their waitress.

"We'll have to figure out arrangements," she says. "You know, who's going to live where, what Zach wants."

"Ah. I suppose you'll want to stay in the house with Zach, then?"

"Not necessarily."

He takes this in, the possibility that he might be able to remain on Oak Drive, while also wondering what the catch is. "And you'll live where?"

"I've been looking at condos over in Lower Mills."

Graham can't hide his surprise. "You've already started looking for a place?"

"Yeah, well, you know, just to get an idea for what's out there. And there are some really nice two-bedrooms over by the old chocolate factory. Completely renovated. It's only about a mile from our house. I think Zach would like it."

"Huh." So much information flies at Graham right now that it's unclear how much he's actually retaining. He wishes he'd thought to turn on his phone to record the conversation so he can go back and listen later. See if he sounds as flattened as he feels. If the death knell of his marriage can be detected ringing in the background. But one thing is clear: Leslie has thought this through right down to the extra bedroom. He glances over their bill.

"Oh, and one more thing," she says. Graham's heart stops momentarily. In his forty-one years, he has learned that the phrase "one more thing" almost never means anything good.

"I'm launching my own marketing company."

He sits back. "Oh, wow. Seriously? Since when?"

"Since the bank approved my start-up loan last week."

For once, Graham is speechless.

She grins, as if she's been waiting all weekend to break the news. "It's something I've wanted to do for a long time. And if I don't leap now, I'm not sure I ever will. I'm certainly not getting any younger. A handful of my clients have agreed to come with me. And a few people from my department. I'm giving notice next week."

"Oh boy." He shakes his head, searching for a way to slow down the runaway train that's headed his way. *Did I know that Leslie always dreamed of launching her own company?* He can't recall. Either way, it's probably not a good sign that it lands as a surprise. "And you didn't feel like it was important to maybe share this with me sooner?"

"Like I said, the bank approved my loan just last week."

"Oh. Okay. Uh-huh. I see." He can't, however, quite bring himself to congratulate her. It's as if she's placed a blindfold over his eyes and spun him around fifty times.

"I know it's a lot to take in, but I hope you'll be happy for me. It's a chance for me to finally be my own boss. A chance to start fresh, start over, you know?"

Start over. Start fresh. As if the chance to escape their marriage, their lives together has been something she's been dreaming about for a long time.

So this is it, he thinks, while signing the bill. *The long sojourn of a marriage.* As he closes the leather check holder, an incredible sense of loss falls over him. Both for their twelve years of marriage, many of them wonderful, and for all the time they've already wasted while waiting for the next chapter of their lives to begin.

"It will be hard to tell Zach." His voice catches.

"Yes, but it's not as if either of us is leaving him. He'll just see us at different times. We'll love him just as much."

"Uh-huh." Graham suspects she's underplaying the effects of their separation on their son for the sake of her own sanity. But he can't blame her entirely; he recognizes his own culpability in the dismantling of their family unit. He's hardly innocent, after all—coveting his friend's wife, one of the Ten Commandments broken! Not spending enough time with Zach. Not doing enough with Leslie. But neither is Leslie entirely innocent. Her heart hasn't been in this marriage for at least a year. Not really. In some ways, she's finally admitting what they've both known to be true.

"All set?" their waitress perkily asks. Graham looks up and feels inexplicably disappointed that it's not Maya, their waitress from Friday morning. It seems as if *someone* they know, even marginally, should be present to bear witness, to confirm that this pivotal moment in their lives is happening.

"All set," he says and hands over the bill.

$\sim$

On their ride to the airport (no sign of Nate or Drew), Graham's cell phone dings with a text from Betsy. They exchanged numbers at the Derby yesterday, and he's been keeping her apprised of Nate's health. She and Della have already boarded their plane, headed back to Minnesota. The text is a photo of her and Della in their hats. Della's is the centerpiece. Loved hanging out with you all! it reads below. It turns out that Betsy *does* own a cell phone but prefers using her trusty Kodak for keepsake photos. She's promised to send Graham duplicates of all the photos once they get home.

Wouldn't have been the same Derby without you two! he taps back, adding a heart emoji.

Eventually, he and Leslie check their bags and prepare to board the plane. Graham offered to request a new seat assignment so that they wouldn't have to sit together, but Leslie declined. "That's silly," she said. "We're going to see each other as soon as we get home, anyway." He shrugged. Couldn't argue with that.

Now they make their way toward the back of the plane, Row 19, but not so far back, thankfully, that he'll feel as if he's sitting in the bathroom. Leslie sends a quick text to Zach, telling him their flight is on time and they'll see him soon. About ten minutes later, he watches Drew and Nate hurry onto the plane and locate their seats, a few rows up. Nate spots them and gives a quick wave before sitting down. They've no idea what he and Leslie discussed back at the hotel.

As if reading his mind, Leslie pats his hand, resting on the armrest, and says, "We can tell them later." He nods. On this, they agree.

While they wait for the plane to depart, the minister's sermon from last Sunday pops into Graham's head. He doesn't consider himself particularly religious, but last Sunday, for whatever reason, church had called to him. It was the children's sermon, actually. While the kids fidgeted around up front, the pastor talked about popular magazines over the years. He described a magazine called *Life*, which published amazing photos of the world around us. Then he mentioned a magazine called *People*, and: *Guess what that one was about?* he asked.

People! the kids shouted, delighted by their brilliance.

Right. And after that, there was a new magazine called Self. *And what do you think it was about?*

Yourself! they yelled without missing a beat.

The minister paused, waiting for the dots to connect in their young minds. *Do you see what's happening here?* he asked. He held up his fingers. *Life. People. Self. Our world keeps getting smaller and smaller. Sure, I know there's this thing called the internet that you kids like to use, but that's not real people. The internet keeps us locked inside our houses, keeps us from talking to our neighbors and helping out. We need to keep our world BIG. You understand? BIG.*

The kids all nodded very seriously.

But the notion stuck with Graham. Probably because it so aptly captured what he's been feeling lately. A narrowing of his world, a shrinking of his social circle, a loss of community. A palpable loneliness.

He'd been pulling out of events, shirking the symphony and museum, retreating more and more into himself. Leslie noticed it first, but Graham dismissed it. Claimed he was too busy with his students and reading papers to stretch his days beyond that. But it wasn't true. They both knew it. He'd simply lost his motivation to go beyond what was required of him. The shine, so to speak, was missing; aside from Zach (and, for a little while, Drew), his world had lost its shimmer, its light.

But as the plane's engines roar to life, Graham feels a little of that shine returning, despite all that's come to pass this weekend. Maybe *because* of all that's come to pass. Because he feels alive again, as if he's made it around to the other side of the eclipse, his own personal eclipse. For too long, he's been hanging out in the darkness, worrying that it would never disappear. But now that he's on the other side, his globe spinning on its axis at full speed, his face to the sun?

Man, oh, man. The light that shines through?

It's bold and brilliant—and bursting with hope.

26

DREW

After leaving Nate behind in their room, Drew roamed the hallways of the hotel, wandered into the gift shop, contemplated buying a hat that cost four hundred dollars, then stepped outside and walked around the block for some fresh air.

We'll be okay. We'll figure things out, she counseled herself. Now that she knew what was going on, their problems somehow felt easier to solve, not worse. Forty thousand dollars was a formidable number, but it was tangible, something she could work with. She knew how to do math, how to subtract numbers until four followed by four zeros became only zero.

She could pick up a few extra summer school classes, add tutoring sessions to her evenings and weekends. It wouldn't be a windfall of cash, but it would certainly help chip away at their current debt. And she's fairly confident that Nate will need to find a new job, preferably before his current employer lets him go. Again, though, that strikes her as an easier fix than a gambling addiction. For that, they'll need to call in the big guns, the experts who can steer her husband back to his old self. Strangely, Drew wonders now if, when Nate quit smoking a few years ago (something she was on him to do), he'd simply swapped out one addiction for another. If somehow, she'd inadvertently instigated this entire mess.

Once she returned from her walk, Drew decided to head back up to their hotel room to grill Nate on anything else he might be hiding. Because she needed to know. The thought of discovering next week, for instance, that he and Leslie were secret business partners—or something worse—would break her.

But Nate swore that the loan was the very last secret.

On the way out to grab their Uber (they'd ordered their own when it became apparent that they wouldn't make Leslie's 1:30 deadline), a woman's voice called out to them. *Nate, hold up!* When Drew spun around, an attractive woman with long, dark hair was waving at them, her silver Arlo Skye suitcase in tow.

"Hey!" Nate cried back. "What are you doing here? I didn't know you were staying at the Brown, too."

And Drew thought, *Are you kidding me, universe? Haven't I already paid back my karma this weekend? Now I have to be nice to one of Nate's old girlfriends?*

"Yeah, I've been here the whole time," the woman said. "Weird, huh, that we never bumped into each other?"

"I know." Drew watched her husband do that thing he did whenever he was nervous—rake his fingers through his dark, curly hair.

"Hi, I'm Drew," she said, extending her hand.

"Philomena." The woman smiled, took her hand. "Phil for short."

"Honey," Nate said. "Phil and I went to high school together back in Newton. She's in the horse business now, handicapping."

Oh. That's when Drew connected Philomena with Phil, Nate's betting adviser this weekend. Phil was a woman! The one who told him to put all his money on Horse Cents. Drew stepped back.

"I know this is bad form," Phil said. "But I'm having a heck of a time reserving an Uber. Would it be okay if I share a ride with you guys? I'm assuming you're headed to the airport? I'll pay my half, of course."

Nate cast a nervous glance in Drew's direction, probably trying to gauge if she was about to throw a punch.

"Actually," Philomena added. "How stupid of me. Happy to pay for the whole ride, considering I cost you a win yesterday."

"Aww . . . not your fault. Not really," said Nate, and Drew glared at him. "I mean, not your fault that I bet so much money."

"Why? How much did you bet?"

Nate hung his head. "Fifteen grand."

"Ouch! I never told you to bet *that* much."

He shrugged. "Whatever. Water under the bridge. So do you want to hop in with us? I think our driver is waiting."

"Are you sure it's okay?" Her eyes focused on Drew when she asked.

"Yeah, come on. Get in," Drew obliged. "Especially if you're paying."

Saying that last part felt good.

Now, finally, she and Nate are sitting on the plane, a few rows ahead of Graham and Leslie. Nate gave a wave in their direction, but at the moment, Drew feels less than charitable toward their friends. She doesn't appreciate that Leslie and Nate were keeping yet another secret from her, namely Leslie's generous loan of ten grand.

In light of all that's happened, though, her husband's hookups with Leslie have lost much of their sting. In fact, Drew's a little embarrassed for what even she can see now was a colossal overreaction. They'd kept a college secret from her, but it happened so far in the past, could she really be upset? Hold a grudge over it? Maybe for a day, but not much longer. Nate was right: it was a white lie. One that paled in comparison with everything else they've learned about each other this weekend. As angry as she might be over how out of control Nate let their finances get, she also understands that he has an addiction, and that he's promised to get help.

And perhaps most important: she still loves him.

As for Graham, well, her heart breaks a little for him. That she maybe took advantage of his advice and his company, which she genuinely enjoyed, only to inadvertently lead him on. It wasn't that she was lying. She was attracted to him that night; *she'd wanted to kiss him!* Ever since the chocolate-cake incident. And the endorphin high of flirting with him the next day at the track had been a welcome ego boost. Knowing that someone other than her husband found her attractive and considered her interesting had opened her mind to new possibilities. Such as that being in her forties wasn't all that terrible.

She would never leave Nate; she knows this deep in her bones. But Graham has reminded her that an intellectual life can be just as important as an emotional one—even more so. Because through books and music and art, you could always escape from the real world when you most needed to. She suspects that their private book club of two is now defunct, but Drew will continue to read and recommend books to Graham. She hopes he'll do the same, and that once this weekend becomes a distant memory, the four of them will return to their easy rhythms, a friendship that has sustained them all for over a decade. She doesn't know what will happen between Leslie and Graham, but Drew hopes for Zach's sake, that they'll figure it out, find their way back to each other, even if, as Leslie hinted the other night, they spend some time apart.

When the flight attendant comes by, offering today's newspaper, Drew grabs a copy and spies atop the fold a photo capturing all three horses, Horse Cents, Sheer Luck, and Good Enough. The headline reads:

Huge Upset at the Kentucky Derby! Good Enough Wins! Horse Cents, Sheer Luck Disqualified

Nate reads over her shoulder. "What could have been," he says wistfully.

"Yeah, would have been nice, that's for sure." She reads a little about the race, the foul, and the ruling by the stewards. How no one could believe that Good Enough, who'd initially placed third, surged to first, thanks to the other horses being disqualified. "Not bad for a horse with 30–1 odds," writes the journalist.

Then she stops. "Hey, listen to this." And she begins to read aloud. "Despite all the upsets in yesterday's race, it seems as if the universe might have been trying to send a message to the fans: if a horse named Good Enough can win the Kentucky Derby with such dismal odds, then maybe the rest of us should consider easing up a bit, too. It's tempting to think that if Charlotte (the spider in E.B. White's *Charlotte's Web*) were around today, she'd celebrate the occasion by spinning a web in the horse's honor. One that might simply read, 'Some Horse' or 'Good Enough Wins.' Perhaps we should all take note."

"Wow," Nate says. "Quite an article. Maybe a little overdone, though, don't you think?"

Drew shrugs. "I don't know. I kind of like it. Suppose that's why I bet on Good Enough. The idea that you don't always have to be the best, you know? That sometimes good enough is plenty." On the other side of the fold, there's a lineup of photos captioned with the following:

Spitting Image Scratched. Illegal Drug Use Detected. 15 Owners Charged

"Wow." Her eyes scan the photos, only to discover in the second row, two familiar faces. "Honey, check it out!"

"Holy cow." Among those charged are Trixie and Benton Fairfax.

She and Nate read the brief article together, but there doesn't appear to be much information beyond the fact that prerace testing revealed the presence of a banned substance. It explains that fifteen different people own a share of Spitting Image, and that at the moment, everyone is under investigation.

"Guess it wasn't a bum knee after all, huh?"

"I thought there was something too good to be true about those two."

"You did?" Drew is surprised. "Really? Why?"

"I'm not sure. Guess they struck me as fake."

"Huh." She considers this. "I thought they were entertaining. And maybe a tiny bit annoying." She pauses. "But they're *criminals*. Or alleged criminals, I should say. We hung out with criminals! On Millionaires Row!"

Nate shakes his head. "We seem to attract danger, don't we? At least, this weekend we did."

"Attract it or create it, you mean?"

A crooked smile darts across his face. "Touché. Hey, I'm sorry it wasn't the birthday weekend you were hoping for. I'll make it up to you."

"Nate, honey," she says quietly. "Please stop thinking that you have to make anything up to me, okay? I have a feeling that's how we got into this financial mess in the first place."

"*Okaaaay.*" He pauses. "It's just that I want you to be happy."

She squeezes his hand. "I *am* happy. As long as I have you and Owen, I'm happy. We're gonna figure out all the other stuff. Hey!" On his finger, where the pale, exposed flesh beneath his wedding ring used to be, there's a gold band. "You found your wedding ring! Where was it?"

"Would you believe me if I told you it was in my toiletry kit the whole time?"

"But I thought you'd left it somewhere back home?"

"So did I. Turns out I had it all along."

"Huh, that's weird."

He shrugs. "No weirder than anything else that's happened this weekend."

She laughs. "Well, make sure it stays on your finger this time, okay?"

"You bet." He buckles his seat belt. "Hey, do you mind if I close my eyes for a few minutes? I've got a wicked headache."

"Go ahead. I was planning on reading my book, anyway."

A few minutes later, when Nate begins to snore, she digs in her bag for Steven Rowley's *The Guncle*. Her hand latches on to the book, and when she pulls it out, she notices her program from Oaks Day stuck between the pages. She yanks it free, which is when a small piece of white paper flutters onto her lap, like a butterfly. Her heart in her throat, her fingers slowly begin to smooth the paper out.

Her winning ticket for Good Enough.

She forgot that she tucked it into her program on Oaks Day. The entire time, it's been sitting there. *Three thousand dollars found!* Relief spills over her. When she gets home, she'll have to research how to cash it in, if she can even do that from afar? *Well, there must be some way to get the money,* she thinks. For the time being, she slips the ticket into her wallet for safekeeping.

"Ma'am, can you please slide your bag under the seat in front for takeoff?" the flight attendant asks, carrying out her final check of the cabin.

Drew does as she's told.

The engines start to roar, and the plane begins to gradually roll backward.

"See you later, Louisville," she whispers through the window. Beside her, Nate's forearm already hogs the armrest. Typically, Owen claims it first whenever they travel. She's tempted to gently slide her husband's arm off in order to give herself more room. What will he care? He's already asleep.

But then, in a sudden moment of clarity, she lays her arm and then her hand over his, threading her fingers between Nate's. His wedding band sparkles with specks of light from the sun pouring in through the window.

There's no reason, she thinks, why they can't share it.

And every reason why they should.

Acknowledgments

Every book, as the saying goes, takes a village. My thanks to agents Annelise Robey and Meg Ruley for their early reads, enthusiasm, and endless support. Thanks to Selena James for brainstorming on what would make a compelling Derby story—and for her patience and grace when it came to deadlines. To Ronit Wagman, this is our second book together, and I wouldn't have it any other way. Without your editorial wisdom, there would be no novel. And to my copyeditor, Karen Brown, who lent her careful eye to these pages, and to Rachel Norfleet, proofreader extraordinaire, my enormous thanks for your time and effort. To all the other talented folks at Lake Union Publishing, critical to getting authors' work out into the world, my sincere thanks: Rachael Clark, Adrienne Krogh, Nicole Burns-Ascue, and Angela Elson.

I did a fair amount of research for *Betting on Good*, not the least of which was traveling to Churchill Downs to witness the Kentucky Derby in person in 2023. My warmest thanks to the people of Louisville, Kentucky, who made our stay such a pleasure and who answered my many questions, both around town and at the racetrack. A special thanks to my husband, Mike, who helped orchestrate the trip (and who downed many a cocktail in the name of research).

Several books and newspapers were useful in providing an overview of both Churchill Downs and horse racing, in general. These include the following: Laura Hillenbrand's bestselling *Seabiscuit: An American Legend* (Random House, copyright © 2001 by Laura Hillenbrand); *Kick the*

Latch, an incisive novel about life at the track, by Kathryn Scanlan (New Directions Books, copyright © 2022 by Kathryn Scanlan); *101 Reasons to Love America's Favorite Horse Race* (Stewart, Tabori and Chang, copyright © 2010 by Mary Tiegreen and Sheri Seggerman); *The DK Smithsonian Handbooks: Horses* by Elwyn Hartley Edwards (Dorling Kindersley Handbooks, copyright © 2002); *The Kentucky Derby: How the Run for the Roses Became America's Premier Sporting Event* by James Nicholson (The University of Kentucky Press, copyright © 2014 by James Nicholson); *The Official Program of the Kentucky Derby 149* (copyright © 2023 Churchill Downs Racetrack); and *The Official Program of the Kentucky Oaks 149* (copyright © 2023 Churchill Downs Racetrack).

Various articles in the *Lexington Herald-Leader*, the Louisville *Courier-Journal*, *The Wall Street Journal*, *Vox*, the *Los Angeles Times*, Kentuckyderby.com, ChurchillDowns.com, and TwinSpires.com provided invaluable information on the history of women in the industry, the history of disqualifications and inquiries at Churchill Downs, the dangers of racing, what to look for in a racehorse, how betting works, and general racing trivia, among other topics. I'm grateful to these publications for their insights. Any mistakes in the book are my own. All the main characters in the book are fictional, and although I tried to remain true to the details and spirit of Churchill Downs, there are places where, for purposes of the narrative, fictional license has been taken. Also, to my knowledge, Shania Twain has never sung the national anthem at the Derby (although she would be amazing).

On a more personal note, this book was written during an exceptionally difficult time for my family. My younger brother, Peter, only forty-four years old, passed away unexpectedly in February 2024. Peter was beloved by all who knew him, funny and fun-loving, a devoted dad and husband, a wonderful friend and brother. A car fanatic, he liked to ask me, "When are you going to put a car chase in one of your books?" Although it's not a car chase, a mention of one of Peter's favorite sports cars appears in the chapter on Millionaires Row. I hope he knows that the world will never be quite the same without him. Rest in peace, little brother.

About the Author

Photo © 2024 Claudia Starkey

Wendy Francis is a former book editor (Houghton Mifflin) and the author of seven novels, including *Feels Like Summer*, *Summertime Guests*, *The Summer of Good Intentions*, and *Three Good Things*. Her writing has also appeared in *Good Housekeeping*, the *Washington Post*, and NPR's *Cognoscenti*, among others. A graduate of Harvard, she lives outside Boston with her husband and sixteen-year-old son. For more information, visit www.wendyfrancisauthor.wordpress.com or find her on Facebook or Instagram @wendyfrancisauthor.